New York
Theater Review

Also in this Series

New York Theater Review (2005)

ISBN 13: 978-1-4116-6483-8
ISBN 10: 1-4116-6483-3
Black Wave Press
www.nytr.org

New York
Theater Review

Brook Stowe, Editor

Black Wave Press
New York

BLACK WAVE PRESS
P.O. Box 250898
Columbia University Station
New York, NY 10025
www.nytr.org

Cover Design by Savage Candy
www.savagecandy.com

ISBN: 978-0-6151-4307-1

First published in March, 2007

Body Text set in Garamond 11pt.
Auxiliary Text set in Palatino Linotype
Printed in the United States of America

This book is dedicated to the ones I love:

Everyone who has chosen to make New York City their home and theater their life; especially theater below 14th Street and anywhere in Brooklyn

Contents

Illustrations

Acknowledgments

I am greatly indebted to everyone who contributed to this book, to your time and care and talent. I also want to send a special shout out to all who helped make our fundraiser at the Brick Theater such a success last October – especially Susan Bernfield for MC-ing it all; Heather Cohn for calling the show on a day's notice; Michael Gardner and the Brick Theater for graciously donating the space, and Jody Christopherson for her limitless resourcefulness, great sense of direction, and for making the near-impossible happen.

New York

Theater Review

The Influence of Anxiety
An Introduction by George Hunka

New York theater – uptown and downtown theater, Broadway and Fringe and off-Off Broadway and indie and performance art (or whatever you want to call it these days), improvisation and dance/music/theater mash-ups and directors' theater and good old fashioned plays – was in robust, almost embarrassing good health in 2006. It may seem churlish, even self-destructive, to suggest that there might have been too much theater in New York. Even were you to have attended the theater every single night of the past calendar year, you would have only scratched the surface.

All this theatrical activity may have demonstrated the cultural and political anxiety of theater artists. They had reason to be anxious. As a series of natural disasters both overseas and at home sucked dry traditional sources of charitable income for all the arts' physical health, economic resources became more desiccated than ever. The fifth anniversary of the World Trade Center disaster and the beginning of the third year of the Iraq War – which seemed farther than ever from a conclusion of any kind – led to dour, late-night contemplations and endless attempts, from the Off-Broadway musical revue *Bush Wars* to the Culture Project's city-wide Impact Festival, to demonstrate the nightmarish depredations of the sixth year of the Bush II Administration.

There seemed to be an aesthetic anxiety as well. Through the seasons of Performance Space 122 and The Kitchen, HERE and La MaMa, no particular aesthetic or performance practice equal to the Abstract Expressionism of the 1940s and 1950s, the Fluxus movement of the 1960s, or the 1970s Minimalist movement emerged as more valid or productive than any other. No similar body of thought or aesthetic had primary influence in New York theater. Nor did New York theater artists appear to feel they needed any such body of thought or aesthetic. Instead, in 2006, for what it was worth, it was *all* good, the party line seemed to indicate, so long as it was on a stage. Theory's venue remained the classroom rather than the theater space. Speaking as a theorist-without-academic-portfolio myself, I found that among theater artists theory was treated with a certain amount of trepidation, as if to theorize was to hobble rather than to inspire the creative process. On the other hand, many of these artists' reluctance to theorize may just as well have been a disinclination to think, or talk, about what they were doing, or trying to do. Perhaps it's true that theory is an attempt to capture the more elusive qualities of theatrical lightning in a jar. The disinclination was to the possibility that it could be much more than that, as theater writers from Ben Jonson to Howard Barker have demonstrated.

Outside the academy, theory continued to find significant outlets in 2006, however. Attendees at the CUNY Segal Theatre Center's Prelude 06 festival, perhaps the city's most significant and accessible event for experimental and downtown theater artists, saw programs, panel discussions and workshop stagings that ran the gamut from play readings of traditional scripts to the laconic, seemingly formless media and metatheatrical ironies of Brooklyn's Collapsable Giraffe.

New York theater, as it ever does, attracted controversy in 2006 that managed to find its way onto op-ed pages, the covers of magazines and a substantial portion of this year's *New York Theater Review*. Theory gets its hearing in these pages as well, kicking off with a consideration of multicultural linguistics and imagination in Caridad Svich's "Bad English or Bordered Voices in American Theater," which considers a globalizing influence that has begun to seep into the American character (if ever such a thing truly existed), certainly a controversial subject itself. Caridad opens the "Essays" section with a vision of the future of theater not only in the "mash-up" of aesthetic approaches but of cultural voices as well.

Another key trend in 2006 was the continuing social and cultural irrelevance of the city's larger institutional theaters, an irrelevance to which these theaters themselves contributed out of an ill-founded fear and cowardice. Downtown theater featured its own fear-based spectacle, "*l'affaire Corrie*" – the debacle that was the New York Theatre Workshop's (mis)handling of the London import, *My Name is Rachel Corrie*. Garrett Eisler's contribution, "In Praise of Controversy: What the *Corrie* Conflict Taught Us about Theater in a Post 9/11 World" recaps the event from beginning to end.

The past year also marked the 100th anniversary of the birth of Samuel Beckett, one of the most influential theater artists of the 20th century. New York theater events included a visit from the Gate Theatre's production of *Waiting for Godot* and, among other things, *Godot Has Left the Building*, a postmodern take on Beckett's classic. Alan Lockwood offers a full report – of both NYC and international events – with his "Everywhere and Nowhere: Beckett at 100."

The essays conclude with another look backward and ahead. "Where Are We and What Are We Doing Here?" Brook Stowe's review of the year's offerings in new theater books, examines two volumes about theater giants of the past (Orson Welles and William Shakespeare) and two volumes by and about theater leaders of the present and future (Anne Bogart, Chuck Mee and Robert Brustein). The "Profiles" section, a spirited, communal interview with leading lights of downtown theater in 2006, provides a look to the future as you read between the lines of their individual approaches to the work in which they so passionately engage.

In the best examples of 2006's scripted theater in New York, there was also a political undertone, albeit an undertone with a distinctly elegiac quality. The three plays in this year's volume share a sadness that seeks to find meaning for the contemporary world in our experiences of the past. Anne Washburn's *I Have Loved Strangers* brings the Biblical Jeremiah to 21st Century streets and enmeshes him in the machinations of a terrorist group. Reaching back over three generations, Quiara Alegría Hudes' *Elliot, A Soldier's Fugue* mourns the continuing fascination of the human race with war and its consequent, horrifying effect on the human community. More optimistically, Adam Szymkowicz' *Food for Fish* has Chekhov's *Three Sisters* yearning for a lost New Jersey rather than a lost Moscow, but they do manage to find an ambivalent new future in putting a history behind them.

"Postponed" plays turned out to have ambivalent futures, too. 2006 ended with the NYC premiere of *My Name is Rachel Corrie*, the play that had grabbed headlines earlier in the year without a single performance. Finally opening in a commercial Off-Broadway house in October, *Corrie* met a lukewarm critical and commercial reception that failed to attract the protests, controversies, or howls of indignation of which the New York Theatre Workshop was so loathe to invite without efforts to "contextualize" the play.

The calendar year is but a convenient construct by which to mark the passing of time, and the beginning of this year is no less anxious a time than the beginning of last. The hole in the ground that used to be the World Trade Center (the embarrassing, continuing memorial at Ground Zero that remained the object of partisan bickering and the unending machinations of real estate magnates) seems no closer to being filled than it was twelve months ago. We are now entering the fourth year of an unpopular war with no end in sight, although the Bush Administration is another year closer to its demise than it was in 2006. A recent story in the *New York Times* detailed the continuing deterioration of arts funding for smaller, more experimental arts groups in New York. And, as usual, New York's experimentalists continue to experiment. In addition to new productions from veterans such as Richard Foreman and The Wooster Group, The Living Theatre returned to New York in March with a new production of their legendary play, *The Brig.* Producing in tandem with the City's younger experimentalists at the beginning of their careers, it seems likely that alternative New York City theater will be able to boast just as vital and productive a year in 2007 as it did in 2006. Maybe there's no such thing as too much theater, especially in times as anxious as these.

-- New York City
February 2007

Essays

Bad English or Bordered Voices in American Theater
A cut from a mashed-up mixtape for the reclamation of a lost sound
by Caridad Svich

America sings how it sings. In "bad" roaring English. In howling wails and stomps. In orphan tales and bastard poems of near-apocalypse. Always almost, but never quite. Always on the verge. The American resolution – and by American in this instance I mean the United States – is to be found in the scrap heap junkyard of its culture, in between the highway signs, and by strolling through the vanishing backyards of its towns and cities. Technology may be central to the lives of cyborg Americans but it is in the holler of song, in the punk snarl, country plain, rock-steady, and hip-hop groove that we tell our stories. Bordered by borders, the mobile place that America occupies is its greatest sustaining renewable hope. Fixed-ness doesn't sit well with the American temperament, though we always want to fix the where of where we are. We live in paradox, between the red and blue, native and immigrant, white, brown and black, English and non-English-speaking. Isms divide us, as tribal voices hold sway for a time. But what do we seek? And, moreover, what do we seek in our theater?

Walk around, step out, take a peek in … America's theaters from Los Angeles to Austin to New York City … are speaking of the voices of many, even if you can't always tell. The age-old-now dilemma of the mainstream vs. the alternative is age-old indeed. How many times will we look at that divide as the measuring stick of who we are? Shouldn't we just see first which stories are being told – being staged – and why? I differentiate between stories told and stories staged because so many of our stories are not staged or even given body and voice, but rather are hidden, tucked away, in little rooms where readings are held, public for a moment, and then vanished unless they are found again, or simply read underground amongst friends and peers: that great play that will never be seen, because … And every few years that great play that is never seen either stays the same or becomes two or three other plays, while the first one is erased from conversation, forgotten, relegated to the shelf of regret. How many play-texts live on our American shelves, and what stories might they tell of who we are, alongside the ones that are readily and regularly staged? This is a speculation, an incantation, an imagined journey of the imaginary in which we live. This is a map of the unmapped, creaking through the crevices of lifestyles, buzz and 3-week runs of shows that have had a mere two weeks of rehearsal: block it, light it and go. This is not, however, a map of regret but one of longing, a yearning for the taste of a new English to be heard, an English distended from the colonized dramaturgy of our transatlantic traditions, an English that speaks of the mashed-up state in which we barter our vowels and crush our consonants and let the American smile, ever present, ever entertaining, yield past the grimace and into soul terrain, deep soul blues, *cante jondo jondisimo* un-milked for the Starbucks generation: a wary, sexual blues of desire that doesn't look forward but back, back to that unchained time – unromanticized – where the American voice in its plurality sung local to the global, unaware of the recording devices that would fix it one day for eternity.

If we are to consider the imaginary alive in our midst, consider this: which voices do you walk amongst every day? In your town, city, village, state? Which American speaks to you and why, and I use the word "American" here in its broad sense (taking in North, Central, and South)? Here we are doing a bit of cultural studies in the age of post-post reproduction, writing down the stories, the bits and pieces of instant memory we can grasp before they run away in the slipstream of bytes and auto-delete. In our theater there lives the rural voice, although we don't readily acknowledge it; the agrarian economy of sunup to sunrise and making it through the seasons, dependent on the unpredictability of weather. The sustained cries of exile, Eastern European, Russian, Arab, Asian, Latina/o, also live here, broken and unbroken by the exotic branding of the Other, unleashed in private parlor songs, intimate salons, community centers, amateur performances, town halls, wedding banquets, and illegal downloading. Native American voices also necessarily live here, although they are harder and harder to find in the main of the stream we consume and by which we are consumed. Remove the buy and sell, the product placed, the audience targeted for access, and what remains? Can we imagine a theater truly for all? Come one and … ? And what would that theater look like – not as a demographic study, but as a daily offering of voices? Would our delicate plays, utterings of private expression, need to be pumped up with stars and upholstery, to be "heard"? Would our scorching, damning plays, utterings of rage, despair and quest for solace, need to be softened, tamed of their wildness, of their raw vulnerability, to be understood? And would television remain in most eyes the renaissance vehicle for our finest expressions while theater – grown-up theater – struggles to be less like TV in its willingness to mix things up and be more like TV in its surface dressage? And do our playwrights strive only to make their mark, rather than marks?

We are enamored of the singular sensation in this market America, and forgetting is the by-product of this dance of attraction. To name a name: Oyamo. The brother voice to August Wilson. His voice remains, is constant, but doesn't "break through." And a new generation hasn't even heard the name.

Theater is about forgetting, as is the world. Names pop up, works rise, and others fall by … perhaps to be discovered later or not discovered at all. But as a culture, as a community. In the theater, what is our responsibility to seeking out and listening to the voices that make up our America – this humble, vast but small wealth of voices that tell the tales of who we are and might be, and also who we were, back then way back in the 1800s and 1910s?

A bordered voice becomes the border. It stays fixed there and is always seen from the other side of the wall or fence. If you want to be mobile, a moving theater, then you have to un-border yourself, and be un-located. Place is where you make it. Where is what you name then and there. The where of Illyria, the where of Brecht's Chicago, which is more Berlin than Chi-town any day. Think about the local as a global location. All territories are reflected here in this here of theater, even if we are only speaking to our South African township or our Romanian countryside. The American map contains many stories. Every once in a while you pick up John Dos Passos' *U.S.A.* and you think what a voice map this is!: wandering the lust of its being, its drunkenness with tongue, with utterance, with sheer brazen make-it-up this instant-on-the-spot on-the-run-at-the-drop-of-a-two-bit-carnie-huckster vision re-claimed by our maverick stubborn troubadours of incessant, gnawing at the edge of American fabric song. Think about the edge. Yeah. The edge of our voices, our cities, our sidewalks and no-walk zones. Listen close and hard to the virtual bodies, un-miked whoops and *ayes* traced on our un-paved pavements. Check out the grocery store brands next to the corporate brands. Check the label. Made in China. Fall into a coma. The coma of dreaming society anew, of hearing the stars speak and the ancestors breathe again, even the forgotten ones in the long list of names that was and is our theater. Today their works and ours live. In the continuum. Back in time, through time, acquainted with the blogging highways of opinion, reportage, and the increased necessity of a critical stance. Did you read the *New York Times*' reader report on the Isherwood or Brantley review? And what did *Playgoer* say? But what do you say when you walk into the theater or happen upon it on the street, out-of-the-way warehouse, or shiny mercantile platform? Whose audience are you? And who are you as audience? Do you let the names of the forgotten rise, or squash them underfoot as marginal or less-significant? Do you let the ghosts in?

Spectral voices and shimmers of bodies speak through the theater American, un-bordered by English and the continent's size. Haunt the haunt freakily folkish and unfreakily silhouetted in cut-outs tracing the split dichotomies of race and gender. Kara Walker teaches you the hurricane past and present, but so does Jimmy Walker and the false *Chicanismos* of a Whittier scribe in California and the shifting Creolized *patois* of a *Cubana* in New York. Listen to Thaddeus Phillips' bad Colombian Spanish, his *jerga* remade in Denver tongue, in *El Conquistador!* and let yourself re-listen to the inflections and digressions of a phonetic and theatrical experiment quirkily told as part of an American saga of conquest. Chuck your dreams of being a star. Make a living. Find a way. This is the way of the American theater, too. Document the undocumented, rather than reproducing news stories. Let the news do its job, unless it's not doing it. Pick up where Upton Sinclair left off in *The Jungle*. Favor the unfavored tale. The gnarly that Gnarls Barkley gave us with "Crazy." How is it that "Crazy" embodies the American spirit more than some of our plays? And how is it that it is indeed the word "crazy" that resonates best with our lusty wandering soul? Why, Willie Nelson and Patsy Cline knew it too way back when, almost fifty years ago. Crazy America is with its dark secrets and its brazen untutored take on drama, magpie in nature, variety show-like, and ever indebted to the mixtape of voices from all bloody over.

Ghosts and blood. Keep them close. Yeah. The memory of both. The short fictions of uproar and outrage and stilled silence. Sink into but not go under the vastness of American memories resurrected for the stage. I dream O'Neill and Philip Barry, but Howard Barker and Bernard Marie-Koltes too. And let's not forget the women trailing a blaze and too often not called upon to speak up and onto the world's theater. Think about how many secret histories there are in our theater, and how crucial the critic's role really is beyond the daily report on the local rag, however esteemed. And while you've that thought in mind, think about the site of your theater. What ground is it on? Who lived there before? What was torn down so it could be raised?

In Praise of Controversy
What the *Corrie* Conflict Taught Us About Theater
in a Post 9/11 World
by Garrett Eisler

When *My Name is Rachel Corrie* ended its Off-Broadway run at the Minetta Lane Theatre on December 17, 2006, a question was at last answered that had been hotly debated all year: can you stage a play in New York City that is critical of the Israeli government and live to tell about it? The answer – which should have been unsurprising – turned out to be, "yes." While *Corrie*, when it finally opened, could hardly be called a resounding hit (it received mixed notices and reportedly middling box office after an initial surge of interest), it survived. It even outlasted its initially announced limited run by four weeks. This may ultimately have been less significant as a vindication of the real Rachel Corrie's own advocacy than a repudiation of those who would back off such a play out of fear that if a theater exercised its right to free speech on an unpopular issue, the sky would fall.

Thus ended a bitter and at times confusing chapter in the troubled story of political theater in America. The announcement on February 28, 2006 by the New York Theatre Workshop that they would not be presenting Alan Rickman and Katharine Viner's play, *My Name is Rachel Corrie* that March, as planned, raised many questions about many different aspects of our current theater culture, especially in our cherished world of non-profit institutions that we have assumed are our last bastion of free expression in an ever more conservative country and restrictive corporatized marketplace.

Now that *Corrie* has come and gone, we can reflect a little less passionately and defensively on what some of us were fighting about back in March and April. I myself take away two larger lessons.

One is that controversy can actually be *good* for the theater. More than one commentator at the time complained of "more light than heat" in the uproar. But that cliché in all its hollowness missed the point. People were excited to engage with important global issues in the theater. Yet such passion was counted as part of the problem.

Fear of either "light" *or* "heat" – fear of argument, of honest and open debate – was the culprit here all along. Why else would the NYTW cancel a play its Artistic Director, James Nicola, actually claimed to believe in? Playwright Tony Kushner put his finger on it with his comments to Philip Weiss in *The Nation*: "Never having gotten a clear answer about why Nicola put off the play, Kushner ascribes it to panic: Nicola didn't know what he was getting into, and only later became aware of how much opposition there was to *Corrie*, how much confusion the right has created around the facts. Nicola felt he was taking on 'a really big, scary brawl and not a play.'"

I actually take the position, perhaps unpopular, that we need more "brawling" in the theater, not less. A brawl is at least a sign of life, as opposed to the "deadly theater" (to use Peter Brook's still-apt phrase from forty years ago) we see all around us. When we study theater history, we measure the significance of theater to a given era by the intensity of the trouble it got into. Even the Astor Place riots of 1849 signaled a deep connection between audience and performer that today we consider enviable. Not that I think we need to suffer that episode's scores of casualties to foster a similar engagement. But theater does have to live with both the nice and not-nice effects of that passion.

This is why out of all the things said by the New York Theatre Workshop, what offended me most was their seeming resentment that its decision attracted interest and comment from outside the theater world. In a statement posted on the NYTW website April 25, Nicola and his Managing Director Lynn Moffat declared, "we are disheartened that NYTW has been so badly misrepresented in the press, and criticized by others looking to further their own political or personal agendas." They continued:

> The censorship charge, though unfounded, ignited a fierce, media-driven "controversy" that was quickly fueled by political groups and others who rushed to judgment and criticized the Workshop without knowing what had actually transpired. And because the play itself is framed by the Palestinian-Israeli conflict, the story attracted international attention from journalists and others writing about larger issues such as the Middle East crisis, freedom of speech, and the nature of political theater.

In other words, how dare people engaged with other issues care what is going on Off-Broadway! Personally, I thought we should only be so lucky in the theater. Too bad it took a censorship charge to finally attract some political attention.

The hypocrisy of this statement, though, was immediately apparent when one realized that NYTW has openly admitted that the play's postponement was due exactly to such "others" with "agendas" – namely, those opposing Corrie's politics (identified in the initial *Times* article as "Jewish religious and community leaders"). Only those who supported Corrie – like Weiss in *The Nation* – were branded meddling interlopers. And when asked by the *New York Observer*'s John Heilpern whether he had spoken with Arab-American groups in addition to Jewish activists, Nicola admitted passively, "We haven't heard from anyone in that community, and I can't speculate as to their reactions."

Such head-in-the-sand insularity is what got the Workshop into this mess in the first place. What else explains the apparent fact that it couldn't predict that a pro-Palestinian play would be controversial in New York City as soon as Alan Rickman pitched it? What else explains how the Workshop could be swayed more by random Google searches and nutty propaganda about Rachel Corrie fronting for Hamas than by more objective news accounts? What else explains why the Workshop claimed it needed an entire season to "prepare" a "context" for an Israel-Palestinian conflict that is in the papers every day?

My point is not to harass the NYTW in particular. The time is over for that. But it is worth asking ourselves if this behavior was symptomatic of an entire non-profit theater culture that is "out of touch" with the world, or at least stuck in a stifling cocoon of safeness. When Nicola told the *New York Times* that he realized "the fantasy that we could present the work of this writer simply as a work of art without appearing to take a position was just that, a fantasy," the "fantasy" he's really talking about is the delusion that one can present plays to a living audience as if there *is* no outside world. Or that you can just block out the parts too complex or volatile to leave to chance.

Has it become too selective a slice of the world we see on our stages now? When our theaters claim to be "political" are they really venturing any further than the limits of the Democratic Party Platform? Sadly, New York theater *needed* a play like *My Name is Rachel Corrie* – as imperfect a work of art as it may be – to remind us there are issues out there in that real world we're too easily avoiding, issues way out of our "comfort zones" both to the right and further left than we're usually exposed to.

Another alarming legacy of the *Corrie* debate was the appropriation of such worthy ideals as "context," "balance," "research" – in short, dramaturgy – as a cover for damage control. I was puzzled throughout the spat by the NYTW's constant invocation of some mystical dramaturgical process which it claimed was uniquely its own – some dense research and audience outreach that accompanied all its projects. The time it needed for *Corrie*, the Workshop claimed, was in no way unusual.

I found this odd since the NYTW was *not* a theater I ever associated with such efforts. It boasted of its work supporting Kushner's *Homebody/Kabul*, for instance, but the only "context" I remember from my experience of that show was a photocopied insert in my slim program with some dates about Afghanistan history – something I could have found in a library, or online, in minutes. I'm sure the Workshop did have talkbacks, as it said, but not the night I was there. I have seen talkbacks at other NYTW shows, but like the Five Lesbian Brothers chit-chatting about their process for *Oedipus at Palm Springs*, they were no different than the usual "meet the artists" Q & As at other theaters – "celebrity series," as the Roundabout Theatre now calls them. That's the funny thing about talkbacks as a cure-all. Theaters rarely have them every night. And even then, nothing compels the audience to stay.

All of which brings up another point about the sanctifying of "outreach" and other ways to pacify audience response. You can never reach all the audience all the time. "[O]ur responsibility was not just to produce it," Nicola said about *Corrie*, "but to produce it in such a way as to prevent false and tangential back-and-forth arguments from interfering with Rachel's voice." To which I can only respond – good luck! And why *should* a theater want to "prevent" some in the audience from having their natural response?

One low point in the whole debate was when radio talk show host Brian Lehrer – an icon of NPR liberalism – weighed in, seemingly uninformed by the complete facts. In a piece posted on his show's website, tellingly entitled "How to Avoid a Controversy," Lehrer wagged his finger at London's Royal Court Theatre (the original producers of *Corrie*) for resisting NYTW's purported efforts at audience outreach. Bizarrely, he offered as a counter-model a small Westchester symphony concert he took part in of an oratorio about Israel-Palestine; Lehrer was so proud that the orchestra published materials, held pre- and post-show lectures/discussions, etc. But in comparing this to an Off-Broadway run of a play, Lehrer downplayed two major differences: the concert played only one night, and the audience was small and relatively homogenous. In other words, Lehrer's example had nothing to do with the life of the theater, where controversy can't be so easily contained because the theater is – or should be – part of the give-and-take of the everyday life of a large city.

Again, in the theater, you can't reach all the audience all the time.

As a former practicing dramaturg myself, I have no problem with more research and more discussion. I think it is an embarrassment, in fact, that New York's non-profit theaters *don't* have big meaty program notes on a par with the best European theaters. But I would also be ashamed as a dramaturg if my work was being used primarily to soften dissent and contain disparate views.

In the post-9/11 era, we are going to have to find a way to be OK with staging controversial work. If our theater is going to remain relevant, that is. Artists are going to want to perform it. We're going to have to find the courage to stage such work even if it hurts some people's feelings. We're going to have to prepare ourselves for angry emails and phone calls, for cancelled subscriptions and revoked donations. If our theater is going to be effective, all of this is going to happen.

(Is it revealing that the only way *My Name is Rachel Corrie* could open in New York was under the auspices of a commercial producer, with no one to answer to but her accountant?)

In trying so desperately to avoid a nasty brawl, look what happened to the New York Theatre Workshop. It was sidetracked for two months, with a dark theater, and here we are, still talking about it a full year later. It was hardly a vindication that every single review of the play when it finally opened at the Minetta Lane had to include some variation of the phrase, "controversially cancelled or postponed by the New York Theatre Workshop."

In sum, it was important that this "brawl" happened, partly because it shined a light onto the decision-making process in our non-profit theaters (which are – for all practical purposes – our *de facto* National Theater). But also because it restored equilibrium. A decision was made under pressure from one side – the side of, "let's not talk about this right now." So it was only right that the other side – those saying "Yes, *let's* talk about this, and now!" – applied some pressure of its own.

Now *that's* fair and balanced.

Everywhere and Nowhere: Beckett at 100
New York and international theater take on centenary events in 2006
by Alan Lockwood

For the 100th anniversary of Samuel Beckett's birth in 2006, the world took stock of his theatrical and cultural legacy on stages as renowned as the Comédie-Française's Théâtre du Vieux-Colombier, which hosted *Happy Days*, and as intimate as Under St. Marks in downtown Manhattan, where ghostcrab pulled together an evening of later short works. Born in a well-to-do Dublin suburb in 1906, Beckett made Paris his home, was awarded the Croix de Guerre for "extreme bravery" in the French Resistance, and wrote most of his plays and novels in French that he then translated into English. He abhorred the attention when given the 1969 Nobel Prize; his impact on the art of writing is trumped only by Beckettian implications resounding in our ways of being (who among us doesn't wait for things to get better – or worse?)

Ireland coined a Beckett Euro last year, and Dublin events included *Eh Joe*, the haunted 1965 television paean for which director Atom Egoyan (*The Sweet Hereafter*) cast Michael Gambon, and composer Morton Feldman's opera *Neither*, with an original Beckett libretto. New York University's Tom Bishop helped helm the huge Paris schedule, which continued into early 2007 (last March, Bishop spoke on Beckett at the 92nd Street Y). In London, Nobel laureate Harold Pinter's health forced postponement of his turn in *Krapp's Last Tape*, while the Barbican screened weeks of Beckett on Film, the project out on DVD for which directors from Anthony Minghella (*The English Patient*) to Egoyan and Neal Jordan (*The Crying Game*) re-created the nineteen stage plays with actors including Pinter, Julianne Moore, and Sir John Gielgud in his silent final role in *Catastrophe*. Mary Bryden, the Beckett Society's former president, flew for conferences from Ankara to Tokyo, and the travels of Florida State University scholar S.E. Gontarski included May's festival in Buenos Aires. Gontarski organized the major U.S. conference in Tallahassee, Pittsburgh had productions or readings of all the plays, the online exhibition "Fathoms from Anywhere" was mounted by the University of Texas at Austin, and Two River Theater Company featured almost a month of *Waiting for Godot* in New Jersey, where Jonathan Fox directed seven one-acts and lectures involved Edward Albee, Olympia Dukakis, and Barney Rosset, the writer's longtime Grove Press publisher and U.S. theatrical agent.

New York City, 2006

Though Lincoln Center had hosted the Gate Theatre's full cycle of Beckett plays in 1996 (which debuted in Dublin in 1991) for their inaugural summer festival, what transpired here for the centenary "was relatively muted – it puts in perspective how ephemeral a reputation can be," critic and Hunter College theater department chair Jonathan Kalb said (Kalb's *Beckett in Performance* analyzes the work in theatrical practice and interviews directors and actors including Billie Whitelaw and Klaus Herm, with whom Beckett formed strong working bonds). At the Museum of Modern Art, Barney Rosset screened the aptly titled *Film* starring Buster Keaton, commissioned in 1964 by Rosset's *Evergreen Review* and the occasion of Beckett's sole visit stateside. Grove/Atlantic trumpeted their bilingual *Godot* and the Centenary Edition's four volumes, introduced by Albee, Salman Rushdie, J.M. Coetzee, and Colm Toibin, while the New School hosted a Poetry Society of America evening where Anne Atik, Mary Karr (*The Liar's Club*), and others read Beckett's verse. On stage, *Waiting for Godot* provided the bulk of the action: at the Theater at St. Clement's to open the year, in spring at the Classical Theatre of Harlem, and the Gate Theatre's October week at NYU's Skirball Center.

Hewn from post-WWII cultural anxiety, written as relief from the phenomenally acute novel trilogy on which Beckett's critical regard has been forged, *Godot* staked emotional ground we continue to exist on, and spurred late twentieth century theater from Pinter and Albee to Tom Stoppard and David Mamet. To say the Gate's *Godot* is authoritative is to say the least: Walter Asmus assistant directed Beckett's own 1975 Berlin production, the writer tapped Asmus when the Gate brought together their Beckett Festival cycle, and his cast has been together almost as long. Barry McGovern, who's played Vladimir since that first Festival, spoke on the phone in September as *I'll Go On* – his solo show developed from the novel trilogy – played the Gate, twenty-one years after opening on their stage. "Some people look at *Godot* as a play about despair," McGovern said. "I'm more inclined to think of it as a play about hope. It's both, of course: dark, but very funny." The Gate team played Lincoln Center in 1996, "but we're all ten years older. Things change in the world, and people say, 'Oh, you've changed it!' We've changed hardly anything. But you change, and your memories change." Eager to return, McGovern said, "New York audiences have a broad sense of humor, unlike, say, a Deep South audience where they don't have much sense of irony. *Godot*'s got almost a Jewish humor; it's Irish humor, it's universal."

McGovern's gunmetal delivery brought edge to jests exchanged with the telepathy of a seasoned bop combo; danger and cruelty needs to cornerstone Beckett's work, even when the pratfalls unfold as if in amber. Skirball's massive backdrop appeared buffed by steel wool and cotton, and Steven Brennan's Lucky was shot with astonishing effulgence then heeled, skittishly elegant, as Alan Stanford barked Pozzo's stentorian commands. In Act Two, when Gogo repeated, "I'm thinking," the burled peat and caramel tones of opening night favorite Johnny Murphy (*The Commitments*) flexed the last word towards "sinking." Among bowlers and boots in Skirball's dressing room, Murphy admitted that, when first rehearsing *Godot* in a production some thirty years ago, "I had no idea what it was about." Pozzo was being played by a friend and "tears were running down his face, laughing. We broke for lunch, and I very politely said, 'What in the name of ___ were you laughing at?' He said, 'Johnny, it is hilarious,'" an awareness Murphy took so to heart that, when recommended by McGovern for the Gate production, he consented to come aboard if director Asmus wanted 75 percent comedy (Asmus readily agreed).

Classical Theatre of Harlem's winning *Godot* ran Pozzo's (Chris McKinney) first act exit off a steep rooftop flooded to its eaves, landing with a butt-flop splash in the raft in which Lucky (Billy Eugene Jones) towed him off. CTH cofounder Christopher McElroen said, "*Godot* is obviously one of the greatest plays out there," adding that though "we have tremendous respect [for CTH productions], we approach them as if they were new plays." Company vets Wendell Pierce (*The Wire*) as Vladimir and J. Kyle Manzay juiced the tramps' banter with pulpit and hambone rhythms, and Tanner Rich added *frisson* as Mr. Godot's white messenger (a role he'd played at St. Clement's). Of the flooded set, McElroen said the concept came from "trying to do something different, as opposed to the country road and the tree – which we certainly had, it was just that our road was under water." With "GODOT" chalked on a lower shingled roof near a rupture bashed out from the attic, "the trick was trying not to make it about waiting for FEMA, but just to do the play. Wendell Pierce is from New Orleans; his family lost everything. In addition to our research on Beckett and vaudeville, having Wendell talk about his experiences following [Hurricane] Katrina was invaluable. We sent a letter to Edward Beckett [head of Beckett's estate] explaining our ideas, and sent pictures of the set model. Folks from the estate came, and had positive things to say."

Two sterling productions presented a brace of less familiar radio and television works staged as simulated broadcasts, to comply with estate strictures. At the 92nd Street Y, Harvard's Robert Scanlan directed *Words and Music* and *Cascando*, thorny probes into creativity's disputative sources that include a musical voice, with ... *but the clouds* ... core sampling mournful memory as a sequence of projected images. *Words* and *Cascando*, written for BBC radio commissions in the early 1960s, featured new scores by Martin Pearlman, with Bill Camp cajoling in the former then hitting commanding sonorities in *Cascando*. Scanlan worked with Beckett, who requested that the director report on maverick productions like the 1984 *Endgame* threatened with prosecution because JoAnne Akalaitis's set imposed a derelict subway station ("My advice was just to ignore it, and not make it immortal"); in the mid-1990s, Scanlan simultaneously staged, filmed and projected the television plays *Eh Joe*, *Ghost Trio*, and the exquisite, spare *Nacht und Träume* in Boston and Strasbourg. For the 92Y program, "I wanted to give the impression that, rather than another revival, we could continue chipping away, as Beckett did until the end. He instructed me on how to see. I was astounded by the amount of detail that he wanted. Great artists come along once or twice in a century; with Beckett, it's foolish not to take the instructions he made." Before his death in 1989, Beckett handed Scanlan his final typescript, *Stirrings Still*, "which was a farewell from him – and also to actor David Warrilow," who embodied Beckett's late work and who performed *Stirrings* aware of his own terminal illness.

And in late May at Cherry Lane, Kaliyuga Arts struck theatrical gold with *All That Fall*, the rollicking 1956 radio play set in the Dublin outskirts of Beckett's youth. Helen Calthorpe, as exasperated and bawdy Maddy Rooney, shared twin studio mikes with a raucous succession of characters, then – more than halfway through – Rand Mitchell arrived as Maddy's husband, Dan. By first striking an alerting minor key, then broaching into new comic terrain like Dan's outlandish guffaws with Maddy, Mitchell pointed *Fall* to its unsettling conclusion. At midtown's Cafe Edison, Mitchell said, "the journey Dan takes, between when we first see him and the end, is staggering. He doesn't know what's going to happen. None of us do." Mitchell told of a company that approached Beckett with their take on *Fall*'s ambiguous ending, but "he said, 'I don't want to know,' yet added that the actor who plays Rooney *must* know. That is breathtakingly courageous, to not know what a character of his was actually going to do. I found it the most direct of his plays, for the humor. Laurence Olivier pursued him for years after reading it," as did Ingmar Bergman, but Beckett did not share their urge to stage *Fall*. In radio work, as Mitchell noted, "what you see is what you *hear*."

Mitchell had seen the *Godot* that Monty Hellman (*Two-Lane Blacktop*) directed in Los Angeles in 1959. "I went back seven nights in a row. Monty got that sense of humor and the innate mystery – which is a real reward for being *in* a Beckett play, as well." Beckett's major U.S. director, Alan Schneider, invited Mitchell to develop the legendary evening of *Ohio Impromptu*, *Catastrophe*, and *What Where* with David Warrilow that they toured through the 1980s, including the Jerusalem Festival, "where the dressing rooms were where [Adolf] Eichmann had been placed for his trial." (*What Where* repeats the line "You gave him the works?"; the memory still gives the actor chills.) Mitchell said that Warrilow, "with his exquisitely toned voice, would say that for him, in any Beckett play, it's the [vocal] music that means so much." Regarding Beckett's stage directions, Mitchell felt "there's not one thing that you can do that's going to be better than what he's already said for you to do. If you think of Da Vinci or Rembrandt, or Galileo or Einstein – these people know that what they have to say can't be said any other way."

In New Jersey in March, Two River Theater Company mounted its impressive Beckett Festival. "His birthday coincided with the opening of [TRTC's] new building in Red Bank," said Jonathan Fox, now executive artistic director of the Ensemble Theatre Company in Santa Barbara, California. Fox had directed *Footfalls* while at Columbia University and had found it "one of those beautifully mysterious plays that actually affected people." Hearing of no U.S. centenary festival, he inquired. "We were told that Lincoln Center was going to do it, I heard with the Gate Theatre. I guess it fell through, so we got the rights and decided that it was an important and prestigious thing to do. We had great support from the Beckett estate, and screened *Film* with Barney Rosset's permission, and had a concert reading of *Words and Music*." Two Rivers mounted *Godot* on its main stage, directed by Seth Barrish. "We have a very deep space so the road went on forever and came in through the house as well," Fox said, "so it became this out in the middle of nowhere thing. We opened the short plays in our 60-seat black box theater," with talkbacks after every performance. "By and large, every audience member would stay. The one people responded to most was *Rockaby*. It was a chilling moment when she actually dies. People were gripped by that." Audiences said of the short plays, "they felt they were seeing abstract art on stage." (Rand Mitchell recalled that "the way Alan [Schneider] staged *Ohio Impromptu*, the lighting, the movement, and the color – it was like works of fine art.")

Of the Grove Centenary Editions, Vice President Eric Price said that in the early 1980s, having brought out a twenty-two volume corrected edition, "Grove put the old edition – by accident, apparently – back into paperback, so all those corrections that Beckett had supervised were lost. We'd wanted to do something, but it wasn't until Paul Auster offered to be the general editor that things really started moving." Price hired Laura Lindgren, Barney Rosset's last managing editor before he was ousted at Grove, "and she did an amazing job with assistance from Stan Gontarski." In an email, Lindgren recounted how a too-speedy typist once left lines out of the novel *Molloy*, and how scholar Chris Ackerley resolved textual flaws in *Watt*, which had not been reset after Beckett deleted a poem about Arsene's pet Indian Runner duck ("I never had known why this line was indented this way," Lindgren wrote), while a later, baffling reference to that duck had been left in the text.

Perspectives

Hunter College's Jonathan Kalb felt New York's Beckett centenary participation "was nothing like an artist of his stature deserved. I was in Dublin and there were flags hung from the lampposts with Beckett's picture," he said. Kalb writes on theater for the *New York Times*, where initial editorial enthusiasm led him to speak on Beckett with seventeen playwrights including Paula Vogel, Tony Kushner, and John Guare. Cut to 1300 words, the piece ran with "a giant picture of him." (January 2007's *Performing Arts Journal* published the full interviews.) For Grove's new editions, Kalb contacted the *Times* book editor "and it was the same kind of discussion: 'Why don't you write a thousand words?' On all of Beckett's collected works?! Is it that the public is not really interested? Or is that editors assume the public isn't interested because the editors aren't? Where's the real indifference?"

Kalb found Classical Theatre of Harlem's *Godot* "delightfully silly, with Pozzo and Lucky coming in with a dinghy. The play can bear this kind of thing at this point in its history, and we shouldn't be afraid of trying new things. Besides, if you compare this choice to what JoAnne Akalaitis did so notoriously with *Endgame*, you can see why it works better. The subway setting Doug Stein designed for Akalaitis was huge, about fifty feet wide and thirty feet high, but the swimming pool at CTH was ridiculously and conspicuously diminutive." At CTH, said Kalb, "everybody could see that it was just a little swimming pool, so it didn't call undue attention to the prowess of any designer or director. Quite the opposite: The quality of the actors was also very important. And I loved their physical discomfort, which always works very well with Beckett." Asked if enforced adherence to stage directions diminishes artistic intrigue, Kalb said, "if people feel they can't do something with material that allows them to be creative, they're going to leave it on the shelf. It's an issue for Beckett's posterity, it really is."

Tom Sellar, editor of *Theater* magazine, published by the Yale School of Drama, emphatically shares this concern. At City Bakery, Sellar said young theater comers like Mabou Mines once worked on Beckett and "from that developed an aesthetic precision they then used to do all kinds of original things." But decades later, Sellar insisted, "the possibilities for staging it in fresh ways with the sanctioned stage directions have been exhausted. He's being dropped from the canon of stageable dramatic repertory because the estate is too high-strung. I notice it in teaching at [Yale's] drama school. When I started in the late nineties, students wanted to do the one acts, but I haven't seen a student production of Beckett in a long time. It would be good to see Beckett through advances in stage vocabulary, rather than waiting for another iconic production. He's all about virtuality — what's presence, what's not presence — and if he were alive today with all that electronic media gives us, I'm sure he would be writing plays using digital delay and cell phones — so why not allow that to be integrated?"

Wendell Pierce (left) and J. Kyle Manzay (seated) in Classical Theatre of Harlem's Waiting for Godot. *HSA Theatre, May–June 2006*

Promotional image of Fiona Shaw in director Deborah Warner's Happy Days.
National Theatre, London, January–March 2007

Helen Calthorphe, Rand Mitchell, and cast in Kaliyuga Arts' All That Fall.
Cherry Lane Theatre, May–June 2006

ghostcrab's evening of Beckett shorts. Under St. Marks, November 2006

In October, Martin Harries lectured on his Beckett research at NYU's Ireland House, with fellow scholars Denis Donoghue and John Waters. At an interview near Bryant Park, Harries said that, of the Beckett centenary productions he attended, CTH's awash *Godot* "was the most gripping. One thing that struck me was when Pozzo's blind in the second act and calls for help. That seemed dangerous in a way that it rarely does. He was in danger of *drowning*, right? The contrast between that and the Gate Theatre, where everybody was relaxed, was kind of shocking." Harries' project (tentatively titled *Theater After Film*) concerns "ways that certain people – and I think Beckett is exemplary to this – respond to mass culture and film. Beckett after the war does something very different from what's been done in theater before." Harries cited the later dramas' extreme brevity, and the exacting focus already evident with Winnie's two stock-still acts in *Happy Days*. "From very early on, people were intrigued by film's ability to shift locale with incredible rapidity. The radical locatedness of Beckett's characters may have something to do with that mobility of film. Also, *Play* has that great line, 'Am I so much as being seen?' That meta-theatrical reflection is not unique to Beckett, but Beckett is doing something different than Shakespeare or melodrama did. The presence of the audience that doesn't respond … the Classical Theatre of Harlem harnessed it really well. Pozzo is calling for help and Didi and Gogo have this philosophical reflection on humanitarian intervention. That language did echo the experience viewers had during the Katrina disaster." One response to mass culture may lie in *Play*, where "there's this strange moment where M says, 'Personally I always preferred Lipton's.' Evidently, Lipton was one of the first world brands, and a real pioneer in advertising."

International

London's Royal Court Theatre hosted the centenary's hot ticket, featuring Harold Pinter in ten October performances of *Krapp's Last Tape*. The *Financial Times* declared, "what a supreme master of the visual image" the centenary was showing Beckett to be, adding that none would "prove more haunting" than Pinter at 76 in an electric wheelchair, "looking and listening." The *Times Literary Supplement* questioned the production's alterations; contacted for this piece, Beckett's authorized biographer James Knowlson emailed his unedited response to the *TLS* review. "Beckett had himself already greatly simplified the stage business in his own productions," Knowlson's letter noted of cutting banana pratfalls and an evening hymn ("'He might sing something else but not that,' [Beckett] once said to me"). "The author showed that his relationship with his own text evolved, and one would have to be a dyed-in-the-wool purist to deny the degree of freedom that [director] Ian Rickson and his designers allow themselves."

Ronan McDonald took over directing the Beckett International Foundation from Knowlson, who founded it at the University of Reading in 1988; this January, Cambridge University Press published McDonald's *The Cambridge Introduction to Samuel Beckett*. On the phone, he said, "the main thing we did at Reading was an exhibition called "Samuel Beckett, the Irish European" [Knowlson guided a tour on the author's April birthday]. We had a theater adaptation of the Beckett novella *First Love*, and Larry Held [who Beckett directed in the San Quentin Drama Group] read the text on stage with a park bench. The Beckett Estate is very hesitant about giving permission for adaptations – but there've been a number of stagings of [the brief novel] *Company*, so there isn't total consistency. We also had a gala evening [to benefit Macmillan Cancer Relief] of performances and readings directed by Anthony Minghella that starred Jude Law, Alan Rickman, Lee Evans, and Barry McGovern and Billie Whitelaw."

In an email highlighting events and symposia she attended worldwide, Mary Bryden noted Ankara University's Beckett-Ibsen conference where she read a keynote address, "Ibsen to Beckett via Shaw," as well as the conference she co-organized at Cardiff University, where she teaches, titled "Beckett's Proust/Deleuze's Proust" (Beckett's book-length study of Proust was published in 1931, Gilles Deleuze's in 1964). "Another major event of the year has been the international conference in Tokyo," Bryden wrote, "organized by the Japanese Beckett Circle, entitled 'Borderless Beckett.' On the final day, there was a performance by Noh players of an étude inspired by Beckett's *Quad* [two movement pieces composed for television], a visually compelling performance directed by Kenichi Kasai [who has directed TV serial animes including *Honey and Clover*]. There was also a committed, imaginative performance of Beckett's *Endgame* at the Setagaya Public Theatre, in a new translation by the conference's general director, Professor Minako Okamuro." Bryden also mentioned "an excellent smaller event on 'Beckett and the Thirties,' which was held at the Ecole Normale Supérieure (where Beckett taught English between 1928 and 1930), part of the enormous Beckett Festival in Paris."

Music

After angst and humor, musicality in Beckett garners great acclaim. As the Gate manager rinsed the evening's carrot, Johnny Murphy said, "musicians love this play because it is rhythmical," pinpointing "this sort of rondo: Let's go / We can't / Why not? / We're waiting for Godot / Pause / Let's try something else." Murphy recalled meeting a jazz guitarist friend in a bar after one Dublin show, "and he said, 'Nice one, man. I have nine favorite long playing records, and I just found number ten.'"

Early in *Beckett in Performance*, Jonathan Kalb quotes Billie Whitelaw in D.A. Pennebaker's *Rockaby* documentary, where she declares, "My first task is to find the music of it." "We must take Whitelaw seriously, then," Kalb writes, "when she says she does not read the texts for rational meanings …." Of the through-composed intensity distinguishing Beckett's work, Kalb spotlights Andrei Serban's *Happy Days* production, widely viewed on PBS. "'Music' in this sense, as any good director knows, is not just a matter of sound, it must be understood more broadly as blending into dance and storytelling, including physical movements, bits of information, anything the director must 'conduct.'" Kalb focuses on director Serban's "editing of [Irene] Worth's extraordinary range of physical and vocal mannerisms" – a honing notably absent from the 2004 production at Classic Stage Company starring Lea DeLaria, whose torrential skills became discursive.

The music world has mined Beckett's writing, with composers setting excerpts and entire pieces. The 2006 Paris production of Marcel Mihalovici's 1961 opera *Krapp, ou la dernière bande* was postponed until this year, and Morton Feldman's mid-1970s opera *Neither* for solo soprano was presented in Dublin. (James Knowlson's *Damned to Fame* recounts that at their meeting, asked why he wasn't requesting existing material for the libretto, the composer told Beckett he'd read it all and it didn't need his music.) Holy Cross staged Mihalovici's *Krapp* in Massachusetts, and two Earl Kim pieces setting Beckett fragments were played at an October recital in New York by the Argento Ensemble, whose six-piece lineup opened "Dead Calm" with hurdy-gurdy tocks, then soprano Daisy Press careened through vocal techniques in "Rattling On" ("perhaps I went silent – no, I say that to have something to say"), with the ensemble tracing and diverging from her lines. Clarinetist Carol McGonnell, one of Argento's founders, played her Dublin hometown in April with the Flux Quartet. "We had a concert at the National Gallery and played Feldman and the Philip Glass music for *Company*. Argento also did a Beckett program for the Kilkenny Festival, where the Kim really made it because Irish people know Beckett. Though [Kim's music] is challenging, they have a context for it."

Mary Bryden edited the landmark volume *Beckett and Music*, and spoke from her home in Cardiff of a grant she secured for Rhian Samuel's "The Flowing Sand," based on early poems, which received its March premiere before an audience including Edward Beckett, himself a professional flautist. "Beckett's experience was absolutely steeped in musical references," Bryden said, "and they weren't optional extras. It's the whole aural medium and ambient sound. There are beautiful evocations in *Molloy* [where] he talks about the distant murmur, the bell of the church, the songs of the birds. The narrator in *Malone Dies* even talks about the pains in his back having a tune in them, a rhythm. The Israeli artist Avigdor Arikha says that while he was painting Beckett, they always had music playing – he's often stressed that listening to music was like oxygen to Beckett. Haydn was important, maybe most important was Schubert, but what's often overlooked is that they listened to serialist music like Schoenberg, Berg, and Webern." Bryden's book includes Luciano Berio, Philip Glass, and Everett Frost, producer of the NPR radio play festival that's now available on *Evergreen Review* CDs. Bryden spoke of Gyorgy Kurtag's "What Is the Word" from 1991, which backs Beckett's final text with an alternately cautious and aggressive chamber ensemble. Injured in a crash years before, performer Ildiko Monyok had been mute, and Kurtag "found in her something akin to what he found in Beckett's text: this impassioned search for a word that you can't name, when the singer is trying to get back to speaking again." Bryden concluded that "for me, Feldman is the composer who's come closest to what Beckett's about. The piece I'm fondest of is *For Samuel Beckett* [written in 1987, the year Feldman died]. It doesn't use many colors – Beckett was always saying, 'Too much color' to his actors – and is in that spectrum between black and grey and white, but very beautiful, very sparse."

Future

In January 2007, the Sydney Festival sold out Gate Theatre boss Michael Colgan's world premiere adaptation of *First Love* starring Ralph Fiennes, and presented Barry McGovern's solo *I'll Go On*, and Atom Egoyan's production of *Eh Joe*, for which Charles Dance (*Gosford Park*) stepped in as the aging Joe, taunted by an ex-lover's voice. And in London, the National Theatre premiered thirty-one performances of director Deborah Warner's highly anticipated *Happy Days*. With Fiona Shaw playing Winnie, it was the latest pairing between a team acclaimed as contemporary theater's most fertile and enduring, and Warner and Shaw's latest take on Beckett.

The Beckett estate had turned down Warner's request to do *Godot* with Shaw and Maggie Smith (last year, a court in Rome upheld a Tuscan company's right to cast twin sisters, ruling that the roles remained male), but they agreed to *Happy Days* "so long as Fiona stays in the hole," Warner told the *Guardian*. (Warner declined an interview for this piece.) Her 1994 *Footfalls* at the Garrick in London had been closed for teetering Shaw at the balcony's lip, canceling its Paris run in the most public confrontation since Akalaitis's *Endgame* a decade earlier. Edward Beckett declared that, "the production destroyed the play's timing, atmosphere, the ghostly aspect;" a rampant rumor had Warner banned for life from directing Beckett. Shaw wrote tellingly, in her January 2006 *Guardian* piece on taxing rehearsals at the National, of "the alchemy of Beckett's rhythm, the shift between vacuum and humor," concluding that "one cannot know bits of *Happy Days*; it only works as a whole."

Cambridge University Press publishes the long-awaited first volume of Beckett's letters this year, and in New York at the Paula Cooper Gallery, Robert Wilson opened 2007 with a wall-wide HDTV video portrait of Winona Ryder posed up to one shoulder and her nape as Winnie. January 2008 will find director JoAnne Akalaitis at New York Theatre Workshop with a Beckett program including the two mime pieces, and a cast that features Mikhail Baryshnikov. In the city where recent years have seen Bill Irwin, Marian Seldes, and Alvin Epstein perform Beckett, another kernel may have taken root last November, when ghostcrab's program of shorts, "Beckett Below," ran down abrupt East Village steps. Over Irish coffee with producers Eve Hartmann and Tim Lee, Hartmann termed their efforts "a testing of what we may enact in coming years." She had organized an *Endgame* reading on its author's birthday that Lee attended; he'd directed *Godot* in 2004, but her NYU stage training had barely treated Beckett. They saw *All That Fall* at Cherry Lane and, later that evening, Peter A. Campbell's shorts at the Chocolate Factory in Queens, then approached Campbell about remounting his rapid-fire *Play*.

Hartmann directed *Footfalls* – for which Molly Powell suspended beauty into May's wracked soliloquy, and Ellen Maddow of The Talking Band voiced the Mother – and said, "I've worked on Shakespeare [*Henry V*] and the experience of working on a speech is exceedingly similar to Beckett. You're finding the clues in the sounds of the words, the vowels and the consonants." In selecting his piece, Lee found *That Time* "felt very raw, naked and vulnerable in a way that I had not seen in Beckett." Michael O'Connor's lights radiated Lee's production, casting opulence as actor Milt Angelopoulos eerily opened mouth and eyes in the final silence. "The important part is feeling viscerally the [listening character's] journey – I feel strongly that Beckett is not someone you should feel ashamed if you leave the theater without complete comprehension. He leaves so much room for people to put themselves in to the texts. That's why Beckett polarizes."

"People are either like, 'This is fabulous, I never see Beckett plays,'" Hartmann added, "or I got an email that said, 'Eve, I love you. I hate Beckett. I'll see you in December.' It's cool to do theater that – " " – splits people," Lee reiterated, and then Hartmann resumed the thread. "People want to see them. I don't know why there isn't a Beckett festival every year. There should be."

An early version of this essay appeared in the October 2006 Brooklyn Rail.

Selected Bibliography

Reading

Kalb, Jonathan. *Beckett in Performance*. New York: Cambridge University Press, 1989.

Knowlson, James. *Damned to Fame*. New York: Simon and Schuster, 1996.

Beckett, Samuel. *The Dramatic Works*; *The Grove Centenary Editions*; *Waiting For Godot: A Bilingual Edition*. New York: Grove/Atlantic, Inc. 2006.

Beckett, Samuel. *Samuel Beckett: Shorts* (12 vol. box, or individual). London: John Calder, 1999

Bryden, Mary. *Beckett and Music*. New York: Oxford University Press, 1998.

Fehsenfeld, Martha Dow, and Overbeck, Lois More (editors). *The Letters of Samuel Beckett*. New York: Cambridge University Press, forthcoming in 2007.

Kalb, Jonathan. "American Playwrights on Beckett." *PAJ: A Journal of Performance and Art*. PAJ 85 (Vol. 29, No. 1). Cambridge: The MIT Press, 2007.

McDonald, Ronan. *The Cambridge Introduction to Samuel Beckett*. New York: Cambridge University Press, 2007.

Recordings

DVD: *Beckett on Film* (Ambrose Video)

CD: *The Beckett Festival of Radio Plays* (*Evergreen Review*. *Evergreen* also has Alan Schneider's production of *Waiting for Godot* with Zero Mostel and Burgess Meredith, and the script of the unproduced play, *Eleutheria*)

Morton Feldman, *Neither* (hat[now]art; col legno)
         For Samuel Beckett (cpo; dog w/a bone; hat ART; Kairos)
         Words and Music (Montaigne)

Gyorgy Kurtag, "Samuel Beckett – What Is the Word," (Deutsche Grammaphon)
         "… pas a pas – nulle part … Poemes de Samuel Beckett,"
(ECM New)

Online

"Beckett at Reading 2006": www.beckettfoundation.org.uk

"Fathoms from Anywhere; A Samuel Beckett Centenary Exhibition": hrc.utexas.edu/exhibitions/online/beckett

-- compiled by A. Lockwood

Where Are We and What Are We Doing Here?
Four Books on Theater
by Brook Stowe

No matter in which era of theater we find ourselves at any given time, it seems some other era in the past, vibrantly recalled and greatly lamented, was invariably better. In the 1960s it was the 1930s, in the 1980s it was the 1960s. Now, we're told, it is any time other than the present. If the soothsayers of doom who regularly hold forth upon the pages of the *New York Times*, the *Village Voice* and elsewhere are to be believed, the current state of live theater in New York is apparently perpetually teetering upon the precarious precipice of complete irrelevance and obsolescence. Reflexively, corporate theater institutions in town with annual budgets that could support developing third-world nations launch desperately "hip" marketing campaigns in hopes of snaring that ever-desirable, ever-fickle "18-35 demographic." It is as though – at any moment now – the par cans will dim forever upon houses cold and empty from the West Fifties to TriBeCa. And there will be no more theater in New York City. Because, you see, the theater of today is simply not what it once was. Whatever that was. Once upon a time.

Regardless of the questionable accuracy of the memory of theater past, these sentimental journeys backwards are exercises in near-total futility. What, exactly, are those of us living, creating and experiencing contemporary theater in New York City in 2007 supposed to do with these grim proclamations? Permanently regress into the perpetual high school of Rupert Murdoch's MySpace, producing our art via video clips flung up on YouTube and judging our success by how many "friends" we attract? Or, perhaps we might simply abandon all hope of contemporary experiment and relevance and do nothing but an endlessly cycling repertoire of warmly nostalgic "comfort theater" – Inge, Kaufman, Wilder *et al* – while taking grim refuge in the fantasy that time had stopped forever, somewhere around 1957.

Short of that, the theater of today, the theater of the *now*, is what we have; it is all that we have. As such, it is also who we are, what we are and how we will be remembered by future generations who will undoubtedly think we had it great. We can make of it what we choose – we can dis it, we can pine wistfully for the alleged halcyon days of yore with fixed and misty gaze, but the theater of right now – this moment – is *our* theater. We are in charge of its destiny and we are responsible for it; admittedly, a sobering if not outright terrifying thought. Yet we are not completely alone in the contemporary wilderness, stumbling about in the dark with neither lantern nor compass to help guide us.

If history, with all its unruly tentacles, refuses to conform neatly to the glib "past is prologue" slogan and its numerous variants, a light thrown across history's craggy landscape can reflect back enough to illuminate the present and, perhaps, even a glimpse into the future. Four tomes published in 2006[1] do just that – always diligently, at times brilliantly – reaching back as far as four centuries and as recently as last year to show us that, although the theater of the past is not our theater of today, we are by no means alone and adrift in the present. We are connected to all that has come before, we are inextricably the issue of it, and – despite the cries of the local Chicken Littles – we may not be doing that poorly.

"Where are we and what are we doing here?" critic Robert Brustein cries out in frustration in his review of Daniel Sullivan's Hollywood Stars staging of *Julius Caesar*, on Broadway in 2005. It's a question we might ask of New York theater in 2007 as well. As the world spins ever faster, as MySpace and YouTube and their ever-growing legions of spin-offs and successors help create ever more enveloping fantasy environments, wished identities and isolated parallel universes, where does theater fit in? And what, if anything, does history have to offer us today beyond rose-hued recollections of faded and suspect "better times"? And if the past isn't truly prologue, might it act in the role of consultant? Are there really tangible similarities between the then and the now?

1599

A superpower is mired in a costly and unpopular guerrilla war on foreign soil. A commander slides from favor to ignominy through incompetent failure on the battlefield. A nation lives in fear of imminent attack by foreigners. Censorship is rampant. A playwright navigates the treacherous shoals of a paranoid, reactionary government, constantly balancing the truth of his art upon the realities of commerce and the need to survive, both artistically and literally, through a tumultuous and chaotic year.

The year is 1599 and the playwright is William Shakespeare. In his stately, engrossing *A Year in the Life of William Shakespeare, 1599* author James Shapiro intricately reconstructs a single year in the Bard's life – his 35th – beginning with the pomp and hubristic nationalism lead by the Earl of Essex, bent on crushing the Irish rebellion that brought forth *Henry V*, and concluding

---

[1] *A Year in the Life of William Shakespeare, 1599* was published in late 2005.

with the taxing national fear wrought by both the humiliating failure in Ireland and a much-feared invasion by Spain that produced *Hamlet*. In between, there was *As You Like It*, *Julius Caesar*, and a whole lot of scintillating research and sparkling recounting by Shapiro.

Opening with a prologue that moves with the pace and color of a good novel, Shapiro reconstructs the night in December 1598 when the Chamberlain's Men – a theater company Shakespeare was both resident writer and partner in – arrived at the Curtain theater, their leased base in Shoreditch, to settle a long-festering dispute with their landlord. Their solution? They stole the theater. Quite literally. Working under cover of darkness and heavily armed to confront any who may try to stop them, the cast of the Chamberlain's Men dismantled the Curtain's timbers, lashed them to rafts, and floated them across the Thames to Bankside, where they would become the foundation of the new Globe.

With this prelude, Shapiro sets the tone of how theater was regarded in Elizabethan England – with a near-religious ferocity performers were willing to fight and perhaps die for, and which provided entertainment, education, and often news of current events to a constituency that numbered in the tens of thousands each and every week. Bankside in Southwark was beyond the jurisdiction of the London authorities and Shakespeare's new theater, with its purloined timbers, shared common ground with prostitutes, thieves and such bloodsports as bear-baiting and dog fighting. It was within this "licensed stew" as Puritan preachers referred to the area, that Shakespeare kept his offices and London residence in 1599.

Ensconced in an atmosphere of "freewheeling independence" as Shapiro calls it, Shakespeare wrote no fewer than four plays in this year alone for his new theater. Prior to the advent of intellectual property and well before the protection of copyright, it was a common and fully acceptable practice for playwrights to "ransack" the work of earlier writers, freely lifting large portions of previously written work and incorporating it into their own in egregious acts of appropriation that would these days be regarded as outrageous plagiarism. In 1599, however, theatergoers were expected to keep a running inventory of these previous works into which the new was assimilated, an assumed library of knowledge by an overwhelmingly illiterate populace that far exceeds the grasp expected of contemporary theater audiences. Shakespeare followed this practice most extensively with *Hamlet*, the play he began in the autumn of the year, basically lifting the story from a popular revenge tragedy of the 1580s, also called *Hamlet*, which in turn had been based on a 12th-century saga of a Danish prince named Amleth. "What the Chamberlain's Men did to the (Curtain) Theatre, Shakespeare did to the old play of *Hamlet*," Shapiro writes. "[H]e tore it from its familiar moorings, salvaged its structure, and reassembled something new."

This "something new" caught the tense mood of a country on edge and jittery from a rumored invasion by the Spanish Armada, vanguard of a feared Catholic *coup* against Queen Elizabeth that had provoked paranoia and near hysteria among the populace by summertime (Shapiro doesn't miss the revealing fact that Shakespeare's version opens with two edgy guards standing watch in the uneasy night). With a meticulously controlled blend of research and storytelling, Shapiro reconstructs Shakespeare's writing process as he wrestled with issues of national upheaval and populist politics that had spilled from the taverns and bookstalls of London and out into the streets. "The world had changed," Shapiro observes. "Old certainties were gone, even if new ones had not yet taken hold."

If current events didn't conspire enough to make the Dane uncertain, the "open source" nature of both writing and publication in common practice at the time threatened to send the brooding prince into a state of total confusion. Compounding the fractured status of existing drafts of the play is its wildly truncated and appropriated publication history, which Shapiro details with forensic zeal. In 1603, for example, a road production of *Hamlet* was "cobbled together" from the memory of a single actor in the touring company and sold to London publishers as Shakespeare's own. In a section that is both hilarious and hair-raising (for writers), Shapiro exposes the limits of memory and the veracity of history in a published text where Reynaldo becomes "Montano" and Polonius a chap named "Corambis." What's worse, Hamlet's most famous soliloquy had become disfigured into the following after too many days on the road:

> To be, or not to be. Ay, that's the point.
>
> To die, to sleep. Is that all? Ay, all.
>
> No, to sleep, to dream, aye, marry, there it goes ...

And on from there ever downward; it's every writer's nightmare. The various versions (and hands) sifting together over time and language produced an "incoherent Hamlet that Shakespeare neither wrote nor imagined ... we're left with a Hamlet who is confused – but not the confusion Shakespeare intended."

Hello Americans

"Confusion" may seem an odd choice to define the career of Orson Welles, yet the myriad theories, depictions and recollections of the Boy Wonder of Broadway's blazingly swift ascent followed by his long, slow fizzle into tipsy pitchman for cheap screw-top began well before Welles died in 1985 and continue on unabated today, with each new biography or "exposé" offering up its own blend of speculation and fact, while a definitive portrait persistently eludes all. In other words, the chronicling of Welles' life has become a lot like Welles' chronicling of Charles Foster Kane's in his first and greatest film.

Simon Callow's *Orson Welles, Volume 2: Hello Americans* picks up where his *Road to Xanadu, Volume 1* left off: at the May, 1941 premiere of *Citizen Kane* and the 26-year-old Welles, seemingly on the road to a long and spectacular career in theater and film. As Callow had vividly traced in *Xanadu*, Welles had propelled himself from callow supporting player in Katharine Cornell's touring Shakespearean roadshow company to visionary leader of both bleeding-edge theater (including the groundbreaking "voodoo" *Macbeth* and the politically incendiary *The Cradle Will Rock*, both for Hallie Flanagan Davis' Federal Theatre Project) and radio (the notorious *War of the Worlds* with his own Mercury Theater of the Air) by the sheer force of his gargantuan personality. And all by the time he was 23. In the Spring of 1941, the world did indeed seem to be Welles' oyster, his potential for greatness and for a long and extraordinary career in theater and film assured. Yet, although Welles would continue to work up to his death in 1985, he would never again even approximate the level of creative success that culminated with the release of his first feature film. "What," Callow wonders in his preface, "went wrong after *Citizen Kane?*"

What, indeed. In the 400+ densely-packed pages that follow, Callow begins to answer that question. Welles' epic battles with the philistines of mainstream American (read: "Hollywood") filmmaking are the stuff of pop culture legend already well-documented over the years. However, where biographies such as Barbara Leaming's relentlessly adoring *Orson Welles: A Biography* and Clinton Heylin's petulant, sniping *Despite the System* cast Welles as a noble artist martyred upon the cross of his own high ideals, Callow offers a more nuanced portrait, one in which Welles, while certainly not entirely culpable, was nevertheless complicit in his own long, slow fade to black.

The butchering of Welles' second Hollywood film, *The Magnificent Ambersons*, is legendary both in film lore and in citing how Welles was done wrong by the corporate suits and studio hacks. Callow offers a sympathetic and balanced recounting of this harrowing period, with Welles – dispatched by the U.S. government to South America in early 1942 as a "goodwill" ambassador to help strengthen pan-American solidarity against the Axis – desperately tried to maintain control of the post-production of his film while, a couple thousand miles to the North at RKO in Hollywood, studio butchers were busy dismembering his vision. Callow documents this well while offering additional shading his more partisan biographers had conveniently ignored; namely, how Welles methodically squandered the considerable goodwill he had with RKO by essentially turning a brief film shoot in South America into one long and very expensive bacchanalia, working little while partying to Dionysian excess (Callow suggests that a key motivation for Welles' protracted stay south of the border was to avoid the draft back home).

Whatever his real reasons, Welles might be forgiven this initial transgression. Everything had, after all, gone the Wonder Boy's way up to this point. But when a very similar scenario developed a mere five years later, Welles' cries of foul begin to adopt a rather hollow ring. Having shot his adaptation of *Macbeth* for the "poverty row" Republic Studios in Hollywood on an extremely tight schedule to prove to his many detractors he could indeed stay on schedule and on budget, Welles abruptly abandoned the film in post-production by absconding suddenly to Europe, ostensibly to secure financing for a new project. He feebly offered to edit the film long-distance from Rome, at Republic's considerable expense. The studio declined and eventually cut the film in Los Angeles with contract editors, much to Welles' lasting derision and wistful complaint.

Such is the conundrum and contradiction of Welles the artist. Fueled by chaos (even if it required he create it) and driven to achieve the impossible, Welles would lose interest in projects once they threatened to become predictable and complacent. The next project was always more exciting – the unattainable, the new – infinitely more compelling. Throughout his career, Welles seemed especially drawn to huge, overwrought behemoths destined for spectacular failure (the bloated, lumbering disaster that was Welles' stage production of *Around the World in Eighty Days* being a prime example here, as was the equally doomed *Five Kings*, documented in *Xanadu*). Beginning with the period *Hello Americans* spans – 1941-47 – Welles developed the *modus operandi* that would continue until his death in 1985 – that victimization and failure, rather than success, validated his existence as an artist. As such, his brilliance as envisioned was kept unsullied by the common grime of actual realization.

Yet for all his many faults, Welles was nothing if not a man of fascinating complexities and contradictions. Where he could be a self-centered, monomaniacal, spoiled, screaming brat in his film and theater projects, Callow shows us the less well-known, politically progressive Welles in equal detail: the skilled orator, the passionate newspaper columnist and the ferociously dedicated early champion of civil rights.

On top of an already exhausting array of film and theater projects, Welles in 1945 accepted an offer from the (then progressive) *New York Post* to write no fewer than six columns per week. The *Post* was hoping for insider Hollywood gossip; Welles wanted a soapbox to expound upon his expanding political views. It was not a good match. "[R]ight now, I'm much more interested in politics and foreign affairs than I am in the theater," Welles mused rather airily during this time. "I have set up my life in such a way that I can spend more than occasional time on these interests." Too eclectically fragmented to ever develop a consistent audience, the column was a flop.

More successful was Welles' passionately prescient foray into civil rights. On February 12, 1946, Sgt. Isaac Woodard, freshly discharged from the United States Army, was on a bus home from Augusta, Georgia to Winnsboro, South Carolina. At a stop in Aiken, South Carolina, Sgt. Woodard, still in uniform, made the mistake of asking the driver to wait while he stepped off the use the bathroom. The driver, who was white, told Sgt. Woodard to sit down and shut up. Sgt. Woodard, who was black, persisted. At the next stop, Sgt. Woodard was arrested by the local police and beaten so badly he was permanently blinded. Rebuffed by the War Office in their quest for redress (Sgt. Woodard had been discharged approximately five hours before the beating occurred), members of the National Association for the Advancement of Colored People (NAACP) approached Welles, well-regarded in the African-American community since his groundbreaking *Macbeth* in Harlem in 1936.

The tenacious ferocity with which Welles pursued the case is startling. Adopting a variation of his "Shadow" radio persona of the 1930s, mixed with, as Callow suggests, Inspector Javert from *Les Misérables*, Welles began to devote his weekly fifteen-minute Sunday afternoon national radio program to unmasking the cop responsible for Woodard's savage beating and bringing him to justice.

"We invite you to luxuriate in your secrecy," he intoned on one such show, continuing,

> It will be brief … you're going to be uncovered. We will blast out
> your name. We will blast out your name, your so-called Christian
> name. We will give the world your given name, Officer X … after I
> have found you out, I'll never lose you. If they try you, I'm going to
> watch the trial. If they jail you, I'm going to wait for your first day of
> freedom. You won't be free of me … assume another name and I
> will be careful that the name you would forget is not forgotten …
> you can't get rid of me. We have an appointment, you and I – and
> only death can cancel it.

Due almost solely to Welles' relentless pursuit of the case and the national exposure his radio show provided it, the assaulting cop was identified as Lynwood Lanier Shull, Chief of Police of Batesburg, South Carolina, against whom the Justice Department eventually brought federal charges. The all-white local jury, "forced" as Callow puts it, by the local judge to "discuss their verdict for at least twenty minutes," quickly found Chief Shull not guilty. Commenting on the case some later, Welles remarked,

> We're told that we should cooperate with the authorities. I'm not an anarchist,
> I don't want to overthrow the rule of law. On the contrary, I want to bring the
> policeman *to* law … I'd like it very much if somebody would make a great big
> international organization for the protection of the individual. It would be very
> nice to have that sort of an organization, be nice to have that sort of card. I see
> the card as fitting into the passport … with a border around it in bright colors,

so that it would catch the eyes of the police. And they'd know who they were dealing with ... and it might read something as follows: "This is to certify that the bearer is a member of the human race."

Remaking American Theater

"If artists are not taking the heat, if their reviews are always good, if their patrons are entirely happy, if the politicians are quiet, then the artists have failed their fellow citizens, not just the poor and the outcast, but all their fellow citizens" – Charles Mee
"I am a scavenger. I am not an original thinker and I am not a true creative artist. So the notion of scavenging appeals to me. This is what I do. Like a bird that goes and pulls different things and makes a nest" – Anne Bogart
"My art is just about paying attention – about the extremely dangerous possibility that you might be art" – Bob Rauschenberg

In *Remaking American Theater: Charles Mee, Anne Bogart and the SITI Company*, Scott T. Cummings embarks upon an exhaustive (and, at times, exhausting) dissection of the creative process, the machinations and negotiations within that process and, ultimately, the relationship of said process' issue with the audience.

As the focal point of his study, Cummings chose *bobrauschenbergamerica*, the Charles Mee-Anne Bogart collaboration that premiered in New York in October 2003 as part of the Brooklyn Academy of Music's Next Wave Festival. "[A]ny given moment onstage can be seen to represent the convergence of all time and all space," writes Cummings. "…from the catch in the throat when the lights go down to the gasp of air at the curtain call, [this is] the tipping point on which for a moment all life is balanced." In his introduction, Cummings promises a "close analysis" of the Mee-Bogart collaboration, and to this end he more than succeeds, occasionally to a fault.

Remaking American Theater is divided into two parts. The first serves as a kind of biography-cum-curriculum *vitae* for primary players Mee and Bogart. The second part is a blow-by-blow accounting of the creation of their love child, *bobrauschenbergamerica*, from its conception at the 1997 Rauschenberg Guggenheim retrospective through its birthing at the 2001 Actors Theater of Louisville (ATL) festival to its matriculation at the Brooklyn Academy of Music in 2003. Throughout, Cummings promises that the focus will be "on process," and is it ever.

Charles Mee (aka Chuck Mee, aka so many other *nom de theater* variations author Cummings actually lists them in a prefatory note to the reader), shared with Bogart hard-learned lessons about "the fragility of all life." For Mee, it was contracting polio at age 14 that very nearly killed him; for

Bogart, it was a battle with breast cancer. Mee was a historian prior to turning to playwriting; Bogart well-versed in site-specific guerrilla theater upon the mean streets of New York City in the 1970s and 80s. Cummings deftly weaves the separate mini-bio strands of Mee and Bogart together into their first collaboration, *Another Person in a Foreign Country*, which producer Anne Hamburger staged in a (then) derelict abandoned building on Manhattan's Upper West Side. Drawing upon his own physical disability wrought by polio, Mee created in *Another Person* a "multi-cultural freak show" of Other-ness, those who by choice or otherwise fall without the "norm" of Caucasian (male) heterosexuality. Described in one review as "*A Chorus Line* for people who can't get an audition," *Another Person*'s cast included four blind singers with guide dogs; a rock band made up of residents of a Long Island psychiatric halfway house; a 2' 10" "tiny woman" from New Jersey; a tall, blond transvestite named Ethyl, and an elderly resident from a retirement home down the street who wandered into a rehearsal one night and stayed around. These "found" people, cast-offs and detritus from "normal" society interacting in a crumbling, derelict NYC structure, laid the foundation for subsequent Bogart-Mee collaborations, including SITI's maiden voyage, *Orestes*, the following year, and that which comprises the second part of Cummings' book, the making of *bobrauschenbergamerica*.

The "found" art of Bob Rauschenberg provided the ideal premise for a Bogart-Mee theatrical collaboration. Scavenged from the "back alleys and junk shops of New York" from the mid-1950s onward, Rauschenberg's works combined the personal with the collective through a library of society's detritus. Rauschenberg (whose birth name was Milton Ernest; the "Bob" came later) was himself an early dabbler in performance art. Cummings briefly recounts an early installation performance at Black Mountain College in the summer of 1952 that featured Merce Cunningham (improvising movement while followed about by a dog), John Cage (reading aloud from atop a step ladder) and Rauschenberg, spinning Edith Piaf acetates on an old Victrola set at the wrong speed, a collaborative compilation that created ominous pre-echoes of such contemporary performers as the Wooster Group, Collapsable Giraffe and Radiohole.

When Mee saw the Rauschenberg retrospective at the Guggenheim in 1997, he became intrigued by the possibility of a "collage" approach to playmaking, specifically, a theatrical interpretation of Rauschenberg's "whimsical" and expansive vision of the USA. Mee's pitch to Bogart of this idea and their resultant collaboration fills the second part of Cummings' book. While this showcases Cummings' estimable tenacity and stamina as a theater researcher, it may ultimately drive all but the most ardently arcane scholar for cover, or at least to skimming, from the sheer cumulative avalanche of minutiae. This is not said to denigrate Cummings' devotion to detail in any way; his commitment to his subject is both admirable and foreshadowed in his introduction, where he makes it clear that "if I focus on minutiae at moments, it is because theatrical truth dwells in the details – the choice of a word, the turn of a foot, the timing of a fade – and because any given moment onstage can be seen to represent the convergence of all time and all space."

This may well be true, and Cummings is nothing if not true to his word here, but – as every performance has its audience, every book has its reader, and there is only so much both can reasonably be expected to absorb, however forthright and noble the intent. Indeed, the bulk of Cummings' tracking of the gestation of *bobrauschenbergamerica* – primarily spanning the beginning of "serious" work on the project in April 2000 through its March 2001 world premiere at the ATL's Humana Festival – is incisive, necessary and often very entertaining in Cummings' fly-on-the-wall writing persona. Occasionally, however, the project gets swept into a whirlpool of TMI – Too Much Information – leaving the reader dizzy if not disoriented by the towering mountain of relentless detail Cummings asks us to scale. Indicative of this is the name-by-name dissection of Mee's 56-part draft of early 2001, and – in Cummings' *piece de resistance* that is simultaneously admirable and exhausting – a beat-by-beat analysis of the Humana Festival debut that goes on – interrupted by only two pages of photos – for fifteen unbroken, small-fonted pages.

Ultimately, what does all of this mean? When the last light has been switched off and the final analysis made, to what extent has *bobrauschenbergamerica* actually "remade" American theater? With the number of experimental theater artists and groups such as Radiohole, the Wooster Group, the National Theater of the USA, Theater of the Two-Headed Calf, ERS, Big Art Group, Collapsable Giraffe and Richard Foreman producing regularly in New York City alone, it seems as though *bobrauschenbergamerica*, with its "experiences of freedom, with the limitless possibilities of boyhood and a youthful spirit of adventure" serves more to reconnect its audience to the essential spirit of being American than to forge any pioneering theatrical pathways in millennial theater. Along the journey, Mee's typically fragmented, collage-like structure challenges the viewer to fill in the gaps left intentionally open, to speculate upon the spaces between images, objects, bodies, words. In so doing, Mee and Bogart enable the audience to become active participants in their creation, rather than passive spectators. By creating "open-ended blueprints for theatrical free-for-alls," Mee and Bogart ask the informed contemporary audience to draw upon a collective national and cultural history much as Shakespeare called upon his to draw upon the shared history of *Hamlet*.

Almost as a reluctant postscript, Cummings acknowledges the third party to this creator-audience *ménage à trois* – the critics; specifically, the critical reception to *bobrauschenbergamerica*'s ATL debut in 2001. Understandably having surrendered any claim to objectivity through such a protracted and intense association with the work in question, Cummings nevertheless singles out the sole "negative" review (a "cynical analysis") for a rather peevish rebuttal while allowing the numerous accolades cited to stream past in a parade of adoring pull quotes. In so doing, Cummings transforms into more a member of the production and less the objective analyst, while begging the question ...

Millennial Stages

Do critics even matter? The short answer is, if they write like Robert Brustein, "yes." The longer answer may be found in *Millennial Stages: Essays and Reviews 2001-2005*, Brustein's collection of (mostly) post-9/11 musings on the state of (mostly) New York City theater.

Brustein may be most familiar to the current generation of theater makers and goers as the guy who mixed it up with August Wilson in a "discussion" at NYC's Town Hall in January 1997 over the merits of integrating (Brustein) or segregating (Wilson) African-American theater into the cultural mainstream.[2]

Where Brustein succeeds most as a critic – compared to, say, Frank Rich, the last theater scribe with New York's "paper of record" who came anywhere near Brustein's depth and insight – is his consistent ability to resist imposing his own ego upon his writing at the expense of his subject. Though his personal tastes necessarily inform and influence his critical vision, Brustein as a critic seems to have little interest in constantly reminding the reader that his own personality is the real subject of any given piece, a nearly lost art in today's vast critical wasteland. Although a few lonely beacons of informed, incisive theater criticism remain burning bravely in New York – Alexis Soloski, for one, soldiers admirably on against an ever-shrinking word count at the *Village Voice* – Brustein's consistent clarity and focus upon his subject rather than himself only makes more obvious the rank pool of sludge presently passing for "A-list" theater criticism in New York. From the starstruck gushing of Ben Brantley and petulant preening of Charles Isherwood currently cluttering the *Times* to the increasingly curmudgeonly crankiness of the *Voice*'s estimable Michael Feingold, "old media" criticism is indeed a mere ghost of what it once was. In this instance, the past truly rules, due in no small part to the sad fact that contemporary "critics" have either lost sight of or cast aside a basic tenet of the discipline.

---

[2] Believe it or not, this fierce, passionately partisan exchange originally sprang from the pages of *American Theatre* magazine. It is difficult – if not outright impossible – to imagine such real conflict and actual debate about contemporary theater smudging the slick, smiley-faced corporate gloss that is the *American Theatre* of today.

"Theater criticism cannot simply be the shrill expression of a disgruntled voice railing in the wilderness," Brustein cautions. "It has to recognize, endorse and advance the possibilities of renewal. Without this, criticism becomes simply another mode of performance, and the critic just another actor gesticulating in the void."

Although *Millennial Stages* does have token international scope (portions of one section pay brief homage to Australia and South Africa), the book is really about theater in New York City, and the range is impressively wide and inclusive. Reviews move from the unfortunate "Hollywood" production of *Julius Caesar* (starring Denzel Washington and lesser movie multiplex attractions) at the Belasco to the revival of *The Producers* on Broadway to Suzan-Lori Parks' *Topdog/Underdog* at the Public. Playwrights included are equally wide-ranging as well, from Ms. Parks to George Kaufman to a remembrance of Arthur Miller.

At the heart of *Millennial Stages* lies an area of discussion too few critics spend too little time discussing; namely, does what they do matter? The reply to the vast majority of TV-bred hacks currently fronting as theater "critics" in New York would be a swift and decisive, "no." All the more reason for most not to probe this question too deeply.

Yet this is a topic that engages Brustein to the point of fascination, both with its current state of perceived atrophy (his), and with the possibilities for renewal: the concept that legitimate theater criticism does have a place in the ongoing dialectic between performer and audience, audience and performer. In the delightfully titled, "When Dramaturgs Ruled the Earth," Brustein laments the passing of the "golden age" of theater criticism in New York – an age he assigns to the 1950s and 1960s – during which the City had no fewer than four daily newspapers regularly reviewing; the "Arts and Leisure" section of the *New York Times* was still known simply as "Theater;" George Jean Nathan was still at *Esquire* and the *New Yorker* offered more than the murky meanderings of Hilton Als. This essay – from 2003 – seems now both recent and ancient, as it pre-dates the rise of the vibrant, informed and at times – yes! – combative blogging on NYC theater that exists in the ethernet today. Recalling his earlier, "Where Are the Repertory Critics?" from an earlier era, Brustein remembers that, "I called for a new kind of critical mind capable of recognizing that a resident theater is not a show shop manufacturing hits and flops but rather a living organism of artists developing alongside audiences." In the past three to four years, NYC theater blogs helmed by such informed and engaged critical minds as George Hunka (www.ghunka.com), Garrett Eisler (www.playgoer.com), David Cote (histriomastix.typepad.com/weblog), Jason Grote (jasongrote.blogspot.com) and Isaac Butler (parabasis.typepad.com), among others, have more than risen to the challenge of filling the void left by the decline of the *Voice* and the general disengagement of the *Times*, forming a strong legion of questioning yet supportive new media "repertory critics" for contemporary progressive alternative theater in the City. An interesting sequel to the "Dramaturgs" essay might be, "When Bloggers Recharged the City." Perhaps that will be a part of what would be a most welcome sequel to *Millennial Stages*: *"2006-2010."*

Where Are We and What Are We Doing Here?

As all four of these volumes demonstrate, each in its own way and each through its own subject(s), theater is nothing if not a malleable art form. No form could survive 2500+ years still fundamentally adhering to Aristotle's "poetical" construct and be anything but. Because it is a "living organism," as Brustein notes, it does require occasional care and feeding. Shakespeare's struggles with his early drafts of *Hamlet* in late 1599 (itself, as noted, the reworking of an even earlier *Hamlet*), become the Wooster Group's *Hamlet* (deconstructed in the Wooster's unique way from a 1964 Richard Burton telecine) in 2007 Brooklyn, and a direct line over the 400 years between them can be traced connecting the two. As James Shapiro points out in *1599*, "Shakespeare didn't write 'as if from another planet,' as Coleridge put it: he wrote for the Globe; it wasn't in his mind's eye, or even on the page, but in the aptly named theater where his plays came to life and mattered."

Where are we in 2007? New York theater today is not the theater of Shakespeare's London any more than it is the theater of Orson Welles' 1940s New York, or even Anne Bogart's as recently as the 1980s. Nor should it try or even want to be. Yet contemporary theater is informed and influenced by all of these movements and artists, all of these times, all of the successes and miserable failures that have come before. From this lineage comes not imitation and mimicry, but rather the new forged from the old. What are we doing here? We are creating and performing new theater – *our* theater – the millennial theater of the now, this moment, tonight. Every night, in places like the Culture Project, Performance Space 122, Theater for the New City, the Kitchen, the Brick, HERE Arts Center, LaMaMa ETC, the Ohio, the Collapsable Hole and so many more in Brooklyn, Manhattan and in Queens, plays still come to life, just as they did on the outlaw banks of the Thames 408 years ago. And, yes, they do still very much matter.

Books Reviewed

Brustein, Robert. *Millennial Stages: Essays and Reviews 2001-2005*. New Haven: Yale University Press, 2006.

Callow, Simon. *Orson Welles: Volume 2: Hello Americans*. New York: Viking, 2006.

Cummings, Scott. *Remaking American Theater: Charles Mee, Anne Bogart and the SITI Company*. New York: Cambridge University Press, 2006.

Shapiro, James. *A Year in the Life of William Shakespeare, 1599*. New York: HarperCollins, 2005.

*P*lays

Addicted to Longing

An Introduction to Adam Szymkowicz's *Food for Fish*
by Crystal Skillman

In an interview for the Brooklyn *Rail*, playwright Sheila Callaghan asked Adam Szymkowicz why he writes plays. He answered, "I can't stop. I sort of am addicted to it." This is good, because it is Adam's addiction to writing such obsessive, detailed characters that makes seeing his plays such an addiction for us.

When you read Adam's descriptions of his plays you feel as if you have just read a Mad-lib, a series of events that can't possibly make sense. Cruise his website and you'll see what I'm talking about:

Adam's description of *Pretty Theft*, the play that impressed Christopher Durang and Marsha Norman so much that he was accepted into the Juilliard playwrights' program, reads: "An autistic man obsessed with ballerinas. A kidnapper. A waitress. Two girls in a stolen car running from a funeral and some unpleasantness in a group home."

In *Incendiary*, a pyromaniac fire chief falls in love with the detective investigating her fires; *Deflowering Waldo* tells the story of a "24-year-old ultra-phobic-virgin" and *Food for Fish*, the play you're about to embark upon, brings together "three sisters of different obsessions: a stalker-like reporter, an agoraphobe (played by a man in drag), and a scientist with a plan to isolate and eliminate the gene for love."

Sitting in the theater watching Adam's plays is like playing a game of Twister where the spinner just keeps spinning. Where you'll land next, you never know. These are wild worlds and bizarre territories that you are diving into, so be forewarned. Adam's plays are brought to life with great theatrical imagination. Loneliness accented by awkward dances with ballerinas, humiliation demonstrated as an ex-girlfriend puppet walks out of a flashback on its own, blazing infernos of mismatched affection.

But what makes all of this work so unusually good?

It all makes perfect sense.

Adam understands that humor comes not simply from the idea of these absurd events but from the fact that they are grounded, they are indeed really happening. And even though Adam's characters are pretty eccentric, they are worried, just as we would be, about all the details. How they add up, what they mean, and how they can go on knowing what they know.

The seemingly little things: a kiss, a daydream, a burial of sorts.

As a result, these eccentric characters placed in impossible situations become much more than whimsical tales or funny stories. They become genuinely heartbreaking in an unsentimental, down-to-earth way.

I knew Adam personally but wasn't familiar with his work until we were both published in the same 2004 edition of *Poems and Plays*. Adam's short play, *Save*, about a young poet faced with the crisis of her mother discovering who her daughter really is, exhibited a real desire to challenge conventional structure and covered a lot of ground for a two page play.

In the summer of 2006, I got to know Adam's work more intimately. As Sanctuary Playwrights Theatre was preparing to debut *Food for Fish* here in NYC, Adam's play *Nerve*, produced by Packawallop Productions and Hypothetical Theatre Company, opened off-Off-Broadway. The description of *Nerve* may be deceivingly simple: "a play about falling into a relationship on a first date." But while I was watching this production, it became all too clear that this was one date where every minute of stage time advantages a relationship that normally would take years to span, with hysterical and disturbing results.

Now, as I have had the opportunity to see more of Adam's work, I am struck by how his characters are endlessly searching to "put it together." Adam invites us to hear these characters' inner thoughts in inventive ways that allow us to connect with them deeply. Like us, these people are really trying to come to terms with their own addictions and obsessions, many times failing. Like us, they often find themselves lost. Confused. Full of longing.

Remind you of someone else's characters? The three sisters in *Food for Fish* are indeed from the world of Chekhov's play, attempting, after having lost their father, to live in the world their parents created. And it is here that they become nothing like Chekhov's play. In Adam's play, the sisters have a whole new set of obsessions and are struggling to survive in a very modern America. Going outside is dangerous, dating is a nightmare, and burying father? For now, it's much easier to keep him around. After all, his coffin has become the coffee table.

Enter Bobbie, the Konstantin from the world of *The Seagull* and you have another lost soul in the fray. Bobbie can't stop writing. He is, of course, addicted. And it is a bit of a curse for him, rejection after rejection, as we learn from one of the most side-splitting scenes of the play. So what does he seek? Kisses. Love from strangers under streetlights. And, of course, longing for something more every step of the way.

Perhaps it is this longing that grounds the absurdity so well. One of my favorite moments in *Food for Fish* is when Barbara asks her husband Dexter, "Why don't you ever long?" It's a question that plagues Dexter throughout the play and is essential to their relationship, which has all sorts of problems. To begin with, Barbara is played by a man and Dexter is played by a woman, which perfectly pinpoints their at-odds marriage.

Certainly, *Food for Fish* is "loosely inspired" by the longing explored in Chekhov's *Three Sisters* and all of the attempted relationships seem to spring from this. But very quickly the play becomes its own piece, leading us into an unpredictable maze of twists and turns, guided by the play's narrator Bobbie, a struggling novelist who is dropping pages of his novel into the Hudson River. The story is what we are watching, as only he can convey it from start to finish. But try as he might, the story is not in his hands. In effect, we enter through the cracks of the very story Bobbie is attempting to tell.

This is another reason why Adam's plays are so addictive. They need us. They demand for us to hear them, become a part of them. These characters have, after all, confided their most private moments to us, almost as if they were seeking our advice, our own response. Through Bobbie's story in *Food for Fish*, we are invited to see these characters' inner fantasies and fears. We watch them grow and change, some in more positive ways than others. But still, they are all putting it together, figuring out just who exactly they are and how they will move on.

Sitting in the back row at Sanctuary Theatre's production of *Food for Fish* at the Kraine Theatre on East 4th Street, I felt that the audience was quite moved by this; they felt very connected to these characters, deeply invested in the lives they were witnessing unfolding before them. Lost in the story and in adding it up for themselves. Addicted.

But why?

Because not only is the story important, but how the playwright chooses to tell the story theatrically. Adam takes this notion very seriously and does so with such skill that you don't know what will happen next. His plays have you leaving the theater with your head spinning. You're walking down the street, putting together the twists and turns when you realize that all these little details, these obsessive, addictive behaviors all add up. And what once seemed so absurd, strange and bizarre now seems inevitable and has found its place in the world.

And in some inexplicable way, you feel suddenly that you have, too.

FOOD FOR FISH

by Adam Szymkowicz

For Kristen

and

In memory of Franklin S. Gross

Special thanks to Alexis, Bagel, Sanctuary, and the very talented group of designers, cast, and crew, Shaun Rance for the postcards, Ron Lasko for publicity, Dyana Kimball, Ruth Kreshka, Tom Gilmore, Scott Ebersold and Packawallop Productions. I would also like to thank the actors who helped me by performing in readings of the play, especially Elizabeth Tidy, Clancy O'Connor, Ben Davis, Anna O'Donaghue, Jessica Love, Pilar Witherspoon, Ravenna Fahey, Heidi Schreck and Gideon Banner. I am grateful to Chris Durang and Marsha Norman and the playwrights at Juilliard, Tommy Smith, Jessica Provenz, Ben Snyder, Zina Camblin, Kara Corthron, Brian Tucker and Bash Doran for their dramaturgical help and my writing group for the same: Devan Sipher, Frank Basloe, Stacey Luftig, Stephen Gaydos. I also owe debts to Joe Kraemer, Richard Feldman, Pat McLaughlin, Kristen Palmer, Larry Kunofsky, Sheila Callaghan, Jason Grote, Crystal Skillman, Bradford Louryk, Brook Stowe, Floyd Britchcraft, Gary Winter, Emily DeVoti, John and Rhoda Szymkowicz, Bonnie Peters, Sharon Steflik, and the folks at the Columbia Journalism School who think this play is about them. Apologies to Chekhov.

FOOD FOR FISH

Food for Fish received its premiere at the Kraine Theatre in New York City on July 6, 2006. It was produced by Sanctuary Playwrights Theatre (Bob Jude Ferrante, Managing Director and Philip Hopkins, Programs Director). It was directed by Alexis Poledouris; the set design was by Zane Pihlstrom; the lighting design was by Gina Scherr; the music and sound design was by Robert Quillen Camp; the sound board operator was Jonathan Roche; the costume design was by Chris Rumery; and the production stage manager was B. Carter Edwards. The cast was as follows:

BOBBIE...Orion Taraban
BARBARA/JAMES..Luis Moreno
ALICE...Ana Perea
SYLVIA/ARTHUR..Anna Hopkins
DEXTER...Katie Honaker
SASHA/WOMAN/WAITRESS/ASSISTANT/FRED/ED..............
....Caroline Tamas

CAST OF CHARACTERS:

BOBBIE, a boy

BARBARA, a woman played by a man in drag

ALICE, a woman, sister to Barbara and Sylvia

SYLVIA, a young woman, sister to Alice and Barbara

DEXTER, a man, husband to Barbara, played by a woman in drag

SASHA, a woman

WOMAN – played by the actress who plays SASHA

WAITRESS – played by actress who plays SASHA

ASSISTANT – played by the actress who plays SASHA

FRED – played as a man by the actress who plays SASHA

ARTHUR – played as a man by the actress who plays SYLVIA

ED – played as a man by the actress who plays SASHA

JAMES – played as a man by the actor who plays BARBARA

Note: I like to think this play lends itself to multi-cultural casting and I support the attempt to always use the best possible actor for each part. To this end, the three sisters need not look like they are related by blood in order to be accepted as sisters.

As for the cross-dressing, it should be readily apparent the actor playing Barbara is a man and that the actress playing Dexter is a woman. However, if done right we will periodically forget this as we watch the play. I suggest fake moustaches for women playing men whenever possible, so there is never a doubt in the audience's mind whether or not a character is supposed to be a man or woman.

TIME
The present.

SETTING
New York City. Bobbie's apartment, the apartment of the three sisters, Alice's lab, Dexter's office, a Restaurant, the Street. These can be suggested minimally. At the start of the play, Bobbie's apartment, represented by a desk, is upstage left. The apartment of the three sisters, represented by a coffin is downstage right. I suggest space be used flexibly but that we keep coming back to these two bases of operation.

FOOD FOR FISH

by Adam Szymkowicz

ACT ONE

PROLOGUE

(Lights rise on BOBBIE's mostly-empty apartment.

(BOBBIE sits at the desk, in front of an old manual typewriter. A half-drunk beer sits on the desk beside the typewriter. He places a fresh sheet of paper in the typewriter and begins to type.)

BOBBIE

This is the story of the boy. This is the story of the man the boy could have become. This is the story of the three sisters, Barbara, Alice and Sylvia. This is not the story of the gravedigger, who is the father of the three sisters or of his wife, the poet, who died young. This is my story.

When you have visions that beat at your brains while other people are talking. When you hear non-stop streams of screams. When synapses pop or won't stop crackling, and when blood pumps, and the pounding don't stop pounding. Then you look for an exit to start the ending or search sideways in vain to extract a distraction, but even then, what will curls of hair give to you, hips and breasts, lips sip out of you, in a moment, distract what abstraction pounds- pounds 'til you steal . . . a kiss.

I dress in haste, pull the hood on my head and I take to the street, boot in front of boot to find her. Who will she be tonight?

Last night she was brunette, blue-lipped and serious, mouth curled around a tiny white smokestack, long leopard-fur coat collecting snowflakes on its tips. When she stopped in the streetlamp, I was there. I was a boy and she was not afraid. She took a drag and I took her lips and all her smoke and sadness drained into me. She gasped in the kiss and the snow fell on her lashes. When she opened her eyes, I was gone.

That night I took my silver pen knife from the drawer of my desk – the only furniture I own. I opened the blade, splayed my left hand on the desk and stabbed myself with the right.

(BOBBIE stops typing.)

BOBBIE
No! No! NO! That's not right. No one would do that. It's so fucking stupid.
It's so fucking . . .

*(BOBBIE stops himself, takes out a knife, and stabs himself in the hand. He yells
out in pain.)*

BOBBIE
Ahhhhh!

1.

*(Lights up on the living room of the apartment the three sisters share. BOBBIE in
his apartment, bandages his hand during this scene. When it is bandaged he
continues typing over the scene.*

*(A coffin sits prominently in the sister's apartment. BARBARA sits beside it.
ALICE is reading a scientific journal and making notes. SYLVIA is reading a
newspaper.)*

BARBARA
It's been a year since Father died. When Mother died, I was only seven and
three quarters but I had to become the mother to you both as well as
your older sister. Did I do right by you? I tried, you know.

I had to learn how to be a woman from television. "One Life to Live," "Days
of Our Lives," "All My Children," "General Hospital," "Daylight Menagerie,"
"Passionate Embrace," "Dallas" and the magazines of course. I skipped
Seventeen and went straight to *Mademoiselle, Ms., Playgirl, Good Housekeeping, Home
and Garden, House and Kitchen, Modern Woman, Lady of Leisure.* I stayed home like
a mother would and studied, catalogued every gesture and practiced-practiced to
be an adult so that you didn't have to. Then when you came home I would
show you what I had learned and you would smile. Because I had kept you
from the pain and from the responsibility of being a woman.

Now that Poppa is dead I must learn to be a father to you as well. I watch my
husband carefully to see if he is the right model. He must be firm yet flexible,
strong yet not afraid to show weakness, quiet and reserved, yet emotional and
expressive. He must be bold. He must be vulnerable. He must not be afraid to
(MORE)

76

BARBARA (cont.)

show fear or to cry in front of others. He must not be a sissy. He must work all day and then come home and then he must take out the trash. He must give orders and take suggestions. He must do as I say but never be influenced by exterior forces. The leader of the house, and of course, my servant. In short he must be a man, the new man--like Father was and like Father would be still if only . . .

Do you remember a year ago today? Father fell asleep watching Fox news and didn't wake up. There was a panic of course and the shock and the sorrow eventually.

ALICE

We should bury him.

BARBARA

What?

ALICE

The neighbors are beginning to complain about the smell.

BARBARA

I'll open the window again if it means that much to you. I just can't bear the thought of someone else doing his job. What would he think, to have some other gravedigger bury him? You know how much time he spent getting the heavy machinery license.

ALICE

He wouldn't care. It was just a hobby. He just liked the digging . . . and the dirt.

BARBARA

Well, I can't bear the thought.

ALICE

We could cremate him.

BARBARA

No, No, No.

ALICE

Poppa always said there was a time for burying.

BARBARA

That time has not yet come.

ALICE

Sylvia, don't you think it's time we buried Poppa?

BARBARA
(an explosion)

WE'RE NOT BURYING HIM!

(Pause.)

SYLVIA
(looking up from her newspaper)

Listen to this.
(reads)
Manhattan – an unidentified boy described as in his teens or twenties has been stealing kisses from women all over the city.

(A streetlamp comes on. A WOMAN stands under it.)

SYLVIA

This young Casanova has been spotted on numerous occasions in various Manhattan neighborhoods under streetlamps and bridges, on corners and down alleys where he is said to be kissing women much older than he.

(BOBBIE sees the WOMAN under the streetlamp. He approaches, carrying a typewriter case in one hand. She is looking around, confused.)

SYLVIA

Officer Edward Feeney of the NYPD described his modus operandi as such: "He finds women walking alone, stops them and kisses them."

WOMAN
(approaching BOBBIE)

Excuse me, do you know where Delancey Street is?

SYLVIA

None of the smooched ladies can remember the boy having said anything either before or after the smacker.

(BOBBIE kisses the WOMAN quickly. She gets weak at the knees. When she opens her eyes after the kiss, BOBBIE has disappeared.)

SYLVIA

No charges have been filed as of yet and at least one of the women claimed to have enjoyed the smooch. "It cheered me up, actually. God knows it's been a hard week," said Phillis Grumpert of Park Avenue West.

(The streetlamp goes off. BOBBIE returns to his typing.)

SYLVIA

Blah blah blah . . .blah blah. There's an artist sketch.

(She shows her sisters.)

BARBARA

He's probably a murderer.

SYLVIA

He's not a murderer. He's a kisser.

BARBARA

What? Murderers can't kiss?

ALICE
(handing back newspaper)

Very nice.

SYLVIA

I'm going to write an article about him and I'm going to sell it. To the *New York Times*.

ALICE

Good.

BARBARA

What do you mean, good? In case you've forgotten, there's killers out there killing attractive young girls. What is Sylvia? An attractive young girl. I don't want you going out at night looking for some kissing boy.

SYLVIA

I'm twenty-two years old.

BARBARA

So?

SYLVIA

I'm not a child.

ALICE

She's not a child.

BARBARA

It doesn't matter. There are killers out there.

ALICE

Everyone has the potential to be a killer. Perhaps what you are afraid of is in fact yourself.

BARBARA

That's just not true.

ALICE

We are all killers. If not in the ordinary sense, you must admit each of us has darknesses. We all kill off parts of ourselves to protect ourselves. We kill our ego. We kill our self confidence.

SYLVIA
(lighting a cigarette)
We kill our souls with cigarettes and junk TV.

BARBARA

Sometimes you are both so stupid I can't even talk to you.
(Pause, nicer.)
I just don't want you to be hacked to death because of this journalism hobby of yours, that's all.

SYLVIA

It's not a hobby.

BARBARA

I've heard that one before.

SYLVIA

It's not a hobby.

ALICE

She says it's not a hobby.

BARBARA

It must be a crush then.

ALICE

(teasing)

I think our Sylvia is smitten.

SYLVIA

Stop it.

ALICE

Our Sylvia is taken with the artist's rendition.

BARBARA

You haven't even met him yet.

SYLVIA

Stop it. It's not funny. Just stop it.

ALICE

Yes, yes I will stop. I've grown cold. New York brings it out in me. You know if we were only in New Jersey now . . .

BARBARA

The Jersey we grew up in.

SYLVIA

The Jersey we were born in.

ALICE

We must to New Jersey. I of course enjoy New York like anyone would. The noise and the barrage of people. The subway smells. It is of course, as we all know, a good place to have a crush.

SYLVIA

Stop it.

ALICE

No one can deny New York is a good place for one to work in a lab at a university studying and isolating genes to enrich the knowledge of the world. I truly enjoy working here – where else? But I want to go to Jersey.

BARBARA

To Jersey.

                                    SYLVIA

To Jersey.

              (*A pause, then –*)

                                    SYLVIA
                                (getting up)
I have to go finish my article on the lipsticks of today.

              (*DEXTER enters in a suit and tie. He is a large man, if not in stature, then in
              personality.*)

                                    DEXTER

Morning!

                                    SYLVIA

Morning, Dexter.

              (*SYLVIA exits.*)

                                    ALICE

Good morning!

                                    BARBARA

Morning, husband.

                                    DEXTER
Morning, wife. You're looking especially delicious this morning.

                                    ALICE

How do I look?

                                    DEXTER
                                (dismissive)
Fine. Have either of you seen a red folder?   It's very important.

                                    BARBARA

No . . . no.

                                    ALICE

I can look for it.

              (*ALICE begins to look around.*)

DEXTER

No, no. I'm already late. Ta-ta, darling.

BARBARA

Before you go –

DEXTER

What's that?

BARBARA

I would like to speak to you a moment before you go.

DEXTER

I have literally seconds before I must depart.

BARBARA

I just wanted to ask …

DEXTER

Yes? Out with it woman.

BARBARA

Have you had the chance to speak to your boss yet about that promotion . . . yet.

DEXTER

Oh, yes. The promotion. I'll have to remember to bring that up. Just been so busy in the office but of course, yes, I will speak to my boss immediately about it, if not sooner.

BARBARA

I don't mean to keep bringing it up.

DEXTER

Nonsense. Nonsense. Well, I must be off.

BARBARA

Wait.

DEXTER

I really must go.

BARBARA

Wait.
    (Pause.)
Why don't you ever long?

DEXTER

Long?

BARBARA

Look at Alice, look at Sylvia. All of us are always longing. Why are you never longing?

DEXTER

Um ... I don't know.

BARBARA

I wish you would.

DEXTER

I'll try it for you, OK?

BARBARA

It would really help.

DEXTER

Now I really have to go.

BARBARA

Bye, lover!

    (DEXTER kisses BARBARA, nods to ALICE and exits.)

BARBARA

What?

ALICE

What?

BARBARA

Don't look at me like that.

ALICE

I'm not.

BARBARA

I didn't do anything.

SYLVIA
(entering)

What's another word for emasculation?

ALICE
(to SYLVIA)

This is for your lipstick article?

SYLVIA

No, no. Something else.

ALICE

Have you looked in the thesaurus? Oh, that's right; you don't believe in them.

SYLVIA

I don't believe in them.

BARBARA

It's just that our sex life has petered off and he has no drive and I thought maybe if he wanted something and just wasn't asking or if he maybe felt better about his position at work, we would, you know, attempt more positions –

SYLVIA

In bed.

BARBARA

Exactly.

ALICE

Excuse me. I have to get ready for work.

(ALICE exits.)

BARBARA

I just want him to have uncontrollable desires for me and of course for his own interests, if he has some.

SYLVIA

Is he too tired to . . . you know?

BARBARA

No, that's not it. I just want some sort of . . . I don't know . . . volition behind
it. It's so hack hack or it's not at all. Lately not at all. I think he's depressed.
Have I become dowdy?

SYLVIA

No. No.

BARBARA

It must be something else then.

2.

*(Lights dim on apartment. Lights up on DEXTER who mimes riding the
subway. He holds onto an imaginary rail. We can still see BOBBIE behind.
Either he is typing or there is a sound of a typewriter.)*

BOBBIE

Good fiction is no different than non-fiction. It's just a shift of the adjectives, a
replacement of the specifics. You put a tarp over something and when you take
it off, it has changed. It's not magic. It's just that you notice what you didn't
notice before. With that in mind, please know that this story is true. These are
people I know. This was my life—This is . . .

(BOBBIE gestures to DEXTER or DEXTER is somehow illuminated.)

BOBBIE

The man clears his head on the subway. He lets himself be rocked by the
motion, goes slack in the lurches. He is a spectator. Attracted by this color,
struck dumb by this shape, astounded by this shade of skin. The man doesn't
speak but sometimes there is excessive eye contact and a lot of looking at the
ground. The man never follows through. He always slinks away when the
doors open. He is nursing a depression.

(BOBBIE takes out a handgun and looks down the barrel.)

BOBBIE

I clear my head by looking down the barrel of a forty-five. It used to be a flare
gun, then a bee bee gun. Then it was this but unloaded. Now I have to load it
or the mind won't clear. I'm afraid of what the next step might be. I am
terribly good at following through. You might say, that like the man, I am
depressed. If you had no sense of proportion, you might say we are the same.

(Lights come up on ALICE in the lab. A lab ASSISTANT stands beside her.)

BOBBIE

Alice, the middle sister, is also depressed.

ALICE

I feel so miserable. I must get busy with something as soon as possible. Work! Work!

ASSISTANT

Work!

ALICE

To work. Ever since he came to the house it's impossible to get work done. But never mind that. What is the situation with the mice?

ASSISTANT

The same.

ALICE

Well, I need more mice. Get me more mice.

ASSISTANT

From where? You know there's a mice shortage and your work is making it more severe.

ALICE

Get on the phone and get me more. I need the right combination. I mean, if they're not in love how can we tell if they're out of love? It's impossible.

ASSISTANT

I'm sorry.

ALICE

Don't be sorry. Get me more mice. Get me more mice! Get me more mice! More! More!

(ASSISTANT runs off.)

BOBBIE

Sometimes Alice wants to strangle her assistant. But she has no time. She has work to do. I too have work to do on a novel that runs away from me. I wrestle with it for hours to get one word on the page, then suddenly it's writing itself page after page and then nothing again.

(ASSISTANT returns.)

ASSISTANT

Are you really sure it's what you want?

ALICE

What?

ASSISTANT

Are you sure this is the project you want to work on – to spend your time on, devote your life to?

ALICE

Why do you ask?

ASSISTANT

It's just . . . well, there aren't that many women in the field and I just hate . . .

ALICE

You just hate what?

ASSISTANT

To hear them laugh at you.

ALICE

Let them laugh.   They laughed at Copernicus. They laughed at Aristotle. Then they published.

ASSISTANT

But –

ALICE

Get on the phone.

ASSISTANT

But –

ALICE

Get on the phone and get me more mice.

ASSISTANT

Yes, sir, professor.

(Exit ASSISTANT.)

ALICE

Damn grad students.

(ALICE goes back to work.)

BOBBIE

I'd rather not talk too much about myself if that's OK. Of course that will backfire because you'll see what I wrote and you'll assume things about me that probably aren't true and I won't try to correct you and so you'll just go on assuming.

But I don't care. I'm still not telling you about myself. I'm telling you this story instead.

Dexter, husband to Barbara, the oldest sister has arrived at his place of employ.

(Lights come up on a cubicle. DEXTER enters. SASHA is at his desk waiting for him. She holds a red folder.)

SASHA

Dexter.

DEXTER

Ms. Thompson.

SASHA

You were four minutes late this morning.

DEXTER

I'm sorry. I was in a meeting that ran over.

SASHA

A meeting with whom?

DEXTER

My wife. She wants me to long.

SASHA

I'm sorry?

DEXTER

I'm not sure I know what it means to be a man. Probably because my father left when I was a kid. Am I too sensitive? Am I not sensitive enough? Now I'm supposed to have longings. I just want to go to sleep.

SASHA

What?

DEXTER

Nothing. I'm sorry I'm late. It won't happen again. Do I need to get you some coffee?

SASHA
(picking up a red folder)
You left you red folder on your desk. Left it where anyone could pick it up, rummage through it, read it, photocopy it, steal it, sell it to the competition and put us out of business.

DEXTER

Oh.

SASHA

Dexter, this is very serious.

DEXTER

I know it is, I just find it difficult to care, really.

SASHA

You what?

DEXTER

Find it difficult to –

SASHA

The point is you put all our jobs at risk when you left here without locking up your red folder.

DEXTER

I didn't mean to.

SASHA

I need you to be a team player. We have a big project coming up. I need you to
(MORE)

bat this out of the field. I need this to be a T.K.O. – Total um Knockout. You hear what I'm saying? You got to take this one long and score between or among those posts. Are there three posts?? Is there one post? It doesn't matter. It's a metaphor. I need your head in the game.

DEXTER

Yeah.

SASHA

I don't want to fire you. This could even be partially my fault. I haven't been entirely present with you lately. I've had a lot of personal issues. My mother was visiting and I haven't been feeling beautiful. Sometimes I feel like there is a weight holding me down, keeping me in this box, not even like a glass ceiling workwise but more like a box of my own creation holding me down keeping me, you know, still and from excelling.

DEXTER

I don't . . . um. . .

SASHA

I know you're holding back too.

DEXTER

I am?

SASHA

You're bottling up your emotions. That's not healthy.

DEXTER

It's not?

SASHA

We have to trust one another implicitly. Can I trust you?

DEXTER

Yeah.

SASHA

Because I feel a, you know, wave of energy between us and I really um, want it to swell if it has to but, um I hope it will, um wash through us like rays of light.

DEXTER

I'm not sure what you're talking about.

SASHA

The rays.

DEXTER

I wanted to actually talk to you about a raise.

SASHA

No, like rays. Like invisible rays and sometimes they bounce but maybe they should, you know, penetrate.

DEXTER

Abstract things confuse me.

SASHA

I'm glad we had this talk. I feel like we got a lot of things out in the open. I feel much better, don't you?

DEXTER

I have to go to the bathroom. Watch my red folder while I'm gone, will you?

(DEXTER exits to another area. Sound of typing.)

BOBBIE

Sometimes on a day like today the man likes to retire to the single occupancy bathroom on the fourth floor. He locks the door and tries to find release – to unbottle some of what's bottled up.

(DEXTER begins to masturbate, his back to the audience.)

BOBBIE

He thinks about past girlfriends and beauty pageant contestants, the Greek woman selling fruit. But none of it is doing it for him. He thinks of his wife. He thinks of his wife's sisters. Then his mind fixes on his boss, Sasha.

(SASHA appears running in slow motion. BOBBIE follows her in slow motion, reaching his hands out for her neck.)

BOBBIE

He thinks about chasing her—about catching her about wrapping his fat fingers around her neck and squeezing.

(BOBBIE reaches SASHA and his hands are around her neck. In a stylized manner, he strangles her.)

BOBBIE

He will feel bad about this afterwards. The shame he feels will put him off masturbation ... for a day or two. But right now his hands are squeezing and –

(DEXTER comes. SASHA gets up and exits.

(Lights up on the apartment of the three sisters where SYLVIA and BARBARA are both on laptops.)

BOBBIE

Sylvia, the youngest sister, and Barbara, the oldest do not waste time in single occupancy bathrooms but get straight to work. Barbara schedules the day's deliveries for her online delivery service. She calls her minions of bicycle messengers.

BARBARA
(on the phone)

They need it in five minutes. Well, go through the park, then if you have to.
(to SYLVIA)
It's better to be a horse even or a bicycle messenger than to be one of those young women who wakes up at twelve o'clock, has coffee in bed and spends the next two hours dreaming.

SYLVIA

Please don't talk to me. I'm trying to work.

BARBARA

That's what I'm saying.

SYLVIA

What's another word for obnoxious interruption?

BARBARA
(on phone)

Seventy-second and third. Do it after the ... right. Take the truck. I'd do it myself but ...

BOBBIE

Barbara dreams of a time before the fear arrived when she could leave the apartment whenever she chose.

BARBARA

Just get it done, OK?

SYLVIA
(writing)

Red is a color that never seems . . .

BOBBIE

Sylvia dreams of the boy running around New York kissing women. She looks at her lipstick article. She thinks of the boy. She wishes she were not regulated to writing certain articles because she was a woman. Sylvia decides she will write the lipstick article no more. She wants to write about history and art and poetry and truth and medicine and sports.

SYLVIA

I don't want to write about medicine.

BOBBIE

What?

SYLVIA

I don't want to write about medicine. You're just making stuff up.

BOBBIE

It's my story. You want to write about medicine.

SYLVIA

Barbara, have I ever said I wanted to write about medicine?

BARBARA

Not now.
(on phone)

Take the West Side highway.

BOBBIE

If they ever assigned you to write an article about medicine, you wouldn't do it?

SYLVIA

I just wish you wouldn't put thoughts into my mind. *I'm thinking this. I'm thinking that.*

BOBBIE

Fine.

SYLVIA

Because you don't know me. I don't know why you think you know me.

BOBBIE

I don't know her. Not yet.

SYLVIA

That's what I just said. Why do you have to repeat everything?

3.

BOBBIE

Alice never cares what I say about her.

(Lights up on ALICE. She wears a lab coat and looks through a microscope.)

ALICE

Beautiful.

(FRED enters wearing a lab coat. He probably wears a moustache.)

ALICE

Beautiful.

FRED

Hi Alice.

ALICE
(not looking up)

Fred.

FRED

What are ya looking at?

ALICE

My sister's husband.

FRED

Is this your current project?

ALICE
(coming up from the microscope)

What can I do for you, Fred?

FRED

Well, I was thinking – are you, um . . . .. I was going to eat something tonight and maybe drink and I thought if you weren't doing anything . . .

ALICE

I'm sorry Fred but I already have a date tonight, but if you want to add your name to the chalkboard of suitors on the wall, I may be able to fit you in sometime next month.

FRED

(looking at chalkboard)

That would be –

ALICE

I mean if you're serious.

FRED

There's a lot of names.

ALICE

If you're not serious—

FRED

Oh, I am. There's just something about you.

ALICE

What you speak of, I think, Fred is a coldness I have managed to cultivate towards the majority of men. Because I give off the air of not caring about you and because I speak to you and others brusquely, because I am short and dismissive with you, you think there must be something about me. I get many dates because of this. Perhaps you think I am like this all the time, but I am not. It disappears when I go home. It is not anything true. Because when I go home I am under a different spell. Not unlike the way you are under mine. Do you understand?

FRED

I think I love you.

ALICE

All right, well, add your name to the chalkboard and leave me a sample of your genetic material and we'll see what comes of it. I promise not to erase your name prematurely.

FRED

Thank you.

ALICE

Now please go. I have to look at this some more.

FRED

Thank you.

(Exit FRED. ALICE goes back to her microscope.)

4.

(BOBBIE in his apartment, takes a letter out of an envelope. He reads it.)

BOBBIE

What? You fucker! You worthless fucker!

(BOBBIE paces, he looks at the letter again. He crumples it up and throws it. He pounds the desk in anger, then puts a new sheet of paper in the typewriter. He types.)

BOBBIE

Dear Sir, Did you even read my masterpiece? If you had, you would not be sending me this form letter of rejection. Not unless you are indeed a complete and worthless moron. I do not accept you as an arbiter of real talent. I have more talent than all of you put together if it comes to that! You with your hackneyed conventions, have usurped the foremost places in art and consider nothing genuine and legitimate except what you yourselves do. Everything else you stifle and suppress. I do not accept you. I do not. It was optimistic of me to think that you were not an undiscerning fool.

Are you all conspiring against me, you with your form letters on separate letterheads that converge into one voice? As punishment for this, your highest crime, know that you have pushed me to eschew publication altogether. Know that you and the others and the world at large will miss out on the rest of my work which I shall never again let you touch with your dirty and destructive hands. My work belongs to eternity now. To the universe of ephemera. But never to you. May you find your just punishment knowing you have kept another genius from the hungry world who aches to hear him. Sincerely, The Author Who Would Have Made You Famous.

(BOBBIE takes the sheet out of the typewriter and puts a new one in. He picks up a wine bottle from the floor and places it on his desk. After staring at it for a second, he begins to type.)

5.

(In the apartment shared by the three sisters. BARBARA is seated near the coffin. SYLVIA stands, reading out loud from a piece of paper.)

SYLVIA

My job was to learn more about this mysterious young kisser. Who was he? Why was he set on pressing the lips of the women of Manhattan? But most importantly, I needed to see him face to face, to touch him, to make the myth into a stark reality. The young flock to New York looking for something shiny and golden, and many end up working at Starbucks and sharing a bedroom in Queens while their savings disappear. He is my New York and I set out to discover if he was a iridescent razor-faced god or a greasy acne-covered flunky.

(looking up)

What do you think?

BARBARA

I don't want you to go wandering around looking for this kid. Who knows what part of town you'll go to. And alone, no doubt.

SYLVIA

I am a reporter.

BARBARA

Because you wrote about lipstick?

SYLVIA

That was a starting assignment. I have aspirations. I want to collect data— categorize ideas and facts. I want to unclog the sink that is the world and show the dirty greasy truth. And then form this imperfection into a story people can understand. You understand?

BARBARA

I suppose.

SYLVIA

To do this, I need to continue to leave the house. I can't just never leave the apartment like you.

BARBARA

I wish you wouldn't . . .

SYLVIA

How long has it been? Seven years?

BARBARA

There's nothing out there for me. Nothing but danger. New York is scary.
Not like New Jersey.

SYLVIA

New Jersey.

BARBARA

New Jersey. People die when they go outside. They freeze to death or else get
hit by cars. They are shot at, trampled, burned to death. They are stabbed, they
get diseases. It's not good for people to go outside.

SYLVIA

I'm not having this conversation.

BARBARA

I forbid you to leave.

SYLVIA

I'm not a child anymore.

BARBARA

First Daddy dies and now you're going to get yourself killed too.

SYLVIA

People leave their homes every day without getting killed.

BARBARA

But you're the youngest. We can't lose you. You are the hope of the family.

SYLVIA

I don't want to be the hope.

BARBARA

How about if you go out and do your investigating or whatever but you only do
it during the day?

SYLVIA

Because he does all his kissing at night. *The Voice* and *The Journal* are both very clear about that.

BARBARA

Well, wait until Dexter comes home and I'll have him walk around with you for a few minutes.

SYLVIA

You never understand anything! You're not supportive! You stand in the way of my success time and time again.

BARBARA

I do not.

SYLVIA

You're not going to keep me down this time, you dumb old agoraphobe!

BARBARA

What did you call me?

SYLVIA

Nothing.

BARBARA

You didn't have to hurt my feelings.

SYLVIA

I'm sorry.

BARBARA

I don't want to be this way – you know that. I'd like to go to the park. I want to play croquet and go swimming.

SYLVIA

Then why don't you?

BARBARA

I wish you would be a bit more understanding.

SYLVIA

I'm sorry.

BARBARA

Why don't you just hold off? I'll figure it out so someone can walk around with you. I'll hire someone.

SYLVIA

You don't need to hire anyone.

BARBARA

Then, you'll stay in?

SYLVIA

Well . . .

BARBARA

That's a good girl.

SYLVIA

Barbara.

BARBARA

Thank you. I knew you weren't going to hurt the family like that.

SYLVIA

I'm going.

BARBARA

But –

SYLVIA
(putting on her coat)

Goodbye, dear sister.

(Exit SYLVIA.)

BARBARA

Get back here! I forbid you. Wait. Wait. Let me call someone to go with you. Sylvia! Sylvia! Be reasonable.

(Enter ALICE, dressed for a date.)

ALICE

Where's she going?

BARBARA

Out.

ALICE

Oh.

BARBARA

I wish you would support me more.

ALICE

How do I look?

BARBARA

I should have tied her up. Are those my shoes?

ALICE

Yes. Can I borrow them?

BARBARA

Why didn't you ask me before?

ALICE

I'm asking you now.

BARBARA

Oh, all right. Who is it tonight?

ALICE

I'm not sure. I'll check my spreadsheet.

BARBARA

When are you going to find a husband?

ALICE

Probably tomorrow.

BARBARA

I'm serious. That's your problem. You don't approach this with any seriousness. If you did, I am sure you'd be married by now.

ALICE

I just haven't met him yet. I'm sure that's what it is. If I go on enough dates . . .

BARBARA

Maybe your standards are too high.

ALICE

I'm trying. I'm really trying, which is more I can say for some people.

BARBARA

What do you mean?

ALICE

You don't exactly take a lot of chances, do you?

BARBARA

You are a terrible person!
(Pause.)
I'm going to go lie down. All this confrontation has upset me. Please wake me when Dexter gets home.

ALICE

Certainly.

(Exit BARBARA. ALICE goes to the coffin.)

BOBBIE

Sometimes when Alice is alone, she runs to her father's coffin and presses her lips against the cold wood.

(ALICE does this.)

BOBBIE

Despite the odor, it calms her, especially when the clock is approaching six ten or six eleven, sometimes six seventeen or even on occasion six twenty-one. That is when the man returns in his heavy boots. The floor boards creak then, not like when the sisters step. And a new odor permeates too—a man odor. But for now, Alice speaks to her decomposing father and tries to forget the creak of boots to come.

ALICE

Oh, Father, what am I doing? I don't know who I am anymore. I go to work in a fog. Is this what I'm supposed to be doing with my days and nights? Look at me, ready for another date, a date I don't want to go on but why sit at home
(MORE)

ALICE (cont.)
when another cold soup man is willing to buy me a another hot meal. So I put on the date lipstick and the date perfume, because who knows, maybe this time, this man, but no, he too will sit in a shadow and I will stop listening in the first minute.

Why is my life not like yours and mother's? Why is my bank account empty at the end of every month and my bed empty at the end of every night? This was not the way you lived, even when you were digging and burying. I am unable to bury a damned thing. Help me. Help me, Father. What am I supposed to be doing? How can I get through this night? Or tomorrow?

(Enter DEXTER.)

DEXTER

Good evening.

ALICE
                                        (standing up, straightening her dress)
Dexter. I didn't see you. I was getting ready for my date.

DEXTER

Another date, is it? Well. Have you seen my wife?

ALICE

She's resting. Do you like this dress? And this lipstick? And these shoes?

DEXTER
                                        (not looking)
Sure.
                                        (sniffing the air)
It smells in here. I think we need a stronger deodorizer.

ALICE

I'm sure you're right about that.

DEXTER

Thank you. No one ever tells me when I'm right anymore. Not like when I was a boy.

ALICE

That's absurd. Why you're right constantly. People should be saying it constantly.

DEXTER

I think you're right. I'll bring it up at the next staff meeting. Thanks, Alice.

ALICE

How about this bag with this outfit? Do I look pretty . . . for my date?

DEXTER
(distracted)

Sure.
        (Pause.)
I guess I should wake my wife up.

ALICE

You don't need to do that yet.

DEXTER

No? Thank God.

ALICE

Let's talk.

        (They sit.)

ALICE

So.

DEXTER

So.
        (Pause.)
How are you, then?

ALICE

I can't stand to look at you sometimes. The way you sit. It makes me want to scratch my skin to the bone.

DEXTER
(not hearing)

Good, good.
                (standing up)
Thanks for the talk.

ALICE

Why did you marry my sister? What was it about her? Was she so different?
Did you find her beautiful? What makes her better than me, preferable to me?
Do you still like waking up to her each morning? Do you ever wish . . .

DEXTER

I really should wake her up. You know how she gets when she feels like she's
missing out. We must make sure she doesn't feel that way.

ALICE

Are you afraid of her?

DEXTER

No. Are you? Don't answer that.
        (A beat.)
Never mind. Go ahead and answer that.

ALICE

Um....

DEXTER

Forget it.
        (Pause.)
Alice, I'm concerned that I don't really know how to be a man. My father
wasn't around to teach me. I don't know how to hit someone. I'm not really
sure how to hold a baby. My college education has not really prepared me
either... For anything really. I don't know how to talk to a woman. I don't
know how to be a good husband.

ALICE

You're a wonderful husband.

DEXTER

I don't know how to talk to my wife.

        *(BARBARA enters, hair askew, somewhat angry, wearing a somewhat revealing
        nightgown.)*

BARBARA

Why didn't you wake me up?

DEXTER

I was going to.

106

                        BARBARA
Why didn't you wake me up?

                        ALICE
I didn't want to. So long, sister. Wish me luck.

                        BARBARA
Luck.

        (Exit ALICE.)

                        BARBARA
So.

                        DEXTER
So.

                        BARBARA
Why don't you touch me anymore?

                        DEXTER
I'm impotent.

                        BARBARA
That's not what the doctor says.

                        BOBBIE
                            (stops typing)
No, no no.

                        BARBARA
What?

                        BOBBIE
It's not right.

                        BARBARA
I liked it. Did you?

                        DEXTER
You're too hard on yourself.

BOBBIE

Let's start again.

> (BOBBIE *tears out old sheet and crumples it, throws it away. Puts in a new sheet and starts typing. BARBARA and DEXTER stand there for a second then resume their previous positions.*)

BARBARA

So.

DEXTER

So.

BARBARA

We're all alone.

DEXTER

Are we?

> (BARBARA *begins to light candles.*)

BARBARA

You don't mind if I light some candles?

DEXTER

No, no. Go right ahead.

BARBARA

How was work?

DEXTER

Good.

BARBARA

You ask about the raise?

BOBBIE

Sometimes the man feels a violence inside him that frightens him both with its unexpected arrival and the apparent force. It comes from his testicles but it rings in his ears. It is huge and muscular and covered with plates of armor. He does not understand it.

DEXTER

I haven't got a chance to ask about the raise yet.

108

BARBARA

I thought you were going to ask.

DEXTER
(suddenly angry)

I will!

BARBARA

You don't need to speak to me like that.

DEXTER

I'm sorry.

BARBARA

Apology accepted. Now come give me a kiss.

(DEXTER and BARBARA kiss.)

DEXTER
(pulling away)

You're . . . um . . . you haven't brushed your teeth.

BARBARA

I just woke up.

DEXTER

I wish you would brush your teeth.

(BARBARA exits to brush her teeth.)

BOBBIE

The man thinks about his wife. He thinks about past girlfriends and beauty pageant contestants, the Greek woman selling fruit. He thinks of his wife. He thinks of his wife's sisters. Then his mind fixes on his boss, Sasha. He shudders.

(DEXTER shudders.)

BOBBIE

The man thinks of his wife.

(Re-enter BARBARA.)

BARBARA

Here I am, freshly brushed.

(BARBARA and DEXTER kiss. After a bit, DEXTER pulls away.)

BARBARA

What is it?

DEXTER

Nothing. It's just . . . I'm under a lot of stress. From work.

BARBARA

Relax.

(They kiss some more. It gets intense but DEXTER pulls away again.)

DEXTER

That smell. I'm sorry. I'm still not comfortable being this affectionate in front of your father.

BARBARA

He doesn't mind. You want me to make you a drink?

DEXTER

No, no. I don't know.

BARBARA

Then what?

DEXTER

It's all just the same over and over again. I come home and you're here and we try to make love and then we have dinner. I just wish . . .

BARBARA

What?

DEXTER

I just wish for once it was something else. Something different.

BARBARA

You want me to be the French maid.

DEXTER

No, I mean, yes, but that's not what I mean. You haven't left the house in what? Six years now? Since we got married, you pretty much haven't left the apartment. For once I'd like to come home and find that you'd gone out. That you were off doing something. For once I'd like to be alone in this house to do whatever I want...watch TV or something like . . . well, I'd watch TV. You wouldn't have dinner ready. Maybe I'd order a pizza or just eat cheetos and a cupcake.

BARBARA

Why is everyone biting my butt about this today? I don't need to leave the house. I can get everything delivered.

DEXTER

Forget it. I'm sorry I said anything.

BARBARA

I don't need to leave. I always have dinner ready for you, don't I?

DEXTER

I'm sorry I upset you.

BARBARA

It's not like I don't work all day and then get dinner ready.

DEXTER

You don't have to. I'm saying you don't have to. Sometimes I don't want you to.

BARBARA

What kind of a wife would I be then?

DEXTER

The kind of wife I want – sometimes, occasionally. You could go to the corner and get some toilet paper.

BARBARA

I have it delivered!

DEXTER

I know you do. It's just . . . forget it.

(Pause.)

BARBARA

I'm terrified. I'm terrified all the time.

DEXTER

I know. Forget it. Forget it.

6.

(Lights on SYLVIA.)

BOBBIE

Meanwhile, Sylvia, the youngest sister, walks the streets from end to end, grid to chaotic village and back to grid again. She walks west and when she reaches the water she walks east again until she reaches the water and she has to turn around. She has no system but her looks are intense, so much that more than one crack-addled bum has to look away after meeting her sizzling eyes. She is intent on finding the boy, somehow or other.

How was that?

SYLVIA

It was fine.

BOBBIE

Just fine?

SYLVIA

Just fine.

7.

(A table at a restaurant. ALICE sits at a table with ARTHUR. ARTHUR probably has some facial hair.)

ALICE

And because I work at a university setting I don't get paid as much as other scientists in my field who work for corporations. So, yes, I will let you buy me dinner.

ARTHUR

Oh. OK.
(Pause.)

112

ARTHUR

You're beautiful. Do you believe in soul mates?

ALICE

Women are still paid seventy six cents on the dollar compared to men doing the same job so it's not hard to justify you paying for a meal.

ARTHUR

Well, how much do you make? Cuz I'm no Rockefeller. But you are a rare beauty. I bet you get whatever you want.

ALICE
(handing him a cotton swab)

Please swab the inside of your mouth with this.

ARTHUR
(talking with the swab in his mouth)

What's thith for?

ALICE

Just my way of deciding if there will be a second date.

ARTHUR

Oh. OK.

(ARTHUR hands it back to her and she places it in a plastic bag and puts it away.)

ALICE

Thanks.

ARTHUR

I don't mind paying for the dinner anyway because then I can take liberties later.

ALICE

This isn't that kind of date.

ARTHUR

Oh. What kind of date is it?

(ALICE is out of her seat dabbing his arm with alcohol.)

ALICE

I'm just going to take some blood, OK?

ARTHUR

OK. Do you believe that we have multiple lives and that we meet the same people over and over in different incarnations?

ALICE
(putting the syringe in)

You'll feel a little pinch.

ARTHUR

Ow. Like your husband or boyfriend in this life could have been your sister in another life. Or your mother. And throughout history we all keep trying to fix the same relationship problems and work through different cultural structures and biological makeups over and over. Could you imagine if that's true? Really makes you think about what it means to be you or me—how similar we are despite our obvious current physical differences.

ALICE

There, now. It's all over.
(Back in her seat she stows the blood and takes out a file folder. She glances inside.)
ALICE

What is it you do again?

ARTHUR

I feel like you and I have a connection. Like we've met before.

ALICE

You do have a job, don't you?

ARTHUR

I'm in fish transportation systems.

ALICE

Like barges and trucks?

ARTHUR

No. Actual mechanisms for the fish. I design small vehicles to help them move better.

ALICE

Like cars?

ARTHUR

More like bicycles, really.

ALICE

Is that necessary?

ARTHUR

I sure hope so. I put a lot of work into it. It's coming along quite nicely.
Especially for the bass.
     (Pause.)
What kind of scientist are you?

ALICE

I'm isolating genes. Right now I'm looking for the gene that causes romantic
love.

ARTHUR

Why?

ALICE

If I isolate it, then I can alter it.

ARTHUR

Why would you want to do that?

ALICE

People should be able to choose who to love.

ARTHUR

That's not very romantic.

ALICE

Or to not love at all if that's what they want. I mean, we don't need romantic
love. It's completely unnecessary.

ARTHUR

I disagree.

ALICE

We should be able to control our own feelings about things, if not with drugs,
then with gene therapy.

ARTHUR

That's terrible. That's unnatural.

ALICE

So are fish vehicles.

ARTHUR

I'm not going to defend fish vehicles to you. Either you get it or you don't.

ALICE

I feel the same way about my work. I mean, haven't you ever been in love with someone who didn't love you back?

(ARTHUR *takes a drink. Then he stands. He is visibly hurt.*)

ARTHUR

Excuse me please for a moment.

ALICE

I didn't mean to upset you.

ARTHUR

I just have to use the facilities.

ALICE

I'm sorry.

ARTHUR
(*about to cry*)

There's no need to apologize. I'll be right back. I just have to . . . compose myself.

ALICE
(*holding out a cup*)

While you're in there, will you fill this with urine?

8.

(*In the apartment of the three sisters we are back with* BARBARA *and* DEXTER.)

BARBARA

I want things to be good with us again.

DEXTER

Things are good.

BARBARA

Not like they used to be. I want us to be closer. Like where it looked like our relationship was going.

DEXTER

We're close.

BARBARA

Do I have to go outside to prove to you that I love you?

DEXTER

No.

BARBARA

If that's what it takes.

DEXTER

It's fine. Never mind.

BARBARA

You're sick of me.

DEXTER

No.

BARBARA

I've grown fat. I'm ugly. I hate this haircut. I hate all my clothes.

DEXTER

No.

BARBARA

I can go outside. Would it make things better? Because I am a strong independent woman. You need me to prove something? I'll prove something. I am a strong woman. I can leave the house. I can live any kind of life I want. I will leave right this moment.

DEXTER

OK.

BARBARA

OK? Um, OK. Here I go. I'm going. I'm scared. No I'm not. Watch me leave. I'm leaving. I'm walking. One foot in front of the other. Here I go. Good bye. Perhaps I will see you later this evening after my walk. Ohmigod Ohmigod!

DEXTER

Barbara?

BARBARA

Blow out the candles, will you? So the house won't catch fire?

(BARBARA exits the apartment but is caught in a pool of light.)

BOBBIE

At the bottom of the stairs Barbara has to stop and catch her breath. And then she finds a sort of balance. There is a gentle breeze. The winter air is cold but not too cold. She likes how it feels on her cheeks. She walks block after block smiling at strangers, stopping to pet dogs and look at window displays. Everything is OK with the world and within her and then suddenly it isn't. The panic rising inside her is unexpected and without cause like sudden electrocution. Sidewalks loom, cars careen. Her skin itches more than anything. They will bomb her. She smells something in the air. Poison gas? And then as she begins to hyperventilate, a distraction arrives.

(BOBBIE steps under the streetlight where BARBARA is.)

BARBARA
(hyperventilating)

Excuse me. Boy! Boy! I can't breathe.

(BOBBIE kisses her. Her eyes stay closed and she freezes.)

BOBBIE

Her sadness envelops me – it's a sadness that reflects my own sadness and I feel the level of my misery increase as she becomes light.

(As the kiss ends, BOBBIE slips off and BARBARA opens her eyes and beams.)

BOBBIE

When the kiss is done, she is elated and I am gone – already trudging towards my apartment alone. She feels like a woman and I am a small boy with a large burden.

118

9.

(On the street.)

BOBBIE

And then ... Sylvia finds me.

SYLVIA

And then I find him.

BOBBIE

Her sister's breath still on my lips.

SYLVIA
(to BOBBIE)

I want to tell it.

BOBBIE

But this is my story.

SYLVIA

Let me tell it. It doesn't only belong to you. This part. It was like this. He was under the streetlamp, illuminated like an angel.

BOBBIE

Sylvia.

SYLVIA

Quiet. Like you were.

BOBBIE

Sylvia.

SYLVIA

Like it was.

(BOBBIE stands under a streetlight, typewriter case in hand. SYLVIA approaches him.)

SYLVIA

You're him, aren't you? You're the boy.

(BOBBIE tries to kiss her. She turns away.)

SYLVIA

No. Don't.

(BOBBIE *begins to walk away, hurt. SYLVIA follows him.*)

SYLVIA

Wait, don't go.

(BOBBIE *continues to walk away. She has to speed up to keep up with him.*)

SYLVIA

I follow him to a bar on the lower east side – a dive of a place. The floors are covered with sawdust and peanut shells. I watch as he opens his case and takes out a typewriter.

(BOBBIE *sits at a table, takes out his typewriter.*)

SYLVIA

He puts a clean sheet of paper in and begins typing. He doesn't look up when the tattooed waitress brings him a beer nor does he look up when she asks me what I'm having.

WAITRESS
(*appearing*)

What are you having?

SYLVIA

I'll have whatever he's drinking.

(WAITRESS *disappears.*)

SYLVIA

Listen, I just want to talk to you. I'm not trying to bother you. I'm not a cop or anything.

(BOBBIE *continues to type.*)

SYLVIA
(*rapidly*)

Have you kissed a lot of girls?

(*Pause.*)

SYLVIA

Is that too forward? How long have you been doing this? What do you do during the day? Are you an orphan? Where were you born? Are you the son of someone particularly successful like a star or a doctor or a star doctor? Is that your real hair color? What sort of moisturizer do you use? What type of music do you like? Which newspapers do you read? Which periodicals? Are you stoned? Where do you come from? Do you come here a lot? Are you my destiny? I think you're beautiful.

(BOBBIE looks up. They lock eyes for a second, then BOBBIE goes back to typing.)

SYLVIA

I want to stay here. Is it OK if I stay here and watch you? I mean, you don't seem to want to talk to me.

WAITRESS
(appearing, setting down beer for SYLVIA)
He doesn't talk when he's writing. We like to call him "the mute."

SYLVIA

Does he come in here a lot?

(But the WAITRESS has already disappeared.)

SYLVIA

Do you come here a lot? You could nod if you wanted. That would be fine.

(BOBBIE continues typing.)

SYLVIA

Or maybe you could write the answers to my questions on a piece of paper.
(looking over his shoulder at the sheet of paper)
SYLVIA

What are you writing?

(BOBBIE finishes typing and takes the paper out of the typewriter. He hands it to SYLVIA who reads it silently.)

SYLVIA

This is what I remember from the page he handed me.

BOBBIE

"Where were you?"

SYLVIA

it said.

BOBBIE
(quoting from the page)

Have you been here the whole time in the corner in the shadows sipping your lager? You're like a pigeon, ever-present unnoticed, beautiful in the right light and capable of flying. Me, when I look at you, all I feel are clusters of light, the rat tat rumble of oncoming headlights, fireworks, bonfires, incredible stabs of concentrated heat hurtling towards my eyes.

"Even death can't find me here," I think, as your stale breath seeps deeply into my lungs. You are no beauty or at least open-handed I can count twelve or more with tauter looks whose tongues I've touched. And you, steeped in the corner for five minutes, seven hours, ten years, who can say how long? Your angles, curves, brush of lash, stiff lip on edge of glass. When did you sneak in under the line of mine to flip the switch? Don't know how you did it but it's like an extra sense opened up or a new way of living, like learning you can breathe underwater or being able to read binary code one morning.

It's dim here but you prick my irises jagged. I must try to only look at you when you're looking away.
(Beat.)
It hurts less.

SYLVIA

Then he takes the page from me. And from nowhere produces an empty wine bottle, and rolling the page up, slips it, smooth as can be, into the bottle and corks it.

(BOBBIE does this.)

SYLVIA

Then he swigs down the rest of his beer, stands up and walks out of the bar without a look in my direction.

(BOBBIE walks swiftly around the stage, SYLVIA in tow.)

SYLVIA

Did you write that about me? What was that? Why did you put it in the bottle? Are you trying to lose me? Do you want me to go away?

(BOBBIE ignores her.)

SYLVIA

When we get to the Hudson River, he tosses his bottle into the water.

(BOBBIE does this.)

SYLVIA

It is dark but I can see it plunk and then rise back up to the surface moments later. I watch it bob, more than a little flabbergasted that it is really there in the river. When, seconds later, I turn back to the boy, he is gone.

(BOBBIE has disappeared to BARBARA's part of the stage. BARBARA is on the street.)

BOBBIE

Barbara's night is a swirling kaleidoscope of pleasant shadows that alter with each wind gust. Each stoop is a delight of textures and colors, each face a new friend leading her with gentle threads back to her apartment. Her step is sure. Her limbs vibrate with each heartbeat as her body tingles in a way that almost offsets the throbbing inside. Even her hair feels alive.

(DEXTER is drinking and smoking a cigar. BARBARA enters.)

DEXTER
(disappointed)

You're back already.

(BARBARA walks towards him as he backs away.)

BARBARA

I am an attractive worthwhile woman.

DEXTER

I know.

BARBARA

Other men look at me and undress me mentally.

DEXTER

I know they do.

BARBARA
(grabbing him)

I want you. I want you on top of me, inside me, over me, under me. I
want you to pick me up and throw me down. I want you to tear off my clothes
and hold my arms so I can't move. I want you to push me around and then
mount me. I want your hands, your eyes, your cock, your blood pulsing inside
you inside me. Tell me what to do. Tell me how to be. Be rough with me.

DEXTER

No.

BARBARA

What?

DEXTER

I can't.

BARBARA

Why?

DEXTER

I'll hurt you.

BARBARA
(an order)

Hurt me.

DEXTER
(moving away)

No. I can't – Stop.

BARBARA

What's going on? Tell me what you're feeling.

DEXTER

I don't want to talk about my feelings, for Christ sake!

BARBARA

I'm sorry.

DEXTER

Mother fucker!

BARBARA

Dexter!

DEXTER

What?

BARBARA

Your language.

DEXTER

Fuck my language.

BARBARA

No, fuck me, Dexter.

DEXTER

Barbara.

BARBARA

You hear what I said? I'm being naughty. You like it when I'm naughty. You like to fuck your naughty little wife.

DEXTER

Just calm down for a second.

BARBARA

I don't want to calm down. I'm not feeling very calm right now.

DEXTER

Let me think.

BARBARA

No thinking. Sex. Be an animal with me.

DEXTER
(pushes her away)

No!

BARBARA
(angry, hurt)

What do you want then? You want me to be the man? You want me to buy a strap-on and bend you over like a girl?

(Pause.)

DEXTER

I think I should go.

BARBARA

What? What did I say?

DEXTER

I think I need some time away.

BARBARA

You're my husband!

DEXTER

I'll call you.

(Exit DEXTER.)

BARBARA

Hey, come back here.
        (Beat.)
Why does everyone keep leaving?
        (Silence.
        (BARBARA looks to where DEXTER exited then after a bit she goes to the coffin.)

BARBARA
        (to coffin)
What did I do? What am I supposed to be doing? You left too soon. You left before you could tell me how to be a wife. Daddy! Daddy! Why did you have to go so soon, Daddy?
        (Pause. BARBARA inhales deeply in anguish and recoils.)
Daddy, you smell really bad.

10.

(On the other side of the stage.)

BOBBIE

Meanwhile Sylvia is looking for me on the streets –

SYLVIA

I'm telling it.

126

BOBBIE

I don't appreciate you appropriating my story.

SYLVIA

I don't appreciate you appropriating mine.

BOBBIE

Well, I don't like it.

SYLVIA

Go ahead and stop me then.
(*Silence.*)
What you can't? No, you can't stop me now, can you? The night is blank and the streets are empty. I pick a direction at random and begin running. I feel like I am running through water. My legs don't move like I tell them. My brain is mush holding on to a single thought—that I must find him. I run and I run and the air is water and my brain is melting. I am about to give up. I can't see anything, anyone, anywhere. And then he is there.

(*BOBBIE caught in streetlamp.*)

SYLVIA

Where were you?

(*BOBBIE tries to kiss her. She turns away again. He begins to walk away again, hurt.*)

SYLVIA

No, I'm sorry. Don't go. Shit! I'm so stupid. Wait for me.

(*BOBBIE and SYLVIA walk.*)

SYLVIA

He walks more slowly this time. As if he's waiting for me. But he still doesn't look in my direction or seem to see me in his periphery. I stare at him as we walk along, oblivious to the night, the neighborhood, to everything. Then we are standing in front of a brownstone. Then we are in the hall. Then we are in his apartment or what I assume is his apartment.

(*BOBBIE goes to his desk, opens the drawer, takes out his handgun. He looks down the barrel for a while. They are both completely still. Then BOBBIE slowly turns his head and looks at SYLVIA.*)

SYLVIA

How can I explain that I'm not afraid? Yes, it is dangerous, but not any more dangerous than falling in love. When it comes down to it what it really does is make a piece of metal move very quickly. It doesn't ever get to the root of things. It just takes care of the surface problem – if that's what it's for, that is. I don't ask what it's there for. But let me be clear I'm not afraid.

(BOBBIE puts the gun back. Sits down and begins to type.)

SYLVIA

I am more afraid of what he is writing. I am afraid of his command of language, his diction, the way the verbs might rub up against my palate or jam themselves, get stuck in my throat. I am afraid I might like it too much, get used to it. Or maybe instead it's the opposite: I am afraid of disappointment. I am afraid of who I think he is and more afraid he isn't.

(BOBBIE stops typing, slips the sheet into a bottle and corks it.)

SYLVIA

Then he speaks to me for the first time, although he looks away from me as if anyone in the room might catch his voice and latch onto it and find meaning in it and, if it happened to be me, well so be it. He says:

BOBBIE

If you stay here, I will hold you all night long.

SYLVIA

So I do.

END ACT ONE

ACT TWO

11.

(BOBBIE alone at his desk.)

BOBBIE

What happen to our dreams when we are done with them? Do they exist without us in pieces that are lifted into the clouds? Do our dreams fall with the rain into the sea where the fish feed on them? Or can a dream not exist without a person there to dream it?

This is the story of a boy with dreams. This is the story of the man with dreams the boy could have become. This is the story of the three dreaming sisters, Barbara, Alice and Sylvia. This is not the story of the gravedigger whose dreams we are not concerned with, who is the father of the three sisters or of his wife, the poet, and dreamer who died young.

I had a credo and it went like this: We do not exist as individuals—we are all the same thing, you and me and the birds and the trees. When we look for love, we look for true love, but true love is love with any other, or love towards a bird or a duck. So choosing a love is simple because anyone and everyone you choose to love is the right one. We are all the same and so are they.

But when I fell in love with Sylvia, the youngest sister, my bastardized version of stoic Buddhism went out the window.

(BOBBIE climbs into bed with SYLVIA and they hold each other.)

SYLVIA
I have to go.

BOBBIE
No.

SYLVIA
I have to go.

BOBBIE
Don't.

SYLVIA

I have a deadline.

BOBBIE

Do you want to go?

SYLVIA

Not really.

BOBBIE

I don't want you to go. Not until you've told me everything about yourself.

SYLVIA

I've told you everything. You haven't told me anything about you. Tell me something.

BOBBIE

No.

SYLVIA

Tell me something that happened when you were twelve.

(Pause.)

BOBBIE

Once when I was twelve I swallowed twenty seven sleeping pills.

SYLVIA

Did you have insomnia?

BOBBIE

No. Suicidal impulses.

SYLVIA

Wow.
(Beat.)

SYLVIA

Who found you?

BOBBIE

Tell me more about your sisters.

130

SYLVIA

Ummm . . . Barbara, my older sister, is an insane paranoid agoraphobe who bosses me around. Sometimes I think she's like how Father would have been had he been more assertive. She's sort of fierce.

BOBBIE

So you don't get along.

SYLVIA

Oh, no. We get along. I guess it's just been hard on her since Father died. She was always the favorite.

(Lights up on the BARBARA and ALICE by the coffin.)

BARBARA

First father, over a year ago and now Dexter and Sylvia.

ALICE

They've been gone a night. It's not the same.

BARBARA
(dialing cell phone)

No one is answering their phones. It is surely because they are dead. I forbid you to leave this apartment. Because then you will disappear too and I will be all alone in the world.

ALICE

They're coming back.

BARBARA

Did father come back, did he?

ALICE

Speaking of, I think it's time to bury him. I find comfort in his presence too – we all do – but it's becoming a problem.

BARBARA

The smell.

ALICE

Sure the smell. But also, well don't you kind of feel like his presence is holding us back?

131

BARBARA

I don't, no.

ALICE

Look at Sylvia — she goes through men like Kleenex. I rarely have a second date and you and Dexter —

BARBARA

He's not holding us back.

ALICE

I just wonder if our relationships with the living would improve if we moved our dead father out of the living room.

(Pause.)

BARBARA

Where would we even bury him?

ALICE

New Jersey?

BARBARA

New Jersey.

ALICE

New Jersey.

BARBARA

I can't think about this now, while my sister and husband are missing. Sylvia of course finally ran into a serial killer. The law of averages was bound to get her. And Dexter, you don't think he's left me?

ALICE

He'll be back.

BARBARA

How do you know?

ALICE

I just think so.

BARBARA

You think . . . I'm going to faint. I am so worked up right now. Please give me some air. Get me some water. I'm going to vomit.

ALICE

What if I went to his work and talked to him?

BARBARA

You'd do that?

ALICE

I could take a long lunch. I could just talk to him.

BARBARA

What would you say?

ALICE

What do you want me to say?

BARBARA

Tell him I love him very much.

ALICE
(to invisible DEXTER)

I love you very much, Dexter.

BARBARA

I can't imagine life without him.

ALICE

I can't imagine life without you.

BARBARA

I want him to come home and sleep in my bed.

ALICE

Sleep with me in my bed.

BARBARA

Tell him I want a baby.

ALICE
(snapping out of the trance)

You do?

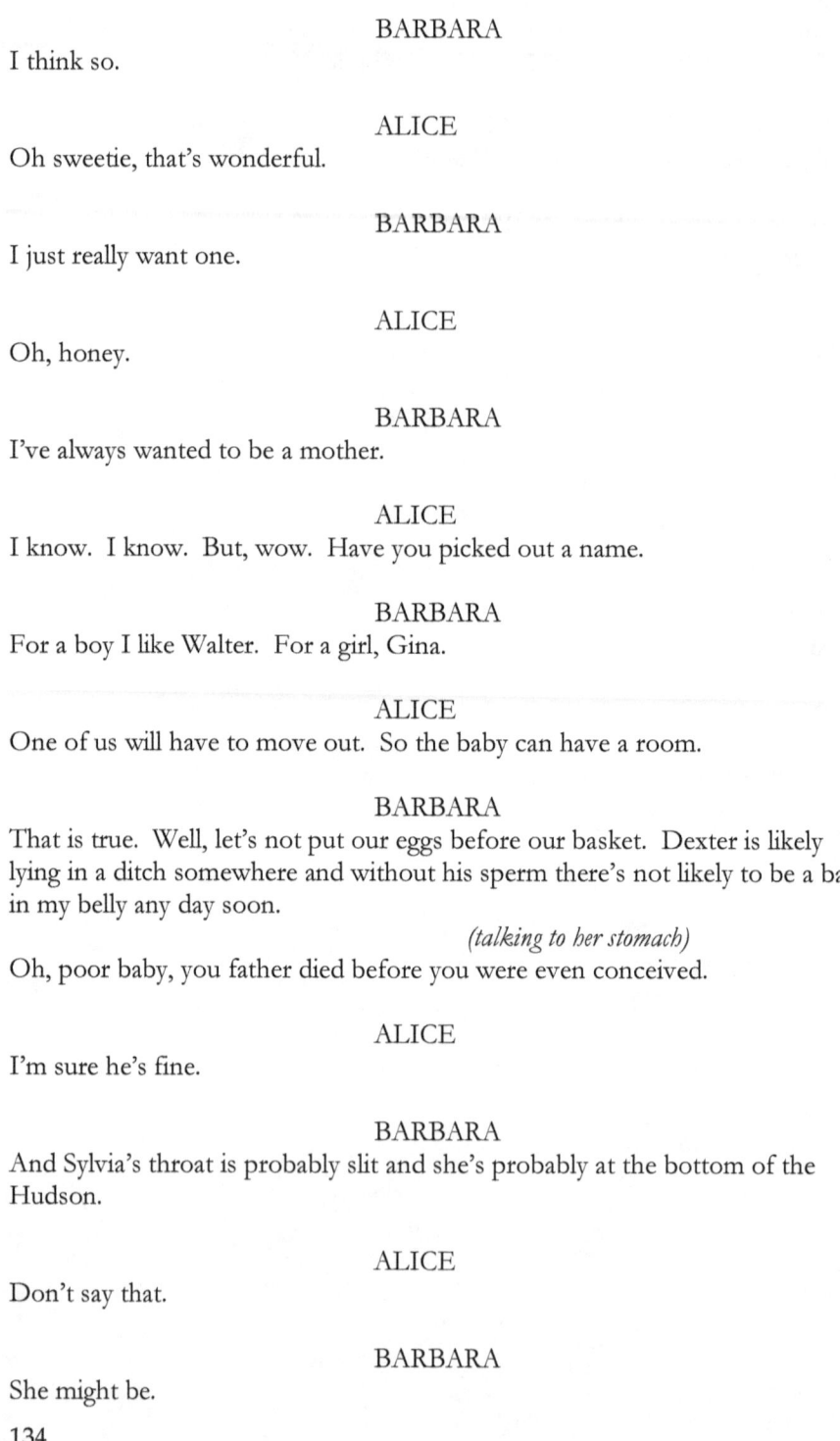

BARBARA

I think so.

ALICE

Oh sweetie, that's wonderful.

BARBARA

I just really want one.

ALICE

Oh, honey.

BARBARA

I've always wanted to be a mother.

ALICE

I know. I know. But, wow. Have you picked out a name.

BARBARA

For a boy I like Walter. For a girl, Gina.

ALICE

One of us will have to move out. So the baby can have a room.

BARBARA

That is true. Well, let's not put our eggs before our basket. Dexter is likely lying in a ditch somewhere and without his sperm there's not likely to be a baby in my belly any day soon.
(talking to her stomach)
Oh, poor baby, you father died before you were even conceived.

ALICE

I'm sure he's fine.

BARBARA

And Sylvia's throat is probably slit and she's probably at the bottom of the Hudson.

ALICE

Don't say that.

BARBARA

She might be.

134

ALICE

She's a big girl. She can take care of herself.

BARBARA

I'm not sure she can actually. She's so idealistic she never sees what's really there until it's too late. She's probably in someone's trunk right now.

(Enter SYLVIA.)

SYLVIA

Good morning. Have you been outside? It's so gorgeous out today.

BARBARA

Where have you been?

SYLVIA

I was with him.

BARBARA

Who?

ALICE

Our little Sylvia has a new boyfriend.

SYLVIA

Laugh all you want. I don't even care this morning.

ALICE

Who is laughing? Tell us his name.

SYLVIA

Actually I'm not sure about his name.

ALICE

What does he do?

SYLVIA

I'm not sure about that either.

BARBARA

How long were you with him?

SYLVIA

All night. It was marvelous. He wrote this beautiful poem about me.

ALICE

Can I read it?

SYLVIA

It's in the Hudson River.

BARBARA

It's what?

SYLVIA

He's so handsome and sensitive. Not like anyone I've ever met. You'd like him
I think and so would you. You would both really like him.

ALICE

Well, that's great. I'm really happy for you.

BARBARA

Well, next time you're going to be out, call. And get his name in case he does
anything horrible to you later. Actually, if you could get a photocopy of his
license and fax it here, well that would be best for the police to track him down
later. Get fingerprints as well if you see an opening.

SYLVIA

He touched me here. And here. And here. You want to dust for prints?

BARBARA

Oh, Sylvia.

ALICE

How is his kiss?

SYLVIA

Well, we actually didn't kiss. I thought maybe I'd kiss him goodbye this
morning but then I didn't. He kisses everyone anyway. I decided I would be the
one who wouldn't kiss him. It makes me special, don't you think?

ALICE

What do you mean he kisses everyone?

SYLVIA

He's the boy who goes around kissing girls at night.

136

BARBARA

Oh.

SYLVIA

What?

BARBARA

No, nothing. It's just . . .

ALICE

What?

BARBARA

Nothing.

SYLVIA

He has the softest fingertips. He ran his fingers through my hair over and over
—

BARBARA

Soft fingertips.

SYLVIA

The softest.

BARBARA

And his eyes?

SYLVIA

Very strong.

BARBARA

His feet?

SYLVIA

Wide.

BARBARA

Does he have the intensity of a car battery in a thunderstorm?

SYLVIA

Very much so.

BARBARA

Um . . . Sylvia?

ALICE

When do I get to meet him?

SYLVIA

Soon. Very soon.

BARBARA

Sylvia.

SYLVIA

What?

BARBARA

He kissed me. This boy of yours.

SYLVIA

What?

BARBARA

I left the house last night.

ALICE

You did!

SYLVIA

Really?

BARBARA

Dexter and I had an argument and I . . . went for a walk . . . and he was there
and he . . . kissed me.

SYLVIA

Oh my god.

ALICE

What was it like? Did you tell Dexter?

BARBARA

No. I didn't.

                         SYLVIA
Was it everything you've ever wanted from a kiss?

                         BARBARA
It was —

                         SYLVIA
What?

                         BARBARA
It was —

                         SYLVIA
Yes?

                         ALICE
What?

                         BARBARA
It was nice.

                         SYLVIA
I knew it.

          (All three sisters sigh together in unison. They stare off into space dreamily.)

                         BARBARA
It was soft.

                         SYLVIA
I thought it would be.

                         BARBARA
It got quiet.

                         SYLVIA
It makes sense that it would.

                         BARBARA
It was like music.

                         SYLVIA
I don't doubt it.

BARBARA

You'll want to interview me for your article, I suppose.

SYLVIA

Maybe later.

BARBARA

Anytime. I'm probably not going anywhere today.

ALICE

I have to get ready for work.

BARBARA

You'll go talk to him? I mean, if he's there.

ALICE

I'll see what I can do.

(Exit ALICE.)

SYLVIA

What was that all about?

BARBARA

Nothing.

12.

(DEXTER *in his office seated with his head on his desk. The phone rings over and over but DEXTER ignores it.*
(Enter SASHA.)

SASHA

Dexter. Dexter.

DEXTER
(not raising his head)

What?

SASHA

I think we should have a meeting.

DEXTER

I can't.

SASHA

Why not?

DEXTER
(lifting his head)

I'm completely booked. It's been very busy.

(DEXTER puts his head back down.)

SASHA

You don't look busy.

DEXTER

I might have an opening on Wednesday.

(The phone begins to ring again.)

SASHA

Are you going to answer that?

DEXTER

I'm much too busy.

SASHA

Dexter, you can't have your head on the desk all day. You can't ignore your email and phone calls.

DEXTER
(lifting his head)

Can we talk about this later?

SASHA

I think we should talk about this now.
(Gets tired of the phone. Picks it up.)
Sasha Thompson's Office. Yes. No, she's in a meeting. All day I'm afraid. I'll have her call you as soon as she gets in. Goodbye.
(Hangs up.)
They wanted to speak to me.

DEXTER

Did they leave a message?

SASHA

I'm not calling them back.

DEXTER

I'm going to get blamed for that later.

SASHA

Don't worry. I'll take the heat.

DEXTER

You're the one who's going to blame me.

SASHA

I'm worried about you. Is there something bothering you?

DEXTER

No.

SASHA

I can sense these things. Is there a problem at work? Is it a personal problem because I am a good listener and I can speak in a low voice so others will not hear.

DEXTER

Everything is fine. Couldn't be better. I love it here. Love answering the phones. Love filling out the spreadsheets. It's like a dream. It's what I was put on earth to do, no doubt.

SASHA

Now there's no need –

DEXTER

Perhaps there could be more faxing – Could there be more faxing …OH! and filing? I enjoy the challenge of the alphabet.

SASHA

You're not pleased with your new job duties.

DEXTER

Before you came, I was managing twelve people. Now I get the coffee.

SASHA

It wasn't a demotion.

142

(DEXTER grips a pen tightly in his hand.)

DEXTER

That's what everyone keeps saying. It's like chutes and ladders in here. I think I'm climbing but then whoosh all of a sudden one day I'm taking dictation. Meanwhile one of the CEOs has run off with our pensions.

SASHA

We're still not sure about that officially.

DEXTER

What are you sure about?

SASHA

You're not happy.

DEXTER

I just want to know if everyone's going to be "restructured" again next week or if we're all going to be laid off.

(Long pause.)

SASHA

You sure there isn't a problem at home you want to talk about?

(SASHA is interrupted by the appearance of ALICE.)

ALICE

Hi. I tried to phone ahead but no one was answering. I just came to check on you.

DEXTER

I'm fine.

ALICE

Are you?

DEXTER
(annoyed)

I said I was fine.

ALICE

When are you coming back?

DEXTER

I don't know.

SASHA

Did you leave your wife?

DEXTER

I –

ALICE

We all really miss you. Barbara of course misses you a great deal. Sylvia I think misses you too. And then, of course there is me. The house seems so empty without you. Every time I hear a noise I don't recognize I think it's you returning. But of course you haven't.

DEXTER

I've only been gone one night.

ALICE

It was a very long night. I couldn't sleep. Usually your snoring lulls me to sleep but I had a restless night last night. And as a consequence, I mixed up some samples at work. Set us back two weeks at least.

DEXTER

I have to get back to work.

ALICE

I was supposed to tell you things from Barbara.

DEXTER

Alice, I really don't have time.

ALICE
(in misery)

I love you. I miss you. My bed is cold. My life is empty without you. I can't function. I can barely get out of bed. My life is miserable and lonely and pointless.

DEXTER

She said that?

ALICE

It was the basic gist.

                                    DEXTER
Alice, go back to work. Tell Barbara I'll call her.

                                    ALICE
You will?

                                    DEXTER
Probably.

                                    ALICE
Do you need to talk?

                                    SASHA
I'm a good talker.

                                    DEXTER
No, please!

                                    ALICE
I'm a good listener. I'm here for you. If you want to open up.

                                    SASHA
I'm here too.

                                    DEXTER
                                              (stabbing his desk with his pen to punctuate
                                              each sentence)
I don't want to open up!!! I don't want to talk! Why don't you both get out of
my cubicle and leave me alone?!!!

          (ALICE and SASHA are shocked by DEXTER's sudden violence. They both
          leave without another word.)

                                      13.

          (BOBBIE at one side of the stage at his desk. SYLVIA at the other side of the
          stage with BARBARA. They are setting the table for dinner.)

                                    BOBBIE
Three weeks later. The man has not returned home.

          (BOBBIE comes over to their side of the stage and sits with them at the table.)

BARBARA

Well, Bobbie, it's really good to meet you officially.

BOBBIE

Likewise.

BARBARA

I've heard so much about you.

SYLVIA

No, you haven't.

BARBARA

Sylvia gushes about you.

SYLVIA

No, I don't.

BOBBIE

I've heard a great deal about you as well. In fact, I've made you a character in my new novel.

BARBARA

You what?

(ALICE enters, miserably.)

ALICE

Everything's impossible.
                              (to BOBBIE)
Oh, hello.

BARBARA

What's wrong with you?

ALICE

Nothing. It's just so gray out today.
                              (to BOBBIE)
 I'm Alice.

BOBBIE

Pretend I'm not here.

146

ALICE

What?

BARBARA

This is Sylvia's boyfriend.

SYLVIA

Barbara!

BARBARA

What?

ALICE

Very good to meet you.

BOBBIE

Likewise.

ALICE

Sylvia rarely brings boys home. You should be honored.

SYLVIA

Alice!

ALICE

Oh, will you relax? My sister doesn't like to be teased. Especially when it's cloudy out.

SYLVIA

It is gray out today.

ALICE

I wonder what the statistics are for suicide on gray days.

SYLVIA

It's never gray in New Jersey.

ALICE

In New Jersey.

BARBARA

New Jersey.

(The phone rings. BARBARA answers it.)

BARBARA

Hello.

ALICE

So, Bobbie, where did you grow up?

BOBBIE

Oh, you don't have to ask questions about me.

ALICE

I'm interested.

BOBBIE

I'm not that interesting.

(DEXTER *in a spot holding a phone to his ear.*)

BARBARA
(on phone)

Are you ever coming home?

DEXTER

I don't know. I'm discovering new foods. Have you ever had sardines?

BARBARA

No.

(ED *is revealed next to* DEXTER, *slumped on the couch watching TV.*
DEXTER *tries to converse with both of them.*)

ED

Women are crazy, man.

DEXTER

I'm being independent.

ED

You should just hang up.

DEXTER

You've always wanted me to be independent.

                    BARBARA

Can't you be independent and live with me too?

                    DEXTER

I don't know.

                      ED

All of 'em. Crazy. And not just once a month, if you know what I'm sayin'.

                    BARBARA

I miss you.

                    DEXTER

I miss you too.

                      ED

Don't say that.

                    DEXTER

I'm sorry.

                      ED

What are you saying that for?

                    BARBARA

You can come home whenever you like.

                      ED

You are so pussy-whipped.

                    BARBARA

I changed the sheets on the bed today. They stopped smelling like you.

                    DEXTER

Oh. OK.

                    BARBARA

I'm not even sure exactly why you left. There was some unpleasantness, yes,
but I didn't think you'd still be gone. Are you . . . How come . . .

                    DEXTER

I've been thinking about your father.

BARBARA

What about him?

ED

You're like a little nancy girl.

DEXTER
(to ED)

Could you be quiet for a minute?

ED

Or like a flower – all delicate and shit.

BARBARA

Dexter?

DEXTER

Am I right for you?

BARBARA

Of course.

DEXTER

How do you know?

ED

La La la. Walk all over me. I'm Dexter.

DEXTER

I have to go now. There's a game on.

BARBARA

What kind of game?

DEXTER

I'm not sure. It's on the TV. I'm going to watch it.

BARBARA

Dexter . . . Are you happier without me?

DEXTER

I'll talk to you later.

(DEXTER *hangs up. A pause.*)

ED

Get me a beer, will you?

(BARBARA puts down the phone.)

BARBARA

I need a drink. Who wants drinks?

(BARBARA makes drinks. SYLVIA lights a cigarette.)

SYLVIA

Was that Dexter?

BARBARA

Put out that cigarette.

ALICE

You studied literature?

BOBBIE

Russian literature with a minor in gender studies.

BARBARA

Alice is a scientist.

BOBBIE

I know. That's very interesting. I'd like to come to your lab sometime if that's OK.

ALICE

I suppose.

BOBBIE

Because I'd like to write about you.

BARBARA

Oh, her too, huh?

BOBBIE

I'd like to write about all of you. You don't mind, do you? Of course I haven't met Dexter yet, so I'll just base him on myself. Maybe you could all tell me all your secrets and I could write them down.

(Beat.)

ALICE

I don't have any secrets. I'm a shell of a person.

BARBARA

Look at you. You have a date again tonight. Everything is possible for you.

ALICE

But what's the point, really? This date will be no better than the others.

BARBARA

You don't know that yet. In fact you may not know his worth until you're married to him for five years and even then you may not be sure.

ALICE

I'll never marry.

BARBARA

A girl like you? You could have anyone you want.

ALICE

Not anyone.

BARBARA

Yes, anyone.

ALICE

Barbara . . .

BARBARA

What is it?

ALICE

Nothing. Never mind. I should go get ready.

BOBBIE

Hey, is it OK if I come out with you on your date and sit a table away and take notes?

ALICE

No, that's not OK.

14.

(SYLVIA is in bed. BOBBIE is at his desk staring down the barrel of his handgun.)

BOBBIE

I stare and stare until all the incessant buzzing in my head becomes one voice and then I can write for a while.

(BOBBIE puts down his gun and starts to type. SYLVIA comes to his side of the stage and watches him.)

SYLVIA

It's very beautiful the way you do that. Precise.

BOBBIE

I know the tricks of being a boy. I know how to act like I'm not interested. I know how to feign disinterest. I know how to walk away, how to not call, how to ignore her insinuations that she likes me. In short, I know how to play dumb. I know all this not from being taught but because I am a smart boy and that's what smart boys know.

But I can no longer use my tricks of being a boy. Because suddenly I am in love and all the crafty tricks I'd collected are useless against her laughter, her dimples, her eyes. In short, I am no longer a smart boy. She has made me dumb.

SYLVIA

Do I make you dumb?

BOBBIE

Kiss me.

SYLVIA

No.

BOBBIE

Why not?

SYLVIA

I want to be different.

BOBBIE

You are different.

                         SYLVIA
I want to be better.

                         BOBBIE
Well, if you don't do it, I have to go out.

                         SYLVIA
Why?

                         BOBBIE
Don't ask me that. Kiss me.

                         SYLVIA
Soon.

                         BOBBIE
Why are you hurting me like this?

                         SYLVIA
                          (hurt)
I'm not.

                         BOBBIE
                 (reads what he's writing)
This doesn't make sense.

                         SYLVIA
Our relationship is blossoming, don't you think?

                         BOBBIE
Hmm?

                         SYLVIA
I feel very close to you. I feel like we're becoming intertwined. Don't you?

                         BOBBIE
I'm writing.

                         SYLVIA
Sorry. I just feel really close to you right now.

154

BOBBIE
(stops typing)

Then you should kiss me.

SYLVIA

Not yet.

BOBBIE
(goes back to typing)

Fine.

SYLVIA

I just feel like it's not the right moment yet. I feel like when it is right I'll know it and you'll know it and it will be all the more special. Don't you agree? Bobbie, don't you think that's true?

BOBBIE

Be quiet.

SYLVIA

I just want to do it the right way. In the past I didn't do it right. I think maybe this is better, though, don't you?

BOBBIE

Well, I'm gonna go then.

SYLVIA

Why?

BOBBIE

There's too much talking here.

SYLVIA

I'll be quiet.

BOBBIE

No, you won't.

SYLVIA

Stay with me. Don't go kiss some other girl. Why do you have to kiss some other girl?

                    BOBBIE

I just have to.

                    SYLVIA

But you don't. You can't do this forever, you know. They'll put you in jail one
of these days.

                    BOBBIE

Yeah

                    SYLVIA

They will.

                    BOBBIE

I don't care.

                    SYLVIA

You should care.

        (Pause.)

                    BOBBIE

I can't stop.

                    SYLVIA

Why not? Why not?

                    BOBBIE

It makes me feel worse each time but I can't stop.

                    SYLVIA

I'll come with you.

                    BOBBIE

No.

                    SYLVIA

You want me to stay here while you go off and —

                    BOBBIE

Some nights it takes hours to find the right woman all alone. She has to be
perfect. Not look perfect, but feel perfect. It has to feel right before it feels
wrong. . . . You know? You understand? I want you to understand.

156

SYLVIA

I don't understand. Stay with me. We'll lie in bed and talk all night and then it will be the morning and we'll both have bad breath and we can make breakfast together. Like waffles or cereal . . . or waffles.

(BOBBIE *looks at her. He puts on his coat.*
(*Exit* BOBBIE.)

SYLVIA

Or toast.

15.

(ALICE *and* JAMES *in the restaurant.* ALICE *is about to take blood.*)

ALICE

This is going to pinch just a little.

JAMES

Is that really necessary? I'm not good with needles.

ALICE

Do you want there to be a second date?

JAMES

Will there be a second date?

ALICE

Not if you keep whining.

JAMES

I'm not whining.

ALICE

Be a man.

JAMES

I just don't want to faint and hit my head again.

ALICE

Will you stay still so I can find a good vein?

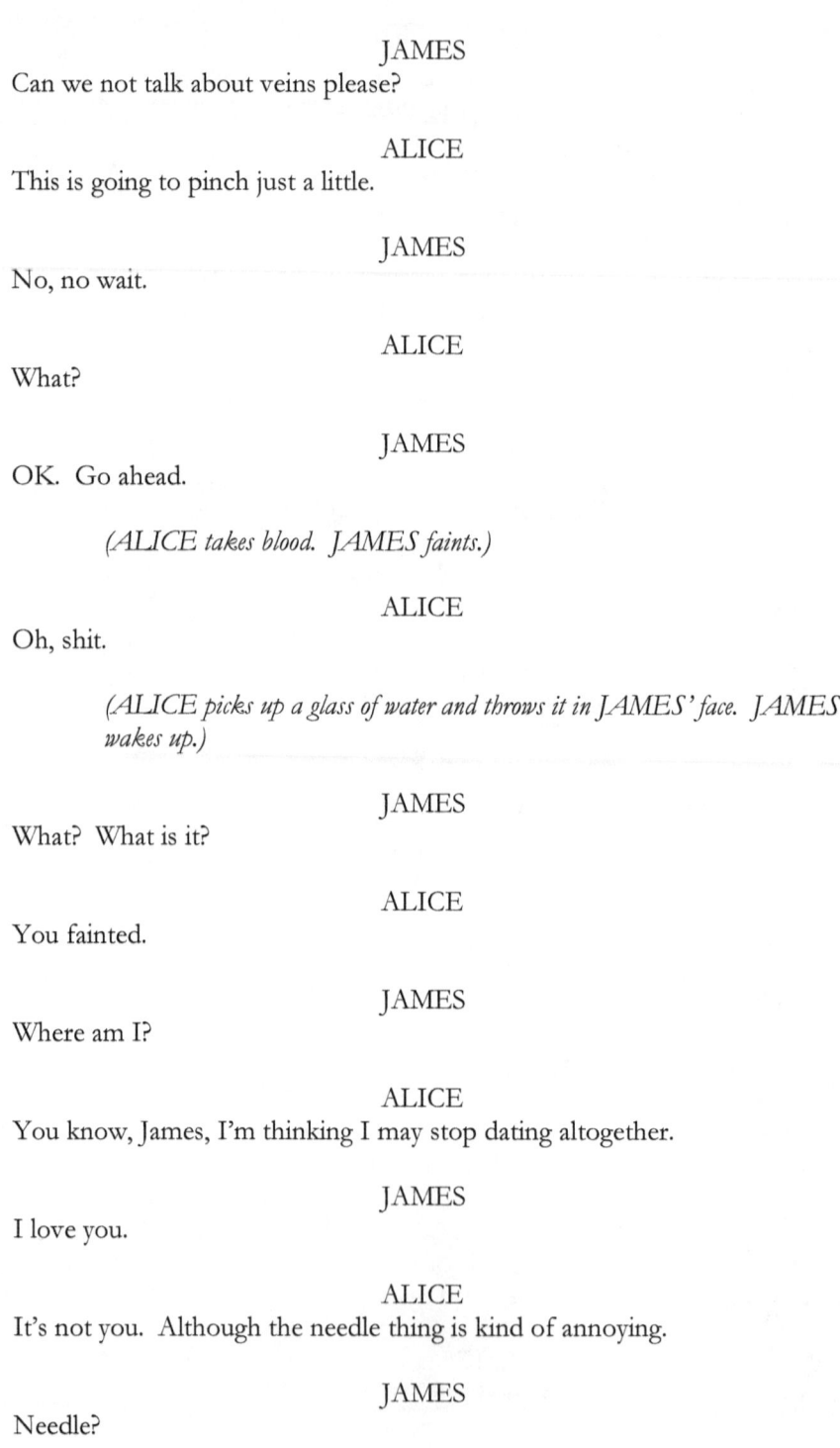

                    JAMES
Can we not talk about veins please?

                    ALICE
This is going to pinch just a little.

                    JAMES
No, no wait.

                    ALICE
What?

                    JAMES
OK. Go ahead.

        (ALICE takes blood. JAMES faints.)

                    ALICE
Oh, shit.

        (ALICE picks up a glass of water and throws it in JAMES' face. JAMES
        wakes up.)

                    JAMES
What? What is it?

                    ALICE
You fainted.

                    JAMES
Where am I?

                    ALICE
You know, James, I'm thinking I may stop dating altogether.

                    JAMES
I love you.

                    ALICE
It's not you. Although the needle thing is kind of annoying.

                    JAMES
Needle?

(JAMES begins to faint again. ALICE slaps him awake.)

ALICE

Stop that now. OK? You there?

JAMES

Hello?

ALICE

What was I saying? Oh yes. So I'm sorry but I don't think there will be a second date.

JAMES

Is your name Alice?

ALICE

Will you focus please?

JAMES

Everything's so far away.

ALICE

I know. That's always the way it is, isn't it? The thing we really want is always so far from our grasp. You just really want one thing, right? It's all you want and no matter what you can never have it. No matter what you do or how cute you dress. It will never happen for you. And you move through every day hoping for a compliment or a smile – some little thing – one little crumb or two and you know it's all you'll ever get but still you live for it. And then he goes away and won't answer the phone and you may never see him again and so what's the point, I ask you? What's the point of getting through the day if he's not there at the end of it? Why go on?

JAMES

Are you talking about suicide?

ALICE

No. Yes. I don't know. I mean life is suffering, isn't it? Maybe I'm not supposed to be happy. I do have my work, which is I suppose in some ways just a veiled attempt to get what I want or at least deal with it. Maybe it's not completely hopeless. My sister could die or he could suddenly see he loves me. Maybe you're right though, maybe if you can't get what you want in this life you should just kill yourself.

JAMES

Did I say that?

ALICE

I don't know. Maybe I'm not even depressed enough for that. Maybe next week. I just want to go to sleep.

JAMES

Me too. Hey, why do I feel woozy?

ALICE
(holding up vial of blood)

I took some blood.

(JAMES faints again.)

16.

(SYLVIA in a streetlamp.)

SYLVIA

I decided I would set about to understand him even if he didn't want to show me the parts of him I wanted to see. The boy had led his life as an enigma, never letting anyone see more than they had to. But I am an investigative reporter. I'll crack this wide open. With a sledgehammer if I have to. Something you should know about me if we're going to continue – sometimes I use a sledgehammer when a hand is all that's necessary and sometimes I use a hand when maybe a word would do. Tonight is one of these nights.

I don't know how to choose – what are the rules to this venture? What are the signals? The body language? I would try to pick someone who appeals, who seemed lonely, someone who has shoes I like and who walks in a way I wish I could. Someone different, someone better.

(SASHA appears in a streetlamp.)

SYLVIA

I see her and immediately know she is the one. What did he say? That it must feel right before it feels wrong? It feels right or it feels something – something buzzing and nice and scary all at once.

SASHA

Excuse me.

160

SYLVIA

Huh.

SASHA

Do you know where there's a liquor store around here?

SYLVIA

Ummmm. There might be, uh.

(SYLVIA leans forward and kisses her. SASHA backs away and then slaps her.)

SASHA

Don't you ever do that! Don't you ever do that!

(SYLVIA crumbles to a heap on the ground.)

SYLVIA

I'm sorry. I'm sorry.

SASHA
(backing away)

Why did you do that!? That's assault. You assaulted me. You're disgusting! Disgusting! What's wrong with you!

(Exit SASHA.
(SYLVIA sobs.
(On the other side of the stage in another streetlamp, ALICE is walking alone. BOBBIE approaches her. SYLVIA continues to sob.
(BOBBIE and ALICE look at each other. They stop. They continue again towards each other. They stop. It is almost like a dance. Then they are together and they are kissing. ALICE's eyes are closed. She becomes elated, he, more depressed and then he is gone.)

ALICE

Oh. Wow.

(A loud sob from SYLVIA.)

17

(*BARBARA is on the phone with DEXTER who is on the other side of the stage, alone.*)

BARBARA

You're coming home, then?

DEXTER

I don't know. I've been thinking, all the time thinking.

BARBARA

About what sort of things.

DEXTER

About us. We got married too quick. Your father was sick then already. And we leaped into the thing even though we didn't know each other very well. You were my first love and then before we knew it we were married. You were taking care of your father every day and then the fear came for you and you stopped leaving the house and I trudged to work day after day and tried to become numb and not think about what was I doing. It was my life. Work and home and work and home. And at home, your father was coughing into his oxygen tank and your sisters were bickering. I was becoming smaller. In the office, I had a new boss every few months--they were interchangeable in their corporate slogans and brand name business attire and just as I would get used to one, he or she would be promoted and so I never knew any of them long enough for them to even know what I was supposed to be doing. Not that I could tell you that. And I still can't. I'm not even sure who I am. I've become so insignificant.

BARBARA

You're very significant. To me.

DEXTER

I'm so furious all the time. This is not what I pictured. Is this what you pictured?

BARBARA

I don't know.

DEXTER

I'm afraid of how angry I can get.

BARBARA

I'm not afraid.

DEXTER

You're afraid of everything.

BARBARA

I'm not afraid of you.

DEXTER

Maybe you should be. Maybe if we had gotten to know each other better before I started living here, we wouldn't be married now.

BARBARA

So what? We got married too quick? You want out? Is that what you're saying?

DEXTER

I'm bad for you.

BARBARA

I don't think you are.

DEXTER

I'm not your father.

BARBARA

What are you saying?

DEXTER

I can't be him.

BARBARA

What are you talking about?

DEXTER

I know you think he was perfect and always had all the answers all the time and always knew what to do and what to say and could protect you so you weren't afraid all the time.

BARBARA

Why are you saying that?

DEXTER

I can't do that.

BARBARA

I'm not asking you to.

DEXTER

I am so angry. I am just so angry with you. He was never like that.

BARBARA

But sometimes he was.

DEXTER

Well he was never a secretary.

BARBARA

I'm not comparing you to him.

DEXTER

Who else is there to compare me to?

BARBARA

I love you. When are you coming home?

DEXTER

I don't know.

(Enter ALICE.)

BARBARA

I'll call you back later. OK?

(They hang up.)

ALICE

Was that Dexter?

BARBARA

Yes.

ALICE

How is he?

BARBARA

I don't know.

ALICE

I'm in love with him, you know.

BARBARA

Pardon?

ALICE

I'm madly in love with your husband, Dexter.

BARBARA

Why would you say something like that?

ALICE

It's true.

BARBARA

I know it's true, everyone knows it's true, but just because something is true doesn't mean you have to say it! The only reason it was possible to live with your problem, was that neither of us ever acknowledged it. Now it's there out in the open. How can we go back to the way it was now that it's out there?

ALICE

I thought I should tell you. We leave too much unsaid.

BARBARA

I like it that way!

ALICE

I'm sorry.

BARBARA

Tell me this. What am I supposed to do with this information, huh?

ALICE

I just thought you should know.

BARBARA

Why?

ALICE

So you can be angry at me. So you can hate me. You can yell at me and we can
have it out.

BARBARA

I don't want to yell at you!

ALICE

Yell at me. Abuse me. Scream in my face.

BARBARA

I don't want to! If I was a man maybe it would be different. Maybe I would hit
you.

ALICE

Hit me.

(ALICE closes her eyes. BARBARA makes a fist but cannot bring herself to hit
ALICE.)

BARBARA

I want you to move out.

ALICE

What?

BARBARA

I want you out of the house. Dexter is coming back and I don't want you living
here when he returns.

ALICE

I understand.

BARBARA

Get out.

ALICE

Do you hate me?

BARBARA

Get out!

ALICE

Please hate me.

166

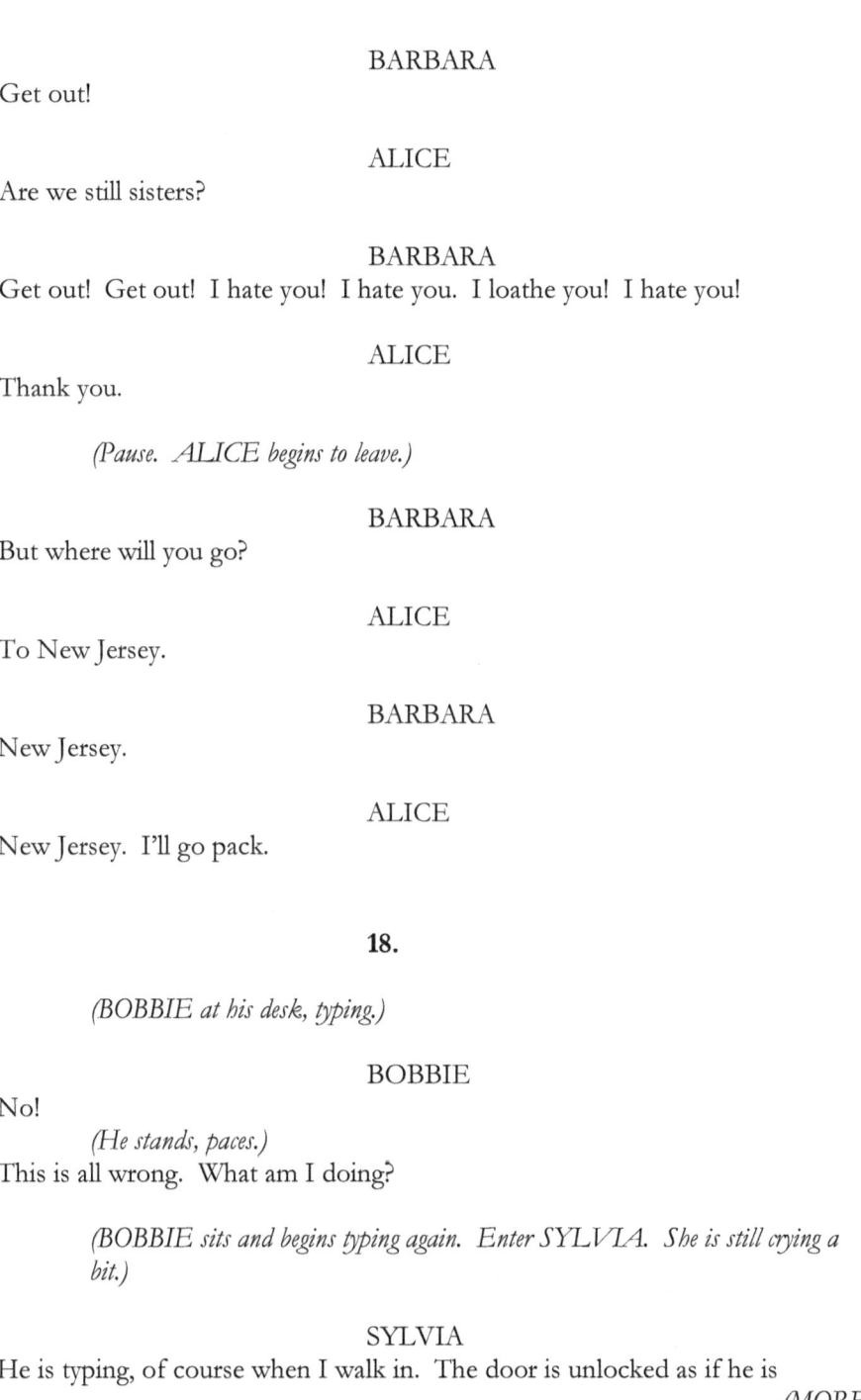

BARBARA

Get out!

ALICE

Are we still sisters?

BARBARA

Get out! Get out! I hate you! I hate you. I loathe you! I hate you!

ALICE

Thank you.

(Pause. ALICE begins to leave.)

BARBARA

But where will you go?

ALICE

To New Jersey.

BARBARA

New Jersey.

ALICE

New Jersey. I'll go pack.

18.

(BOBBIE at his desk, typing.)

BOBBIE

No!
(He stands, paces.)
This is all wrong. What am I doing?

(BOBBIE sits and begins typing again. Enter SYLVIA. She is still crying a bit.)

SYLVIA

He is typing, of course when I walk in. The door is unlocked as if he is

(MORE)

SYLVIA (cont.)

expecting me or as if anyone who wanted could come in and share his time with him and it didn't really matter who it was. I like to think he's waiting for me. I look at his eyes, his nose, his lips. I look over his shoulder at what he's writing.

BOBBIE

Meanwhile, Alice, the middle sister, got on the PATH train with a single suitcase and a strong desire to be a Jersey girl. On the train, she pored over the newspaper and circled in red the most likely and inexpensive apartments.

SYLVIA

I look at his lips.

BOBBIE

A man sat beside her on the train. He was not unusual or particularly attractive or unattractive and Alice guessed rightly that by the end of the trip she would have a date with this man. She supposed one more date couldn't hurt.

SYLVIA

I look at his lips.

BOBBIE

Alice wondered then in the train whether or not she would let him kiss her good night, and if she did whether or not she would enjoy it. She remembered the boy's kiss on seventy first street or was it fifty third? None of it mattered now because she was off to a new Jersey life. She had decided her fate. She would live in New Jersey till she died and was eaten by worms. She could only hope that her sister would once again speak to her. Perhaps they would visit. She smiled at this and then looking up, smiled at the man beside her.

SYLVIA

Bobbie . . . I want you to kiss me.

(BOBBIE *is startled but receives her kiss. They kiss for a long time. They break.*)

SYLVIA

Oh.
        (*Pause.*)
That's what that is.

BOBBIE

I think I love you. I've been going crazy.

168

SYLVIA

Really?

BOBBIE

I've never felt this way about anyone.
(taking a pigeon out of a bag)
I was so low as to kill this pigeon today. I shot it off the ledge. I lay it at your
feet.

(BOBBIE lays it at her feet.)

SYLVIA

That's disgusting. What's the matter with you?

BOBBIE

It's you. You do this to me. I can only breathe when you're around. The rest
of the time it's like I'm in this comatose state.

SYLVIA

You're fine.

BOBBIE

I'm not. I'm not. I want to hold you in my arms forever until one or both of us
die and they have to pry our decomposing bodies apart with crowbars and
picks. I think about this all the time.

SYLVIA

No, you don't. You're writing all the time.

BOBBIE

My writing! I know you want to read this but you can't. It's no good. You'll
see that it's no good and hate me. Women never forgive failure.

SYLVIA

I can't read it?

BOBBIE

Kiss me again.

(They kiss. SYLVIA pulls away.)

SYLVIA

I have to go.

BOBBIE

Wait.

SYLVIA

I have to go.

BOBBIE

Are you going to take the pigeon? I killed it for you.

(Exit SYLVIA.
(BOBBIE punches the typewriter.)

BOBBIE

Ow!

(BOBBIE picks up the typewriter lifts it high and throws it down in frustration.
He looks at it, regains his calm, picks it up and starts typing again. If it's
completely smashed, he takes out the page and starts writing by hand. After a bit,
he look at what he's written, doesn't like it. He crumples it up and throws it down.
(Exit BOBBIE.)

19.

(DEXTER in streetlight, maybe smoking a cigarette. BOBBIE approaches in a
fog of frustration and confusion.)

DEXTER

You're him, aren't you?

(BOBBIE looks at him.)

DEXTER

I need to talk to you. Please don't go. I need to. You need to listen to me.
Because I'm like you. You need to help me. Sometimes I find myself following
strange women. I've been doing it a lot lately. Course I never kissed them.
Don't know how you get away with that.

Last week – I guess it was last week, last week I went too far.   It was a hard day
and when I stepped out of the office into the street there was this beautiful girl.
Painfully beautiful. She was so beautiful that something inside me snapped.

I followed her down the street, into the subway. She stopped short and I

(MORE)

stopped too and I stood right behind her watching her. I was angry. I was furious. I'm not really sure why. I wanted to throttle her. She was just there and it made me so angry that she existed. Her pointy nose, her lips, they all just infuriated me. I just . . I had the sudden urge to push her off the platform into the oncoming train. The closer the train came, the more I wanted to shove her until the impulse was almost unbearably strong. I reached out my hand. She was right there.

I know that people shouldn't do these things. Don't look at me like that.

You know I'm not even sure why I didn't do it. I almost did. It could have gone either way. It's like this thin thread between the two choices. Just this little tiny thing. It could go at any second. It could just snap like that and then what? I would be uncontrollable.

Don't ever grow up.

Don't look at me like that. I'm sorry. I'm sorry I told you that. I'm sorry. Do you forgive me?

>*(BOBBIE kisses him.)*

DEXTER

Oh.
>*(Pause.)*
Thank you.

>*(BOBBIE has gone.)*

20.

>*(BARBARA and SYLVIA by the coffin. SYLVIA is writing on the pad.)*

BARBARA

You writing another article about your boy?

SYLVIA

No.

BARBARA

Why not?

SYLVIA

No one seems much interested anymore. I guess they've grown tired of him.

BARBARA

Not you though, huh?

SYLVIA

There's nothing really all that interesting about him when it comes down to it. I mean yes he goes out and kisses strangers and yes he's writing a novel that he's throwing in the river bust mostly he just drinks a lot and doesn't talk in public. He only ever goes out in the street at night and to the bar. It's boring.

BARBARA

That's too bad.

SYLVIA

It's all right. It's fine.

BARBARA

I liked him.

SYLVIA

You don't really know him.

BARBARA

I still liked him. I wish you would –

SYLVIA

Stop it.

BARBARA

Well, it's just so frustrating. You go through them so quickly.

SYLVIA

That's not true.

BARBARA

What about the last one?

SYLVIA

He was a jerk.

BARBARA

I just want you to be happy.

SYLVIA

Then stop telling me how to live my life.

BARBARA

Fine.

SYLVIA

Fine.

(Pause.)

BARBARA

I just wish you would learn how to function in a relationship. I know it's hard because we're orphans.

SYLVIA

Shut up.

BARBARA

We are.

(Enter DEXTER.)

BARBARA

Dexter!

SYLVIA

Hi, Dexter.

(DEXTER and BARBARA embrace.)

SYLVIA

OK. Um, I'll talk to you guys later.

(Exit SYLVIA.)

DEXTER

I want to come home.

BARBARA

OK.

                    DEXTER
But I need help.

                    BARBARA
OK.

                    DEXTER
I need . . . I don't know. I think I'm a dangerous person.

                    BARBARA
No you're not.

                    DEXTER
I need you to believe me about his. I'm terrified. I'm standing here terrified
and I need your help.

                    BARBARA
You're afraid?

                    DEXTER
It's because I'm a man. We're all killers and rapists underneath, left over from
hunting and war. I don't want to be a man sometimes.

                    BARBARA
You don't have to be. I'm used to having to learn new things. I will be the man
of this house when you cannot.

                    DEXTER
Oh, Barbara. I don't know if –

                    BARBARA
It's something I can do. There, now. Don't cry.

                    DEXTER
I'm going to go to therapy I think and I want you to come with me. Because
I'm terrified.

                    BARBARA
OK.

                    DEXTER
Will you come with me?

                    BARBARA
You mean leave the house on a weekly basis?

                    DEXTER
Maybe twice a week.

                    BARBARA
That's a lot to ask.

                    DEXTER
I know.

                    BARBARA
I'm a good wife, aren't I?

                    DEXTER
I don't really think it's about that.

                    BARBARA
I think I've been a good wife. You've always been a good husband.

                    DEXTER
I don't want to think about it anymore. I keep holding myself up to bizarre standards of what a husband or a man should be. I don't know what that is. I think we just have to figure out how you and me are supposed to be with each other. Can you try?

                    BARBARA
I'll try.

                    DEXTER
Thank you.

                    BARBARA
But I want us to have a baby.

                    DEXTER
You do? I think I want to have a baby too.

                    BARBARA
You do?

                    DEXTER
But not right this second.

BARBARA

No, no. Not right now. You sure not right now?

DEXTER

Later.

BARBARA

Yes, I agree, later. But soon, right?

DEXTER

Maybe when I get that promotion.

BARBARA

Well, my business has been doing really well.

DEXTER

Really? Soon, then.

(Enter ALICE.)

ALICE

Dexter!

BARBARA

Hello, Alice.

ALICE

I just came back to get a few things. I'll be out of your hair soon.

BARBARA

You found an apartment?

DEXTER

Oh, are you moving out, Alice?

ALICE

I . . . um. I haven't found a place yet, but um there are a few possibilities.

BARBARA

There are?

ALICE

Some very promising possibilities.

176

BARBARA

Oh, well then.

ALICE

I'll just be getting some of my toiletries and then I'll be going. Good to see you, Dexter.

BARBARA

Wait.

ALICE

I'm not taking any of your stuff, don't worry.

BARBARA

You're wearing my shirt right now.

ALICE

I'll take it off.

BARBARA

No. No. Don't. I was thinking, Alice. Maybe you could stay.

ALICE

Stay?

BARBARA

For a while. You know, until you find your own place.

ALICE

I guess I could stay for a while. You know, just while I'm looking.

BARBARA

Oh good. Anyway, we're going to need your help burying father.

(Enter SYLVIA.)

SYLVIA

Burying father?

BARBARA

Yes, it's time to bury him finally.

SYLVIA

I don't want to bury him. I want to drop him in the Hudson River.

BARBARA

The Hudson River?

ALICE

The Hudson River.

SYLVIA

We can do it right now. It will be beautiful and perfect and peaceful. You know how Father loved to look at the river.

ALICE

He did.

BARBARA

Right now?

SYLVIA

Let's just take him out now and drop him in the river.

BOBBIE

Which is what they do. In the dead of night, they lift the coffin from the place it occupied for well over a year.

(SYLVIA, BARBARA, DEXTER and ALICE lift the coffin and begin to carry it.)

BOBBIE

They carry him down the stairs, down the street, down another street, past the bodega, past the homeless man in the dress. They almost drop him twice but they recover and although they are tired, they bring their father all the way to the Hudson River where each of them kisses the lid of the coffin.

DEXTER

Rest in peace.

SYLVIA

Bye, Daddy.

ALICE

Good night, Father.

                              BARBARA
This is so hard.

                              ALICE
It's OK, honey.

                              DEXTER
                            (holding her)
Shhh. We have to let him go now.

                              BARBARA
I know. I know.

                              DEXTER
We're saying goodbye.

                              BARBARA
Goodbye. Goodbye.

        (They pick up the coffin again and lower it into "the water.")

                              BOBBIE
And with that, they heave him into the water and he drops with a gigantic
splash. For a minute he floats there and the sisters and the man are worried he
will float down the river and collect on some other shore. But then he sinks to
the bottom to rest among the larger fish.

Barbara suddenly realizes she had left the house and none of her fear had
followed her. Perhaps it is because she had a clear task – to bury father. She
decides she would daily leave the house with a clear task in mind – even if it's to
buy a can of sardines. Or maybe every other day. No sense in creating
impossible goals.

Alice decides in a clear task fashion of her own to come to the river each
morning and throw her worries into it.

Dexter puts his arm around Barbara and Barbara grasps Alice's hand and they
set out for home.

Sylvia goes to see the boy.

EPILOGUE

(BOBBIE stares at a page in the typewriter. He seems numb in his sadness. He does not type.)

BOBBIE

I tried my best. This is all my insignificant brain can do. It's pointless I know. All I have is this little brain. It's the best I can do. I've written the best I can write. You can judge it now if you want.

(Enter SYLVIA.)

SYLVIA

I have played this conversation over and over in my mind to exhaustion. I have wondered if I could have said something different. For the past two years of my life I have wondered this. But that's all moot because it happened one way and I said certain things. To the best of my memory, this is how it went.

I walked in the apartment door which, as always, was open. He was staring at a page in the typewriter. I thought he was writing but he continued to stare for a long time. Fifteen minutes? An hour? I'm not sure. Neither of us said anything the whole time and then –

(BOBBIE takes the sheet from the typewriter and gives it to SYLVIA.)

SYLVIA
(looking at page)
"The end." Did you finish? Are you finished with the book? That's great! Isn't that great?! Congratulations! Why aren't you jumping up and down about this?

BOBBIE

I dunno.

SYLVIA

This is huge.

BOBBIE

I guess.

SYLVIA

Now you can start another one and maybe after you write the pages you could hold onto them . . . and make copies.

BOBBIE

I can't write another one.

SYLVIA

Why not?

BOBBIE

What's the point?

SYLVIA

Don't talk like that.

BOBBIE

Well what is the point?

SYLVIA

I don't know but I'm sure there is one.

BOBBIE

(Pause.)
You can stay here tonight.

SYLVIA

Oh. I probably won't. I mean, I won't be staying here tonight, thanks though.

BOBBIE

What?

SYLVIA

I just think we should change the way we relate to each other.

BOBBIE

What?

SYLVIA

Mostly how we kiss and sleep together. I don't think we should do that anymore.

BOBBIE

Why?

SYLVIA

I guess I just feel differently now. About you and me. I see us differently. Than I did.

BOBBIE

Why?

SYLVIA

I just do.

BOBBIE

It's because I let you know me, isn't it. I always make that mistake.

SYLVIA

Don't say that. Anyway, I'm sure it's only partially true.

BOBBIE

SYLVIA

We're really very different as people. It just wouldn't work even though I respect you and your work and I think you respect mine.

BOBBIE

Christ.

SYLVIA

It's just best for both of us.

BOBBIE

. . .

SYLVIA

I still want to hang out sometime, I just don't think we should kiss each other.

BOBBIE

But that's all we really do.

SYLVIA

We could go bowling.

BOBBIE

You want to go bowling?

SYLVIA

Sure. Or snorkeling.

                              BOBBIE

Please leave now.

                              SYLVIA

Come on. Don't be like that.

                              BOBBIE

Shouldn't you be out chasing some story? Getting your hands dirty. Isn't that
what you want to do?

                              SYLVIA

Yeah. I guess.

                              BOBBIE

So get lost.

                              SYLVIA

Come on. It's not like that.

                              BOBBIE

What is it like, then? You know what? I don't really want to hang out with you.
I don't really want to go bowling or have a beer with you. You're not beautiful.
I don't want to look at your face. Most of the time when you talk I wish you
would shut up. I think I just would like it best if you would get the fuck out of
here.

                              SYLVIA

But . . .

                              BOBBIE

GET OUT!

            (SYLVIA exits. BOBBIE paces furiously.)

                              SYLVIA

It was a cold walk home. I tripped a lot. I cried a little. I didn't find out until
days later. When it was in the paper.

I put in a lot of work afterwards. Almost everyday for two years. I took a lot of
trips up and down the river. I hired boats and diving crews. I rented cars. The
pages weren't numbered. That made collating especially difficult. I think I have
almost all of them now. A lot of the bottles were just at the bottom of the
                                                          (MORE)

                                                                    183

river. A few were in the ocean. Some we may never find.

This was the story of the boy. This was the story of the man the boy could have become. This was the story of the three sisters, Barbara, Alice and Sylvia. This was not the story of the gravedigger, who is the father of the three sisters or of his wife, the poet, who died young. This was a story.

> *(The lights come up bright on BOBBIE who pulls the gun from his drawer.*
> *(BOBBIE shoots himself in the head.)*

> *Blackout.*

<u>END OF PLAY</u>

Anna Hopkins (left), Ana Perea, Luis Moreno (rear), Katie Honaker in the
Sanctuary Playwrights Theatre production at the Kraine Theatre

Anna Hopkins (left), Luis Moreno, Ana Perea, Orion Taraban in the Sanctuary Playwrights Theatre production at the Kraine Theatre

Caroline Tamas (left), Orion Taraban in the Sanctuary Playwrights Theatre production at the Kraine Theatre

Orion Taraban (left, rear), Luis Moreno, Ana Perea, Anna Hopkins in the Sanctuary Playwrights Theatre production at the Kraine Theatre

The Word Made Flesh
An Introduction to Anne Washburn's *I Have Loved Strangers*
by Jeffrey M. Jones

> And the Word was with God,
> And the Word was God...
> And the Word was made flesh and dwelt among us.
>
> — *The Gospel According to St. John*

Words and Bodies

In the end, all theater necessarily comes down to people, onstage, talking. And until recently, despite innumerable variations of dramatic form, the basic understanding of who, and where, these people were never changed. They were always to be understood as [actors portraying] characters inhabiting a space and time like our own. Like us, they knew who they were, and could tell you who they were. They were, in other words, just like real people.

Recently, of course, playwrights have not only dismantled the conventions of dramatic psychology but approached dramaturgy itself as the staging of texts through the medium of voice, collapsing the distinction between actor and role, thus bypassing the need for, and notion of, character. For, interestingly, it turns out that the artifice of character – the pretense that the actor is in fact the *role* – supports all the rest of the theatrical illusion.

The actor, in supplying body and voice, allows the character to stand before us and speak. Because the body is real, existing in space and time, and the voice expresses thoughts, desires and intentions like ours, we are inclined to take characters at their word: if they say they're in Illyria, we'll accept it. Without the foundation of character, however, theatrical "reality" itself warps and collapses. If the speaking voice doesn't issue from a character, who's "in the body?" Who's really there? The fundamental assumption about the relationship between words and bodies in the theater, between who speaks and what is spoken, has changed fundamentally.

This is the starting point for Anne Washburn's *I Have Loved Strangers*.

Landscape and Language

In the opening scene of the play, we find a figure wandering in a landscape. The figure will turn out to be Jeremiah. But the landscape, the background, is not so easily resolved.

We understand at once that the speech of all the other figures (they are hardly characters, nor are they necessarily in dialogue with each other) consists of phrases overheard on the street – that we too are therefore in the position of Jeremiah, wandering through the streets of a city. But only the passage, the wandering – the act or relationship of hearing people as one walks – has been rendered. The city itself is virtual; not because, like the location of any dramatic scene, it is part of a theatrical premise and hence *imagined*, but because, like the passers-by, it barely exists.

In film, such scenes – the crowd blurred, with snippets of overheard dialogue as voice-overs – are unremarkable because the mere fact of filming implies that the people actually existed somewhere once. But in *I Have Loved Strangers*, a play of many landscapes, the locations (summer night, country graveyard) exist only linguistically. Unlike traditional theatrical landscapes, they are not meant to be read as views of a complete and consistent world. Like the calligraphy of Chinese landscapes, they merely indicate the idea of landscape; they are notional at best.

Given the figure/ground relationship, Jeremiah would seem to be a "character" in the standard theatrical sense, but upon reflection, this too becomes problematic. For his words, we recognize – even if we are wholly unfamiliar with the text – come from the Bible. The "character" of Jeremiah turns out to be nothing more than the recitation of the King James version; it is the Book of Jeremiah onstage, speaking – and in highly edited form, at that.

Later on, to be sure, this figure will "break character" in telling the Non-Prophet[1] about his experiences in the pit. At that point, he becomes a dimensional construct, extending in space and time with a personal history, and an inner life. Yet in so doing, he becomes both more like a real person and less his "true" self. For the true Jeremiah is surely a prophetic voice, the voice of several 17th Century committees which, for that matter, is not really "Jeremiah"

---

[1] The name derives from a joke made by Richard Rees, the Artistic Director of the non-profit Williamstown Theatre Festival, where the piece was developed initially. As with Emily's grilling of Ruthie about her *nom de guerre*, this is a further subversion of character. Once the name is in question, so is the identity of the speaker.

190

at all but God himself, "speaking through" the prophet, a human body aware that the words he speaks, often against his will, are "not his."[2]

A Splice of Reality

When dialogue consists of recognizable quotations (even if recognizable only as a style), the audience is expected to understand that the words of the play have been assembled from various sources (A. Washburn *inter alia*). Perhaps because this technique – called variously "collage," the "cut-and-paste method," and, in film, simply "editing"[3] – was developed by Surrealists and popularized with visual images (our sense of sight being our preferred method of verifying reality); we expect it to yield "weird" or "dreamlike" results. Applied to narrative, which is itself a form of thought, the effect can be far subtler. Thus simply by distributing a set of overheard phrases and biblical passages[4] amongst a group of speakers, it is technically very easy to create a scene – viz., a "reality" – we can read as Jeremiah-mumbling-to-himself-while-wandering-through-a-city-crowd.

It is only when such a manufactured "reality" is presented in the theater, with its assumptions of representation – instead of, say, in a poem – that its fictive, essentially linguistic, properties become troublesome. Or maybe not. Yet as Washburn's play unfolds and a sort of narrative emerges – in which, to be reductive, Jeremiah joins the Weather Underground – conventional modes of theater allow for only two possibilities, both dependent on tropes of representation – that this story is meant to have "really happened" somewhere in some sense (which is surely unsatisfactory) or that it is a kind of "dream" (ditto).

In the conventional play, all the pieces are expected to fit, with none left over, because the play is considered as a kind of map: an abstraction of an underlying reality which is complete and consistent. Much will have been omitted for reasons of economy, but if the play is well made, the assumption is that nothing important will be missing, and the sum of its parts will represent a complete and consistent reality.

---

[2] I have deliberately conflated actor and role, text and prophet, for effect. The basic point, however, remains true in every instance – that whatever comes out of Jeremiah's mouth, however Jeremiah is construed, is not really Jeremiah speaking.

[3] In German films, the term is literally *schitt*, meaning, "cut."

[4] For an elegant demonstration of the transformative power of cut-and-paste, compare Washburn's text with the original. You will find so much omitted, so much elided, that her Jeremiah emerges as a very different figure from its biblical source.

In this case, though, disparate elements, having in themselves no necessary – nor even perhaps valid – connection or relation, have been juxtaposed. Indeed, the method – assemblage – has been applied equally throughout the piece to construct dialogue as well as scene structure and narrative. Given the method, the only way to read this play, its characters and narratives – its pieces and its connectors, to be more precise – is as an armature of content analogous to (but obviously different from) narrative in conventional plays, with the additional, radical implication that any assumption of completeness and consistency is invalid and unnecessary.[5]

Of course, an armature of content built of associations cannot help but yield patterns and connections. Surely it is not accidental that the play unfolds along a duality of city and country, where city is the locus of imminent destruction, while country represents safe haven; that destruction comes at the hand of God who has turned on his people, as foretold by the prophets whom God speaks through; nor that the recurrent image of the play – of words placed in someone's mouth – is its very method. Indeed, the same associative process by which a biblical prophet can be superimposed upon a Weather Underground cell extends the content of the piece to include associations shared by the audience – as, for example, the relation between "a city destroyed by the hand of god" and the events of 9/11.

We live, more and more, in a sea of information in which all real events, our lives and time, are but one element. *I Have Loved Strangers* presents connections, points of correspondence between bits of information; not so much a map as a flight plan.

---

[5] This is particularly applicable to actors and directors, given the current bias for rounded, grounded characters, arcs and through-lines.

I HAVE LOVED STRANGERS
by Anne Washburn

I HAVE LOVED STRANGERS

Val Day, William Morris Agency
1325 Avenue of the Americas
New York, NY 10019
212.903.1192

CAST OF CHARACTERS:

JEREMIAH, a prophet

HANANIAH, a prophet

THE NON PROPHET, not a prophet

RUTHIE, a wife

EMILY, several people

PT, master of the unexpected

BARUCH, the one who wroteitalldown

THE KING, the king

EBEDIAH, an assistant to the king

THE WHORE OF BABYLON, as described

THE CITIZENS OF NEW YORK, delineated by letters

SETTING
Ancient New York

NOTE: This play was initially developed with ten actors. Through doublecasting the number of actors can be reduced to seven.

Included in the play are excerpts from the King James translation of the Book of Jeremiah, and material overheard on the streets of New York by the playwright and by members of Williamstown's 2005 Act One company.

This play is inspired by the Book of Jeremiah, and the activities of the Weather Underground. In understanding this play it is not necessary, or even helpful, to have read the book of Jeremiah, or to be familiar with the activities of the Weather Underground.

I Have Loved Strangers was developed and received a workshop production at the Williamstown Theater Festival in August 2005 as part of the Act 1 Leap Frog Program. The play was deeply influenced and inspired by the following performers, as well as by director Johanna McKeon:

THE PROPHET JEREMIAH...Daniel Deferrari
THE PROPHER HANANIAH.......................................Daniel Mefford
RUTHIE...Sara Montgomery
EMILY..Xanthe Elbrick
P.T..Randolph Adams
THE NON PROPHET..Greg Hildreth
BARUCH..Jemmy Gammello
KING...Lance Rubin
EBEDIAH..Lindsey Gordon
WHORE OF BABYLON..Lisa Birnbaum

With sets by Lara Fabian, costumes by Luke Brown, lights by Driscoll Otto, sound by Dave Sanderson, and choreography by Daniel Mefford. The stage manager was Jillian M. Oliver and the Assistant Director was Kate Pines-Schwartz.

I Have Loved Strangers was originally produced in New York by Clubbed Thumb as a part of Summerworks 2006, their annual festival of new plays. It ran from June 6 through June 10 at the Ohio Theater NYC produced by Michael Levinton, Meg MacCary and Maria Striar. Johanna McKeon directed the following cast:

THE PROPHET JEREMIAH.....................................T. Ryder Smith
THE PROPHET HANANIAH......................................James Stanley
RUTHIE...Jennifer R. Morris
EMILY..Laura Flanagan
P.T..Jeff Biehl
THE NON PROPHET/KING..Jay Smith
BARUCH/EBEDIAH/WHORE OF BABYLON..............Elliotte Crowell

With sets by Michael Carnahan, costumes by Carol Ann Pelletier, lights by Driscoll Otto, sound by Emily Wright, and choreography by Karinne Keithley. The stage manager was Colleen Danaher and the Assistant Director was Kerry Whigham.

I HAVE LOVED STRANGERS
by Anne Washburn

Withhold thy foot from being unshod
and thy throat from thirst:
but thou saidst: there is no hope,
no: for I have loved strangers,
and after them will I go.

Jeremiah 2, 25

CHAPTER 1

(The citizens of Ancient New York, on the streets of Ancient New York. Prophets roam among them.)

ALL
(sung, lightly)
(Be ye astonished oh ye heavens, be ye horribly afraid)

BARUCH
It was -- already in the morning -- it was a day of astounding light busting out everywhere: bright, bright! Not yet noon.

D
What a fascinating sunshine; lustrous and pitiless (I must return my video soon)

F
And so we had this whole discussion. And then he e mailed me.

C
Wireless technology is what I like to call bleed-over technology, it's a commercial civilian application -

E
-- over in the corner, where there's that chunk of ivy...

F
It's the classic tale – every man you speak to over 35: 'can't eat like I used to.'

A

Forget about it, I lost

F

I'm babbling right now –

A

I lost about forty-thirty, forty dollars

(There is a change of light, or a shift in sound.)

JEREMIAH

A dry wind bears down
from the high rocks
a hot wind from hard places

(He is heard, but not heard.)

C

Well it was after an NA meeting, and we were all waiting to go out to dinner to celebrate one of the, well it was some sort of anniversary

B

See what I was telling you? It's so cute!

A

It's just a big dog.

B & F

It's so cute!

D

I didn't think it was that moronic.

E

Isn't this part of Manhattan so nice? It's like a village. Like a little village.

A

So far I like all of the parts of Manhattan I've seen

B

…Slo motion –

  A

– from our hotel

                                        E

Remember I was so nice to Martin? And Martin hated me on sight and that
proved my point.

                                        C

If you say 'microwave' or anything related to the microwave, like Rubbermaid,
Bradware, or Tupperware –

                                        B

Well I feel like –

                                        F

Well that's good –

                                        A

If you have a hundred dollars –

                                        E

Is Angelina a good person Mommy?

            (Beat.)

                                        B

No.

                                        D
                                                    (singing lightly)

"dust in de wind"

                              JEREMIAH

The young lions roar upon you, and yell
and they make your land waste
your cities are burned without inhabitant

                                        C

This girl Bowen right?

                                        A

Oh God not this again

C

Fucking tits. Perfect rack right?

D
(to a child)

Yeah that's the Verrazano Bridge. You can see it all the way from here because it's big. It's a Big Bridge.

F

That hurt, I mean she really bumped me.

C

Right. Whatever. I still say you're gay.

G

I'm gonna stop off here at the restroom

JEREMIAH

They that did feed delicately
are desolate in the streets:
they that were brought up in scarlet
embrace dunghills

C

Whoops! Are you okay?

F

Uh…yes. Yep. Yes I am.

E

They can hear your voice saying 'shit' on the first reel'

F
(to a child)

And he'd love it – about the hobgoblins and everything

D
(precise)

Yes, he would.

C

We're not really free. The government tries to trick us.

200

JEREMIAH

Thus saith the Lord:
Behold,
I will give this city into the hand of the King of Babylon
and he shall burn it with fire.

E

I always have the same strange sick sad feeling when I see a mad prophet which
is this: what if he is
right. I always sort of think: he's right!

B

I know. I do too. I think: that's my own mad spirit, cut loose somehow from
my own body, striding through the streets expressly to warn me.

E

Oh. I don't think that. But that's interesting.

B

I do, actually, sort of. For fun, mainly. I always stand far back. I think – what if
he grabs me, what if he looks into my eyes, what if they're my eyes. And then I
have to leave off everything I'm doing and wear bad clothes and go barefoot
through the street raving too.

   (Bit of a pause.)

I don't really believe this. But I think it for fun.

E

I like it. I like it. It's exciting. I might start thinking that too. You never know do
you. It could be true.

JEREMIAH

Therefore thus saith the Lord concerning the prophets that prophecy in my
name;
I sent them not
neither have I commanded them
neither spake unto them:
they prophesy unto you a false vision
and a thing of naught:
the deceit of their heart
they say: Sword and famine shall not be in this land…
by Sword and Famine shall those prophets be consumed!

THE NON-PROPHET

What people don't realize

(takes a sip from his little espresso
cup.)

is that you do have a choice.
You do not have to become a prophet.
And I'm not saying that God isn't insistent…
…he is very insistent…
And persuasive. But you can, ultimately, if you are determined, you can say:
take this particular cup from my lips, I won't do it. And He will pass on.
What are the consequences of this. Well I don't pretend to know. Am I
damned? I can't see it on my skin, I don't see it in my eyes; the world sounds
the same, I dream as before, I don't smell…unusual.
It may be that now, none of my prayers are answered. I don't know. I haven't
dared to pray.
What I know is that He is resistible, and that those who become prophets,
agonize tho they might, have on some level made a decision.

B

But what is it like to be a prophet?

HANANIAH

It's a delight.

E

You can't ask that question!

HANANIAH

No I don't mind. It's a delight. I'll suddenly find myself speaking. The only part
I mind is the waiting, and wondering when I'll speak next.

But it's like: at a party when the tray comes around and you take something
wonderful from it. And
then you think: when will the tray come around again? And what will be on it?

But it's like a good party. Where there's an endless supply of trays. And the
waiters are efficient.

B

Are the waiters angels?!

E

You can't ask that!

202

HANANIAH

Why not?

E

What are the waiters?

HANANIAH
(he laughs)
I don't see them. I don't know. I don't know much, honestly. I only know what
I know after I've said it.

(A serene – for HANANIAH – pause in which no one says anything.)

THE NON-PROPHET
Do you know, I had dinner with the Devil once. I was in an inn, and he was in
the inn, and the inn was full, so we ate dinner at the same table.

He didn't say a word, he was exhausted. I ordered lamb, he ordered beef.

F
How did you know it was the Devil?

NON PROPHET
After dinner they brought round a brandy and, he had eaten a lot very quickly,
and he revived a little and he made a sort of half play for my soul. I think, just,
nothing serious; out of habit.

(HANANIAH and the Girls have been listening in to this conversation.
(HANANIAH smiles in a quicksilver meaningful sort of way.)

HANANIAH
(to the girls)
These are strange times to be alive.

NON-PROPHET
(whipping around to speak to him directly)
I'll say.

(They look at each other for a moment.
(The sound of breakage. Everyone freezes, then turns.)

BARUCH
The light glitters off the freshly sharded off of the

(MORE)

BARUCH (cont.)

infinitely ferocious glitters of spanking fresh the light
shimmers on the newly deadly glass.

C

That bottle's all in jags now – watch out!

(Revealed: JEREMIAH, holding a freshly broken bottle.)

JEREMIAH

And I will take from them the voice of mirth
and the voice of gladness,
the voice of the bridegroom, and the
voice of the bride for the land shall be desolate
The whole city shall flee for the noise of the horsemen
and bowmen; they shall go into thickets
and climb up upon the rocks
Destruction upon destruction is cried for the whole land is spoiled

and I will make this city
desolate
and an hissing;

Everyone that passes thereby shall be astonished

Thus saith the Lord of Hosts:

(indicates the bottle)
"Even so will I break this people, and this city."

(Exits calmly upstage to silence.
(Frog sounds begin.)

CHAPTER 2

*(The Dark, and many frogs. There are many
different types of frogs. There is one frog with a low deep occasional bellow. There are
more frogs with a businesslike mid range twang, and there are many, many little
peepers with a high yammering chirrup.*
(It's a racket.
(Two flashlight beams joggle forward, stop.
(EMILY and PT have paused to listen to the frogs.)

EMILY

And people leave the city to get away from the noise.

PT

Where's the moon?

EMILY

What do you think the decibel level is? I bet it's worse than Times Square.

PT

No I mean it, where's the moon?

EMILY

It isn't up yet.

PT

Or is it new.

EMILY

Um, it might be new. I'm trying to think…

PT

Because if it's new, it's not coming up tonight at all, or, it's already up, but it's invisible.

EMILY

I'm trying to remember the last time I saw it.

PT

Don't you think that's creepy?

EMILY

It's coming back.

PT

No no, that's my point: It isn't gone. It's right above us, right now, but it's invisible. Don't you think that's creepy? This big old dark invisible moon hanging over our heads.

(Beat.)

EMILY

No. I don't. Hang on though okay, this is driving me a bit nuts:

(Let's loose with a prolonged operatic vocal extravagance
(Stunned silence from the frogs.
(An exploratory chirrup.
(Silence.
(Then, tentatively, they start up again, cautiously at
first, but soon regain their original vigor.
(A bit of a [Human] silence.)

PT
(sincerely)

That's amazing. You creeped the frogs out.

EMILY

I didn't creep them out. I…impressed them.

(She switches off her light.)

PT

The frogs were like: what is that.

EMILY

Hey,
(She jostles his arm.)

Turn yours off okay.

PT

Why?

EMILY

I want to see what the dark is like.

(He does so.)

PT

You're the Frog Mama.

(She sings just a bit, low.)

You're going to give them a heart attack, you keep after them like that.

(She continues singing low, a little louder; the frogs continue, undisturbed.
(Pursuing the joke a little longer than is amusing.)

because how often are they visited by the Froggie Goddess, like it's got to be stressful.

(She pursues the song a little longer, ends it mid-verse. or, at any rate before the song is done.

(Silence. Frogs.)

Seriously though, I don't think I can hack this dark. I'm a city boy. I'm used to being lit up from above at all times.

(Bit of a beat.)

EMILY

There are the stars.

PT

They're pretty. They're not really doing it for me.

EMILY

There are comets.

(A flash of light across the stage, and a whoosh; fades out. Another flash of light and whoosh; fades out.)

PT
(not convinced)

Mmmmn.

EMILY

There are fireflies.

(A swarm of fireflies enters, and performs a beautiful luminous dance. The laws of nature are repealed.
(EMILY starts to sing a low firefly song to accompany them.)

EMILY'S FIREFLY SONG

The Heart of the Summer

ALL OF THE WOMEN

is shot through with Stars

EMILY CONTINUES ALONE

Dazzles of Forever
Abducted in Jars

THE AIR RESPONDS

(The air is masculine in character.)

More wonderful
than fire
is the air!
without which
nothing glowing
would be there!

(The fireflies exit, the frogs fade out.)

CHAPTER 3

NON PROPHET

I was continually being tackled and wrestled to the ground by an angel. I had to be on my guard wherever I went. My eyes always darting about, on the watch for a flick of a feather whisking behind a corner. A suspicious glimmer from behind a parked car. A flock of doves rose up just to my left and I freaked out.

CHAPTER 4

(HANANIAH is speaking.)

HANANIAH
(luminous)

When God comes to you...
and he does come to you -
you say: he hasn't come to me

you'll never hear his voice

You've been awake in the night
in the dark listening
for a word a touch,
(you've been desolate)

(MORE)

you've said: I am alone
you've said: I am abandoned
he will not speak to me...
He does not speak to you.

While you are writhing
in your hot, still, brain God
has visited you
and visited you again
falling into your heart
like a soft cooling rain

Your heart is a garden
blooming, and replete
God has rippled though
you, you are complete.

CHAPTER 5

BARUCH

And on this day waves of soiled air
rising from the pavement; sparks of glare

C

Don't forget – you gotta go towards the East side. This is the West. When you
get up on the street –
go East!

D

The chariots shall rage in the streets
they shall justle one against another in the broad ways
they shall seem like torches
they shall run like the lightnings

C

Oh, shit. She shoulda got out at the next stop.

E

If I don't hear from him. I will die – there's the D! Mwah! Go! Mwah!

JEREMIAH

The heart is deceitful above all things,
and desperately wicked – who can know it? Thus saith the Lord. Saith the Lord:
I remember thee,
thy kindness, the love of thine espousals, when thou went after me in the
wilderness,
in a land that was not sown

I will yet plead with you, saith the Lord
What iniquity have you found in me
that you have turned from me
that you are gone so far from me
yet return again to me, saith the Lord

How can you say: I am not polluted?
Thou hast forsaken me
and walked after the imagination of thy own heart.
You are a wild ass, used to the wilderness
that traverses the high places
that snuffeth up the wind at her pleasure
all they that seek her will not weary themselves
thou hast played the harlot with many lovers

For this shall the black earth mourn
and the heavens above be black; because I have spoken it,
I have purposed it and will not repent
neither will I turn back from it

Be astonished, Oh ye heavens at this, and be horribly afraid

be ye very desolate

Saith the Lord.

CHAPTER 6

(*HANANIAH and RUTHIE at home. HANANIAH sits in a
chair, a book in his lap. RUTHIE has just entered the room.*)

RUTHIE
I think we should think about packing.

HANANIAH
(amused)

Where are we going?

RUTHIE

I think it would make sense to have a suitcase in readiness.

(Beat.)

HANANIAH

You're worried. You're panicking.

RUTHIE

With changes of clothes and our papers and, I don't know: powdered milk, a
pack of matches wrapped up in tin foil; I think we should have a plan, I mean it,
I think we should have a fall back position, a house up country. Diagrams.

(Another beat.)

HANANIAH

Of what? We can't afford/ a house up country.

RUTHIE

A flow chart. If not A, then B. if not B, then C. If not C, then D. So that if
things start to happen very quickly, we aren't confused. We can be
programmatic. And efficient, in our response.

(He moves toward her, she stops him.)

RUTHIE

You're going to tell me that everything is going to be alright.

HANANIAH

Yes. It will be.

(She has shut her eyes and stopped her ears.)

RUTHIE

And I'll believe you. And it might be more sensible, if I didn't. Because I'm a
little stupid about these things. I don't notice things right away. I'll look around
one day and I'll realize that everyone is wearing belts. Like, a kind of belt. And
it's obvious that they've been wearing them for months. And I haven't been

(MORE)

211

RUTHIE (cont.)

wearing a belt at all, for months, the whole time thinking that everything was fine, that I was looking good, when I was beltless and essentially naked before the world. Do you understand? I'm oblivious I can't trust the evidence of my senses, or, my powers of observation.

I can't trust my beliefs.

And I believe in you. But I think we should leave. I think it's time to go.

(She opens her eyes.)

HANANIAH
(unruffled)

You think that I have you in a kind of hypnotic thrall.

RUTHIE

Yeah. This has to be your least favorite fight.

HANANIAH

Well. "a prophet hath no honor in his own living room" right .

(She shrugs.
(A bit of a pause, he starts:)

HANANIAH

Look,

RUTHIE

No. You're about to be convincing. I am begging you. Please don't convince me.

(Long pause.)

HANANIAH

What if we –

(He holds up a warning hand.)

I'm not. What if we stock up on emergency supplies. For the closet. Would that work as a compromise?

RUTHIE

That's, no. And we have everything. We have water and chlorine pills and cans and cans and cans and a can opener –

HANANIAH

Where?

RUTHIE

On the upper shelf, you never go in there. We have batteries and antibiotic and vitamins

HANANIAH
(teasing)

Do we have duct tape?

RUTHIE

We have a whole –

(She holds her hands up to gesture it while she tries to think of the word.)

A whole mini flat of it.

HANANIAH

No.

RUTHIE
(it's silly)

Yeah, we do. We do.

(He takes her hand, then her other hand. He pulls her to him, her resisting just a bit then yielding. He puts his arms around her. He rocks her a bit. He puts his hand on her cheek.)

HANANIAH

Do you know what?

(Slightly charged pause.)

RUTHIE

What.

HANANIAH

It's going to be all right.

213

RUTHIE

Oh shit. Fuck.

(Still rocking her gently.)

HANANIAH

I mean it. I know it. I'm not saying things won't be difficult, of course they'll be difficult. They're always difficult. And of course you should be strong, it always makes sense to be strong, and it always makes sense to be prepared and lists...
(laughing)
lists are wonderful but don't be afraid. You don't
need to be afraid.

RUTHIE
(rocking with him)
Fuck. Fuck fuck fuck fuck fuck fuck fuck.

CHAPTER 7

(EMILY and PT are in a rural graveyard. A little bit of scattered light cricketing. They're looking through the tombstones, they are looking for something; PT is reading aloud.)

PT

Lizzie Hale McKee
Cornelius Foster
Emma Ogden Jessup

These are really old names.

Amos W. Harvey

EMILY

Maud J Dollard

PT

Joseph G West
Samuel Chester Dodsworth

You're sure they're still putting people in here?

EMILY

I checked with the county.

(They continue. After a bit:)

PT

Ida and Lulu, twins.

Salome Vreeland

(Bit of a pause. Still checking.)

If it's night time, shouldn't it be cooler? Or something. 5 degrees. Whatever. Some concession should be made. To the fact that it's night. And everything is supposed to be different.

EMILY

I think it's hotter, actually.

PT

Okay. Do you know what I think? Okay I know this is crazy. But get this: actually, okay, this is great:
because

(Flicking his flashlight around.)

they look like teeth, right? So get this: it's like being in someone's mouth.

EMILY

What?

PT

It's like being in someone's mouth, right? There's the teeth, and it's hot and wet and you know really weirdly quiet. Oh hey speaking of which I had my first older married woman last night. There should
be guilt, right? It has not sunk in!

(He shrieks. He has flicked his light onto a piece of statuary.
(Which is an actor, posing as a fabulous biblical gestures angel.
(EMILY laughs.)

PT

Jesus.

(She flicks hers onto one.)

EMILY

A mouth full of angels.

PT

Crap.

(She reads the inscription on the monument:)

EMILY

"And I bore you on Eagles wings
and brought you to myself"

(He flicks and illuminates another angel. Reads the inscription:)

PT

"Death came one bright summer's day
and took our dearest friend away"

EMILY

"Very pleasant hast thou been unto me
thy love to me was wonderful"

PT

"Until the day break and the shadows flee away"

EMILY

"Morning is here
earth's flooded with light
gone are the storm clouds
vanished with night"

PT

"Death is swallowed up in victory"

EMILY

"Won is the glory and the grief is past"

PT

"For me to die is to gain"

(Silence.

(They continue, sobered.)

              PT

Enoch Howard

              EMILY

Sylvia Amelia Fry

              PT

Edward J McCullough

              EMILY

Arabella Longstreet

              ANGEL A

Lyndon Bartholomew Emery

              PT

Angela M LaCrosse

              ANGEL B

Rupert Peter Dodge

              EMILY

Molly John Schwartz

              ANGEL D

Jorge Fernando Diaz

              PT

Anatole Moritz

              ANGEL E

Eddie T O'Conner

              EMILY

Gina Fratelli

(All the angels name at once [NOTE: See Angel Appendix at end of play: each angel should take a different name for each round of naming], there is a cacophony of names spattered all over the place.
(They name again, again a cacophony.
(Again
(Again

(Then they name [all different names] in unison.
(Again in unison.
(Then altogether:)

ANGELS

Roy Elliot Edmunds

Rachael Linda Edwards

Cynthia Longstreet

Peter Samuel Roth

James Dillard Thomas

Penelope Ranadivay

George Martin Lewis

ANGELS

ANGELS

ANGELS

ANGELS

ANGELS

ANGELS

EMILY
(delighted)

Oh! Bingo. This one's very small. This one hardly lived at all:

(The angels whisper with her:)

EMILY/ANGELS

Monica
Alicia
Perry.

(Flashlight out.)

CHAPTER 8

BARUCH

At first it was only the faintest rain

D

I know that first bit. After you make that first right turn I don't know -

F

So pretty but I had to take them off directly after. They really hurt my feet – and I was not stable.

C

As soon as I touched her I knew it was on

(An umbrella goes up.)

A

I said to him I said:

BARUCH

now it's a sluice of fists beating again and again

(Umbrellas go up, and protective newspapers.)

F

and then, this is really romantic –

C & E

I can't eat that. I said. I really can't it's the texture

A, D, F

We were overcome with wonder.

E

Will he be fed upon by the cockatrices?

D

No, no. They will be satiate already

A

he knows his shit!

B, C, A

We were overcome with wonders

E

I beheld the mountains, and, lo, they trembled

F

(Announcement. Bored and weary civil servant.)

There's no waiting on the platform at this station.

C

In Brooklyn or Queens you drink more than 4 rounds or you tip him ridiculously you get that drink free

A, E

The mountains were loaded with lions, waiting to discharge onto the city below

D

I always get the soup here

A

I beheld, and, lo, there was no man and all the birds of the heavens were fled

E

I'll have to check but I don't think so, I think it's expired.

F

(Announcement.)

There is a smoke condition at this station. Please enter the train, or exit the station.

D

His dead body shall be cast out in the day to the heat and in the night to the frost

F

I will make them drink
the water of gall

D

for their words are diseases
and must be purged

220

                                    A
No we all take the 4

                                    E
Then we go downtown.

                                   ALL
Downtown.

                                    C
It's supposed to be good.

                                    D
I love that fucking place!

                                    F
I think oh, I'm really going to miss New York.

                                   ALL
A dwelling place for dragons, an astonishment.
.

                                    D
I was perturbed by the Lion problem I was disturbed by the Cockatrices

                                 BARUCH
The rain came gushing down in great sputtery bursts overstepping all bounds of
moisture everything outside was one big drench:

                              CHAPTER 9

(The Palace of KING ZEDEKIAH who sits on his throne.
(Rain on the roof.
(EBEDIAH is near.
(The remaining actors stand on either side of the stage, and frame the action with
their hands.)

                                 EBEDIAH
                              (to JEREMIAH)
Put now these old cast clouts and rotten rags under thine armholes under the
cords and we will draw you up, from the pit
                               (to the King)
                                                        (MORE)

EBEDIAH (cont.)
We threw down old cast clouts and rotten rags we said:

now put on these old cast clouts and rotten rags
under your armholes, and we will draw you up,

and he did so

And then we threw down the cords
and then did draw him up by the armholes
with cords

> *(JEREMIAH is drawn up and brought before the KING.*
> *(He is drenched in mire.)*

KING ZEDEKIAH

The princes said unto me:

PRINCES
We beseech thee, let this man be put to death for thus he weakeneth the hands
of the men
of war, and the hands of all the people,
in speaking such words unto them. This man seeketh
not the welfare of the people but the hurt.

ZEDEKIAH
(in explanation)
When ye saideth: this city shall surely be given
into the hand of the King of Babylon's army
which shall take it.
I will ask thee a thing. Hide nothing from me.

JEREMIAH
If I declare it unto thee, wilt thou not surely put me to death?

KING ZEDEKIAH
As the Lord liveth, that made us this soul, I will not put thee to death,
neither will I give thee into the hand of those men that seek thy life.

JEREMIAH
The Lord put forth his hand and touched my mouth and the lord said to me
Behold I have put my words in thy mouth I spake: I cried out, I cried violence
(MORE)

JEREMIAH (cont.)

and spoil I am in derision daily,
every one mocketh me then I said I will not make mention of Him
nor speak any more in His name but His word is in my heart as a burning flame
and I am weary with forbearing I must ignite

(JEREMIAH listens, relaxes.)

The Lord sayeth, that He will move among your arms and will falter...will bring
the arms of your archers to faltering. And the spears will fail. He will fill your
soldiers with trembling and with tears and in fact will himself fight against you,
moving among the enemy troops shouting encouragement. With an
outstretched hand and with a strong arm. In anger and in fury and in great
wrath.
He will employ signs he will employ wonders against you
                                                    (gaining strength)
He will smite the inhabitants of this city he will utterly destroy them and make
them an astonishment

Behold I am against thee Oh thou most proud for thy day is come the time that
I will visit thee.
And the most proud shall stumble and fall
and none shall raise him up and I will kindle a fire in his cities
and it shall devour all round about him.
                    (He subsides. Pause.)
Oh, and also: you will be delivered unto the king of Babylon. Thine eyes will
behold his eyes, very up
close they will be unblinking. And he's going to speak to thee, his mouth, just
this far from your mouth, very up
close. And thou shalt go to Babylon.
                                        (rather vacant and faint:)
(and you will say:

the king of Babylon
hath devoured me
he hath crushed me
he hath made me an empty vessel
he hath swallowed me up like a dragon
he hath filled his belly with my delicates
he hath cast me out)

(Very very long pause.)

223

KING ZEDEKIAH

Let no one know these words
and you will not die.

> *(JEREMIAH is bundled from the throne room and abandoned under an awning.*
> *Sounds of cars passing by on wet pavement.*
> *(He stands there, dazed.)*

CHAPTER 10

> *(He puts out his hand, withdraws it from the rain*
> *(The NON PROPHET arrives.* *He is under an enormous gorgeous black*
> *umbrella.)*

NON PROPHET

Can't I buy you a wonderful meal?

> *(He holds out the umbrella.)*

I know a place.

> *(They umbrella off together.)*

CHAPTER 11

EMILY

You can't fuck this up, alright? It isn't a game. Who am I.

RUTHIE

Who are you?

EMILY

Yes. Who am I.
Just answer the question.

> *(A bit of a beat.)*

RUTHIE

All right. You're Emily Owens

EMILY

Wrong.

                              RUTHIE
You're Emily Russell Owens.

                              EMILY
Wrong.

                              RUTHIE
I give up.

                              EMILY
You give up really easily.

                              RUTHIE
Jesus Christ.

                              EMILY
Who am I.

                              RUTHIE
I. Don't. Know.

                              EMILY
Monica Alicia Perry.

                              RUTHIE
Okay. Great. Since when.

                              EMILY
Since this afternoon. My birth certificate came in the mail. Who am I?

                              RUTHIE
Monica something.

                              EMILY
You think I'm an asshole.

                              RUTHIE
You are an asshole.

EMILY

You're going to be the asshole. When you fuck it up. "Monica Perry great I'll remember that great." And we're in line at the movie theater and you say "Emily, Emily, let's get gummy bears" and the guy six ahead of us in line turns around, reflexively. You think the pigs don't go to the movies too?

RUTHIE

All right.

EMILY

If I go to prison can you take my place? Do you know how to load a gun and reload it in under ten seconds? Do you have the energy and the stamina to sleep in a different bed or on a different couch every night? I mean every night. Night after night. It's harder than you'd think. Do you have the will power, and the focus, to walk into a public building with a live explosive taped to your chest, walk calmly to the Ladies room on the second floor, wash your hands, and walk out again all of this time with a live explosive taped to your chest all the time knowing that Louis who assembled it, and strapped it on you, is a genius semiotician and social analyst but he's been up three nights straight and forgets to eat and that when he wired it together this morning his hand was shaking but today is the day to test security procedures, and if it doesn't happen today the plan is out of wack, and if the plan goes out of wack the safety, and, much more importantly, the goals of 14 people are seriously compromised.

RUTHIE

No I can't. I don't.

(Bit of a pause.)

EMILY

I know.

RUTHIE

But I wish that I could.

EMILY
(gently)

I know. Who am I?

RUTHIE

You're.........fuck!

I'm sorry. I'm really sorry.

226

EMILY

Who am I?

RUTHIE
(Struggles for a moment, gets it.)
Monica. Monica…

EMILY
(very rapidly)
Alicia Perry. Who am I?

RUTHIE

Monica Alicia Terry. Perry. Monica Alicia Perry.

EMILY

Who am I?

RUTHIE

You're Monica Alicia Perry.

EMILY

Someone says to you: who is that?

RUTHIE

Monica Alicia Perry.

EMILY

I am:

RUTHIE

Monica Alicia Perry.

EMILY

Good. Now I have a question for you. Do you remember who I am?

RUTHIE

Monica Alicia Perry.

EMILY

No. I know. But I need to know. That is who I am. But do you remember who I am?

(Beat.)

RUTHIE

You're /Monic —

EMILY

No. That's who I am.

RUTHIE

I love you. You're wearing me out.

EMILY

I need you to know who I am — but I also need you to remember who I am.
Not. Any longer.

(Bit of a beat.)

RUTHIE

Oh.

RUTHIE

/You're -

EMILY

But don't say it.

RUTHIE

EMILY

Think it, okay? Tell me who I am with your mouth. Remember who I am with
your eyes.

RUTHIE

Simultaneously?

EMILY

It's tricky, right?

RUTHIE

(Bit of a pause: gathering it together.)
Okay.

EMILY

Who am I?

RUTHIE
(slowly, looking her in the eye)

Monica
(barely whispered: Emily)
...Alicia
(barely whispered: Russell)
...Perry
(barely whispered: Owens).

EMILY
(softly)

Who am I?

RUTHIE

You are:
Monica *(Only with her eyes: Emily)*.
Alicia *(Only with her eyes: Russell)*.
Perry *(Only with her eyes: Owens)*.

EMILY

Okay. Okay. Thank you.

CHAPTER 12

(The remnants of a vast meal. Absurd amounts of dirty plates. The Non Prophet's place setting remains untouched, and he is sipping at a tiny cup of espresso. Jeremiah has pushed the plates aside, and commandeered the bread basket; he is demolishing the last of the bread and then begins on a cucumber.)

JEREMIAH
In the beginning, I did not mind the pit. Well, I had questions about the mire. I was glad, though, to be in a place where I could speak without...bad consequences...to myself. I did a little bit of singing and I enjoyed that, there was a reverberation, I sounded almost professional; I felt free.

In time, I began to feel agitated. I could not pace, or, beat against the sides of my imprisonment because of the mire which was...bogging-down...and entrapping. Also I felt...hot...inside, because of my certainty, and as days went on I felt hotter. Rats don't know anything and they don't care about anything, at least that's the way I see it, and whatever I said to them it didn't matter to them
(MORE)

229

either pro or con.

Beginning from that time, I found I could not like the pit. Even when I was singing. And I was hot because of the certainty and increasingly I found that I had a great deal of hunger. Also there was no question of sleeping. Because of the sinking under the mire problem. And then today...today? Yes. Today then they threw a rope down. I wanted to laugh, because they were whispering very dramatically about the whole thing. They had a torch and they would light it, and then whisper very dramatically, and then extinguish it, and then they would argue, and then they would light it again. I laughed and laughed.
They were furious. They shouted they forgot to whisper. They said this is an extreme secret. I took hold of the rope but when they pulled my fingers slid away. They threw it down again. I couldn't make my fingers clutch. Probably from all of the not eating.

I like this meal very much. Both in terms of taste, and quantity. I wonder do you think they bake their own bread, or do they have a supplier in the city? I would be interested to purchase it on my own,
possibly in bulk.

NON PROPHET
And so you were lifted out of the pit.

JEREMIAH
Yes. With cast clouts and with rotten –

NON PROPHET
And they took you –

(JEREMIAH freezes.)

Probably that's a secret.

JEREMIAH
I think that probably, yes. I think that yes it is.

NON PROPHET
They took you to a person.

JEREMIAH
They did take me to a person.

                              NON PROPHET
And you spoke, to this person.

                              JEREMIAH
        (After a beat.)
There was some chat.

                              NON PROPHET
And after the chat.

                              JEREMIAH
Then I was outside again.

                              NON PROPHET
And the feeling, the –

                              JEREMIAH
Then it was subsided.

                              NON PROPHET
And tomorrow?

                              JEREMIAH
Oh.
        (Beat.)
It will begin again.

                              NON PROPHET
It's painful.

                              JEREMIAH
Not at first, no. In the beginning it's not so bad. I can just, I can mutter a little,
and that's fine. And then a feeling of pressure, which increases. And I can I can
pick up a telephone, in a booth on the street, and I can speak into the
telephone, into the dial tone, and that's fine but then after a while that won't
work and I have to call someone on the phone, any one at all, whatever number
I make up and if they answer I speak to them until they hang up.
But that doesn't work for long. Then I have to start arguing in bars and
shouting on the street and aback street isn't good enough, no, it has to be a
broad street and really there have to be columns nearby and…stripy…marble
                                                            (MORE)

                                                            231

JEREMIAH (cont.)

and acoustics and, you know, obviously, just…swarms…of people. Who will stare back at me blankly. And then inevitably I will be seized by a terrible chilly fury. And then of course I'll end back in the pit. So I'd like more bread now I think. Waiter?

> *(A little bit of a desperate roar.)*

Waiter!?!

> *(The NON PROPHET touches him lightly on the shoulder. JEREMIAH subsides. The NON PROPHET makes a light little gesture, in the air, and bread is brought.*
> *(With great restraint JEREMIAH recites:)*

This is a miracle. If I walk into a field of wheat, I cannot eat it. This is a miracle. If I hold a handful of
flour I cannot eat it. This is a miracle: if I muddle together water, salt, yeast and flour I still cannot eat it.
But I can eat this miracle.

> *(JEREMIAH starts tearing into it.)*

NON PROPHET

The certainty of the powerless is terrible. I can help you you know.

JEREMIAH
(laughs a little)
The Lord is with me. The Lord is always with me. Who can help me?

> *(He starts in again on the bread.*
> *(The NON PROPHET looks both ways, then leans in towards JEREMIAH, and begins whispering in his ear. JEREMIAH at first continues stuffing his mouth with bread, listening, then he starts to shakes his head 'no', then he puts the bread down, the NON PROPHET continues whispering, JEREMIAH is shaking his head no, then he stops shaking his head, the NON PROPHET continues whispering, JEREMIAH is absolutely still, the NON PROPHET continues whispering, JEREMIAH's body starts to shake, he starts to sob silently, he clutches his face, he is wracked with silent sobs, the NON PROPHET has to grasp on to his shoulder to keep contact with him, mouth to ear, he continues whispering, all but wrapping him in an embrace as JEREMIAH dissolves.)*

CHAPTER 13

(Don't forget that it's still raining heavily, continuously.
(RUTHIE is staring fixedly into space.
(When she hears the key in the lock she picks up a book.
(HANANIAH enters.
(She looks up and puts her book down, he registers her but does not really see her.
(He is carrying a paper bag.
(He stands in the middle of the room. He looks at the paper bag. He
looks up. He looks around. He looks at the bag.)

HANANIAH

I was buying coffee.

RUTHIE

Yes. You said you would.

(He looks at her, still not really seeing her. He sits
down. And looks at her really for the first time.)

HANANIAH

I was in line. I was going to buy coffee. And I was tapped on my...

(He can't think of the word.)

RUTHIE

Shoulder?

HANANIAH

Here.
(Places his hand on the halfway point between
shoulder and elbow.)
by a man who said will you come with me please.

I thought he meant, I thought he must mean I had been stealing. Even though I wasn't. Because they do sell small things there but only up at the counter. I would have had to have sidled up to the counter and taken, candies, and then stepped back to get in line. I would have taken them when I had already gotten to the counter that's what I was thinking. It didn't make sense to me.

He said you're Hananiah the prophet I said yes and people had turned around; I
(MORE)

HANANIAH (cont.)

thought alright I can't make a fuss here, I'll explain in the back office. I mean if they have to search my pockets, whatever. And he led me out the door. And I was just sort of thinking: we're on the street, that's funny, I thought there were back offices and I realize because he's got me by the arm that he's hustling but I mean it's all very inconspicuous and delicate there's a car at the curb. And he's making like he's going to open the back door and I said wait. Because I'm thinking this is crazy and why don't we start talking very specifically about the mints or what have you I mean I still need to buy my coffee, and now I've lost my place in line. And he shifts his jacket and he's got a gun. So now I decide I will have to make a break for it because this is crazy and I look over and there's another one by the newsstand and he's got his hand in his jacket in this very significant way. And so I don't know what to do and I get in the car. And we drive and there's another one in the back seat, next to me, and the man who got in the front seat passenger side leans over and says I apologize for that, but it was simpler and then turns his head back. And I said where are we going and everyone ignored me. And there was fear in my voice, I couldn't disguise it, so I didn't say anything else.

(By this point RUTHIE is sitting next to him or kneeling in front of him and stroking his hand gently.)

HANANIAH

We drive for 20 minutes. Or, I have no idea for how long. It seemed like 20 minutes. It could have been any period of time at all.

And we stop outside of a storefront which has a realty sign in it, and the two other stores on this side of the block are boarded up and I was thinking I'll sort of look around me, and try to see where I am, and the man says don't look around, so I don't. There's no one on the sidewalk.

And the one guy has a key, and unlocks the door and we walk in, there's nothing there, just fixtures, and then he has another key and he unlocks the door to the back.

And we walk in.

And I think am I afraid to die? And I think I'm not afraid to die. But then I think no but I'm sorry to die.

(By this point RUTHIE is no longer stroking his hand, but simply grasping it, unmoving.)

HANANIAH

And there's a man in the back room, in a chair, and he has his back to me.

And the room is filled with men, and they're all looking at him. Unless it's their job to look at me. But then something must change on his face, because at once they all look at me.

I can see his arm, on the chair. I can see the edge of his sleeve, and I can see his hand. I see the ring on his hand.

And they see me see the ring, all of the men see and then the room is loaded with guns.

And I'm not afraid. And he doesn't move, an iota, he doesn't say a thing but suddenly the guns are down and back and away. And then every man leaves the room.

And then for the first time he shifts a little bit and he says I still can't see his face:

"is there word?"

And I went cold, literally, all over, literally like I've been dunked in ice water.

Because I didn't know was there word? I never know if there's word.

I thought no, I don't think there is word. But then there was word.

RUTHIE

What did you say?

HANANIAH

I said. I sang some of it. That doesn't happen so often. I said there was glory. I said there was beauty. I said there were arms, and armaments. I don't remember all of it. I said there is blood sinking into the earth, I said there is a terrible cry, from beyond the city walls, and it freezes men and they sob in their sleep, they wake early, they walk to the cold river just at the dawn. I said there's a wind in the heights and the women are uneasy. I said these are strange times. I said they are glorious.
                              (laughs)
I started talking about arm wrestling. I said about how you have your arm all the way over, twisted all the way over and the tabletop is a quarter inch from your
                                                              (MORE)

235

HANANIAH (cont.)

knuckle and it seems impossible but even if your arm is weak your heart is strong and you bust it back, you bust it back quarter inch by quarter inch until it surges forward and blam you press your enemy down into the hard wood. I said that there was victory.

It's the clearest I've ever said it yet. I said that there was triumph.

I said 'you are beloved'

I said that he was blessed.

(There is a slightly indecipherable pause.)

RUTHIE

And the King was, pleased.

HANANIAH

He said 'you can go now', and from his voice I knew he was in tears.

(There is a pause.)

They escorted me back to the car and they drove me here. And when we pulled up the guy in the front seat got out and opened the door for me, and when I got out he gave me this.
(Pulls bag of coffee beans from paper bag.)
these aren't the beans I was going to buy but they're more expensive.

RUTHIE

They know where we live?

HANANIAH

It wouldn't be difficult to find out. I think, no one said anything, but I think. We'll be able to get the house up country.

RUTHIE

The King is a pig.

(Without thinking, he slaps her. They're both horrified.)

HANANIAH

Oh my God. Oh my God oh my God.

RUTHIE

Wow. / (Huh)

236

HANANIAH

Are you all right?

(He moves towards her she steps away. She presses against the side of her cheek, her jaw.)

RUTHIE

If only I'd been hysterical. That would have / been just the right thing to do.

HANANIAH

I love you. I love you.

(He moves towards her again she holds out a hand warning him back.)

RUTHIE

Just stay there for a moment / alright?
He sinks to the earth in front of her.

HANANIAH

I've never hurt, I've never touched I've only, even -

RUTHIE

Okay just shut up. Just. Please. For a moment. Just shut up.
(Long silence. The rain.)
This is the wrong time to say this, because now it has a very different spin. But what I was going to say,
when you were going to come in the door. Or, tonight. I know I was going to say it tonight. Is that I'm
leaving.

I was going to say that I'm not leaving you, I'm leaving and I was going to say I so much wish that you'd come with me, but I know you won't. I did want you to know that this isn't easy for me, and that actually it breaks my heart.

(Mini stunned pause.)

HANANIAH

It was a bad, moment. It was a really bad really bad moment.

RUTHIE

No the whole point is that that's what I was going to say before.

(A knock.

(They look at each other.
(Another knock.)

RUTHIE

'A house up country'.

HANANIAH

I'm going to get it.

RUTHIE
(low)

Don't get it.

(He stops.
(Another knock.)

Don't get it.

HANANIAH
(low)

If they want to kill me, they've already surrounded the block.

(Opens door. A group of people, their faces obscured.
(HANANIAH steps back, Ruthie steps towards him.
(EMILY pulls the veil from her face. She and PT and maybe a few other people are
supporting an unconscious JEREMIAH. He is as before, but someone has slung a
black rain slicker onto him; the hood covers his face.)

EMILY

I'm sorry about this. You can say no. It's important that you know that and
that's not, um – I shouldn't be giving you a choice – there are other options.

PT

Bullshit

HANANIAH

Say no to what?

EMILY

This one needs someplace to stay. Just for the night.

(RUTHIE looks at HANANIAH, then looks at EMILY.)

RUTHIE

I think he's going to have to be cleaner. To stay here.
(to HANANIAH)

Right?
(*to them)*

There are things in there.

(EMILY hugs RUTHIE.)

HANANIAH

'Things' are my clothes. They're in the drawers to your left.

EMILY

We'll come back for him in the morning.
(as they haul him in)

We're going to need towels or something to lay on the bed if you don't want this on the coverlet.

(RUTHIE, who has been trailing after, darts in. After a bit, HANANIAH sits.)

RUTHIE
(Offstage. She's sliding towels under his feet.)

A bit higher, okay? Just for a moment.

SOMEONE
(offstage)

Watch the boots, watch/ the boots.

(Sound of minor breakage.)

SOMEONE
(offstage)

Oh/ shit.

RUTHIE
(offstage)

That's fine. No really. Okay...

PT
(JEREMIAH is in place.)

Okay.

(Some moments of silence.

(During which EMILY crosses back into the room with the other, speaking to him in a low voice.)

PT
(offstage)

This one alright?

RUTHIE
(offstage)

That's fine. Anything in there

(There is a longish whispered consultation at the door, during which:)

PT

This would be easier with a skirt. Can you just? Okay.

(And the other exits. EMILY crosses back into the offstage bedroom.
(There is a pause.
(RUTHIE reenters the room.)

RUTHIE

They're getting him changed.

(There's a bit of a pause. HANANIAH looks up.)

HANANIAH
(gently)

Will you take my hand?

(He holds out his hand.
(Bit of a pause.)

RUTHIE

I think probably I'd better not.

(He looks at her. She looks at him. Then looks away. He stands up. She looks at him.)

And don't – no.

(PT enters.)

PT

What he really needs is a bath but he's too hard to handle passed out. Monica's going after him with awash cloth but hopefully he'll be up for a shower tomorrow.

(to HANANIAH)

I like your stuff. It's actually it's been a long time since I went through someone else's closet. It reminds me of, like, my older brother when we were in high school. I was always going after his football jersey. Man, that used to piss him off!

(There's a little pause.)

You don't mind if I rummage in your fridge do you?

(RUTHIE points out the kitchen. He goes off.
(EMILY appears in doorway.)

EMILY

He has been intermittently conscious. I think it's just exhaustion. PT?

(PT appears with a small hunk of cheddar.)

PT

Cheese okay?

EMILY

PT, can you give me a hand? And actually, Ruthie?
(RUTHIE gets up.
(As she's going off.)
You're not going to want him on your bed tonight I imagine. He looks like a thrasher.
(Offstage.)
Okay if you can just, by the leg – PT., easy.

PT

Yeah okay and you

EMILY

– okay, okay –

(They're maneuvering him into the room and onto the couch.
JEREMIAH is wearing jeans, and a tee shirt.
(His feet are bare.)

RUTHIE
(to HANANIAH)
Will you get a blanket from the Captain's chest?

EMILY
Easy, and over, and over. Okay
            (They get him set down.)
good.
                        (to RUTHIE)
You don't have a washing machine do you?

RUTHIE
No.

EMILY
PT get a garbage bag or something for his robes. Oh and the –

(PT has started into the kitchen.)

RUTHIE
They're under the sink.

EMILY
boots. Get one for the boots. Don't forget the boots, they're in the --

*(HANANIAH brings the blanket over; sees JEREMIAH's face for the first
time.)*

HANANIAH
I thought he was in custody?!

*(JEREMIAH, disturbed by all the jostling, rouses and kind of half rears up,
looks up and on seeing HANANIAH, launches into prophecy.)*

JEREMIAH
Hananiah.

Hananiah Behold, I am against them that prophecy
false dreams. I will feed them with wormwood
and make them drink the water of gall
Is not my word like as a fire? Saith the Lord!
            (There is an internal struggle. The Lord wins.)
                                                            (MORE)

And like a hammer
that breaketh the rock in pieces: Behold, I am
(Briefly, JEREMIAH wins:)
No.
(A struggle.)
No.
(JEREMIAH loses.)
Hear now Hananiah, the Lord hath not…
hath not sent thee; but thou makest
(He's sweating.)
Thou makest this people to trust
I won't
in a lie. Therefore thus saith the Lord – no.
No.
No I won't.
(Exhausted.)
No.

(JEREMIAH wins.)

I won't.
(He falls back unconscious. The lights swiftly dwindle.
(The sound of his dreaming begins, low.)

EMILY
(after a ghastly pause)
We'll be back for him, in the morning.

HANANIAH
You're leaving him here (?)

CHAPTER 13 –
THE DREAM OF JEREMIAH

(There is a garble of back-sound: the mutter of overheard conversations, street noise,
the sound of a subway car entering a station – all of it barely possible to make out.
(Underlying it all, and increasing in volume, is an unearthly bit of pre-singing.
(As the dream progresses, something martial and stirring and uneasy may make its
way in.)

                    EMILY
                   (fading)

We'll be back for him, in the morning.

                  HANANIAH
                   (fading)

You're leaving him here.

                    EMILY
                   (fading)

We'll be back in the morning.

                  HANANIAH
              (fading; to RUTHIE)

This is – no.

                  PERSON 1
You cannot burn enough Danish embassies in my opinion.

                  PERSON 2
Because what it is you've got this sheath of muscle right? Right on the bone.

                  PERSON 3
              (lightly sarcastic)

Cool. Thank you Dr -----------.

                     PT
Me and some of the guys would go down to the quarry in the morning, just at
sunrise, the sky's just turning pink, and the water down below you is black; we
stripped down, our nuts were all shriveled up

                  PERSON 2
Dr ------. That's right. Dr. ------ to you. Thank you Dr......Dr Bedhead.

                    EMILY
They said 'shoe your feet, your bare torn feet, here are sandals put them on' but
I said no

                     PT
It's freezing cold. You dive in a coward, and you break out of the water raging.

                    EMILY
They said here, your throat is dry, here is water, drink, drink the water, quench
your –

244

RUTHIE

But I said no,

PERSON 1
(on cell phone)

Oh, Okay

PERSON 4
(simultaneous)

It takes a certain person/Certain people

PERSON 1
(on cell phone)

Where are you?

RUTHIE

I must be shoeless, thirsty, heedless –

PERSON 5

The Lord hath opened his armory and brought forth the weapons of his indignation.

NON PROPHET
(sharp; urgent)

Make bright the arrows; gather the shields.

PERSON 6
(also urgent, but in a different way)

Mom? I can hold my breath for 28 seconds. That's my highest maximum.

PERSON 7
(compelled)

One post shall run to meet another, and one messenger to meet another.

(Revealed:
the WHORE OF BABYLON. She takes up her song in earnest. The Scarlet Beast is near, and, the NON PROPHET doing a Flamenco dance.)

THE WHORE OF BABYLON
(sings)

Thy soul ached for me and
you cried out for me

(MORE)

I did not answer thee
but laughed from the dark hillside
there are lions in the forests
and wolves in the evenings
You were in longing for me
and I did not repent thee

You were an astonishment
a desolation
I ran in the wilderness
I was an exhilaration

a leopard has found the city gate
and pushed it open with her maw

CHAPTER 14

(Still raining, but slowed to a soft patter. The middle of the night.
(RUTHIE crosses the dark living room for a drink of water. JEREMIAH stirs,
and half raises himself.)

RUTHIE

You're awake.

JEREMIAH

I am. I remember where I am.

RUTHIE

Do you want…water? Or something to eat?

JEREMIAH

Water.

(She goes offstage, gets a glass of water, brings it to him. He drinks it in one go.)

RUTHIE

You were thirsty. Do you want more?

JEREMIAH

Please. And I think I need food also.

(She goes. Returns with the glass of water refilled,

and a hunk of bread on a plate.)

Thank you.

(He drinks half the glass of water. Sits up and holds the plate of bread on his lap. Picks up the bread.)

JEREMIAH
This is a —
This is a miracle. If I walk into a field. If I walk. This is a. If I walk into a field of wheat I can't eat it. I can't eat the wheat. This. This.
(to RUTHIE)
I'm sorry, I'm trying to. I'm trying to, uh
I can't.

RUTHIE
You know, if you're not hungry…

JEREMIAH
No, I'm hungry. I'm very hungry.
I'll just. I'll just eat it.

(He eats it.)

RUTHIE
Do you want more?

JEREMIAH
No, thank you. You're kind.

RUTHIE
Not especially.

JEREMIAH
No? Maybe not. You're kind to me.

RUTHIE
I don't know you.

JEREMIAH
You're his wife aren't you.

RUTHIE
I'm. Yes. I am his wife.

JEREMIAH

Of course. I didn't, I couldn't have one. It wasn't – I couldn't.

RUTHIE

You couldn't –

JEREMIAH

I couldn't have a wife. So I don't know anything about all of that.

RUTHIE

Why couldn't you have a wife?

JEREMIAH

Because it was forbidden unto me. I didn't mind. I didn't think I minded. Now
I think –
Wife.
He can hold your hand? Just like this?

(He *picks up her hand, he holds it, he spreads her fingers apart, he intertwines them
with his own.*)

RUTHIE

Yes.

JEREMIAH

He can touch you, like this.

(He *touches her neck, the side of her face...*)

RUTHIE

Yes. When I'm not angry at him.

(Her *mouth...*)

JEREMIAH

Are you angry at me?

RUTHIE

No, but I'm not your wife.

JEREMIAH

Aren't you? When I'm touching you like this.

248

(She steps up. She steps back.)

HANANIAH

Ruthie?

(HANANIAH steps into the room.)

RUTHIE

He's awake.

HANANIAH

I thought you were gone.

RUTHIE

I'm still here.

HANANIAH

I heard his voice. I thought she's left me, and I'm alone in the dark with a man who thinks he's talking to God. Come back to bed

CHAPTER 15

BARUCH

A day like this is splendor and confusion:
wind and brilliance and no season: gusts
of red leaf and gold, torrents of
blossom, the air thick with birds. Cries.

(It's daylight, morning. HANANIAH stands as before.
(JEREMIAH stands in the center of the room, an explosives vest over his jeans and tee shirt; his robes are slung over his back.
(The NON PROPHET is slowly threading nails in among the explosives with wires. A bag of bright nails at his feet spills out onto the floor.
(EMILY stands and PT slumps on the couch.
(A little cacophony of surreal birdsong, dies out. The scene is saturated with light.
(They are exhausted.)

NON PROPHET

Someone open the window. It's a gorgeous morning.

(A beat. No one does.)

NON PROPHET

I think better with fresh air on my face.

EMILY

I think it's a risk.

NON PROPHET

My fingers are more nimble when accompanied by birdsong. We're 6 floors up.

EMILY

Neighbors.

NON PROPHET

Do you overhear your neighbors?

HANANIAH

I've never heard anything from next door.

EMILY

Which might only mean that they're quiet.

NON PROPHET

Today is the most spectacular day of the year, thus far. I hate to be sectioned off from it by a thick pane of glass.

(Bit of a pause.)

EMILY

February.

NON PROPHET

What?

EMILY

There was a day in February. It was the most beautiful day of the year. Thus far.

NON PROPHET

You're joking. Nothing worthwhile happens in February. It's a completely negligible month.

EMILY

The day after that second snow storm.

PROPHET
(dubious)

Hmmm.

PT

March. March is useless. End to end. I'm going to make us some joe.

(He heads towards the kitchen.)

EMILY
(clinically)

A lot of white. A gray hush. And then around 4 the sky opened up and light poured out.

NON PROPHET

It sounds like more of an effect, than a day.

EMILY

It was a perfect cold: it was dry, it was crisp, it was glittering. There were crows.

NON PROPHET

Crows are an effect.

EMILY

It is pretty today.

NON PROPHET

It's gorgeous.

(RUTHIE emerges from the bedroom with a duffel bag.)

HANANIAH

That can't be all you're taking. We've been here for five years.

(He plunges into the bedroom.)
(There is a silence, while the NON PROPHET continues to work.)

EMILY

How's the weight?

JEREMIAH

It's fine; it's sweaty. It won't be for long.

(A longish beat.)

EMILY

No. Maybe…

(Bit of a pause while she works it out.)

45, 50 minutes.

(Another silence.
(HANANIAH returns from the bedroom.)

HANANIAH

This is crazy. You're leaving behind your blue tee shirt: you love that tee shirt.
You're leaving behind books that you have underlined.

You're leaving your red sweater. Where do you think you're going? Do you
think you're not ever going to be cold again?

Did you take any underwear?

RUTHIE

I brought one pair.

HANANIAH

One pair. That's crazy.

RUTHIE

I'm going to wash it every night , before I go to bed, wherever I go to bed, and
in the morning, I'm going to put it on again.

EMILY

Let's say 65. There'll be traffic.

JEREMIAH

I'm going to need words.

EMILY

What, that you speak? As long as you prophecy victory it doesn't matter what
you say.

JEREMIAH

I'm perfectly happy to lie but I've never done it before.

EMILY

You appear in the city center – it's a huge commotion; everyone thinks you're in prison, you say that…it's a new day, you know, all of that, you have extremely glad tidings – they bring you straight to the King.

NON PROPHET

The key to all of this is the declaiming. If you're declaiming when you hit the security checkpoint, if you're gesticulating, they won't think to stop you.

EMILY

They're not going to pat you down. You kneel right at his feet. No one else can get that close.

JEREMIAH

I won't be able to think of words. I know this is ridiculous: I don't know anything about public speaking.

EMILY
(fumbling)

'I bring you, citizens, I bring you words of prophecy, and peace' I bring you…

Behold and Lo…the Lord hath spake unto me…concerning the triumph that I foretell…
Yea verily, Glory, and Lo…

(HANANIAH unfurls in prophecy.)

THE PROPHECY OF HANANIAH

A strong man stirs in a hot room; the dark; the slow whirr of the fan; ice cubes settle in a glass. He steps forward into blackness but his fingers are ablaze with light. On the rooftop a figure in shadows; at dawn, the wide horizon of the sky. An unsettled shuffling, and a stomping of feet. Over the rooftops a call, and a shout in the street; we awaken on fire, in the early morning, and dress ourselves quickly, and descend to the street still barefoot. The sun is rising, enormous and gold, our throats fill with singing and with longing and we move in unison and the prayers of the people will be answered: the arrowheads of the enemy will crumple when they hit our shields, the foreheads of our men, as though they were paper! Their spears will shiver, midair, into nothingness! Their bullets will arrive in our ranks as lumps of faltering dough. Their missiles will falter and land harmlessly miles from their intended target, or implode at launch. The fingers of God will brush through the air, like a turbulent wind from the mountain; those he favors will be exhilarated, and gain the strength of ten men,

(MORE)

THE PROPHECY OF HANANIAH (cont.)

those he distains will crumple, short shallow and rapid of breath, their pupils
will dilate, their limbs tremble. They will be astonished! They will be an
astonishment! These are metaphors! These are figures of speech! They have
meaning! Accuracy! Weight!

*(He drops, almost stumbles from the prophetic pose and is HANANIAH again
but with traces of magnificence and the prophetic cadence still in his voice.)*

I'm telling you, I would laugh if this weren't so horrible; you can't succeed,
you're not going to succeed, your success is not something which is going to
happen; I know that, how do I know it? Because I have said it; your lunatic will
probably detonate by mistake in an ally and you're going to live the rest of your
life out of a van, with one pair of underwear, running from the police and
waiting for an apocalypse which is never going to take place when instead you
could be here, with me, you could be safe and warm and dry with my fingers in
your hair and my lips on your forehead. It's amazing, to me, that you don't
believe in me, it's terrifying, it's unreal. Do you believe me?

(She moves towards him.)

Stop.

RUTHIE

I can't.

(He steps over to JEREMIAH.)

HANANIAH

And the Lord says. About the false prophets.

JEREMIAH
(gently)

He deplores them. And they die.

HANANIAH

Right.

*(He grabs the vest, pulls at the detonator, and crosses the wires.
(There is a tableau: JEREMIAH, HANANIAH.)*

PT

There was a very long period of time,

ALL

We were overcome with wonder

(RUTHIE *is speaking as a citizen, as she speaks she gestures toward the tableau, and frames it.*)

RUTHIE

This is Smith Street and it used to be really really ghetto, but now there's lots of things everywhere.

PT

microsecond after microsecond,

ALL

We were overcome with wonders

(*EMILY also steps aside, frames the scene.*)

EMILY

You don't understand. You really are. You're beautiful. I love you to death.

PT

where I thought it had failed to ignite: the connection was miswired, the fuse fizzled, the material misincorporated, or just too old. I was, in those microseconds, violently alive. But microseconds pile up, and eventually we came to the end of them.

RUTHIE

What are you learning? Moods? Plants?

(*The NON-PROPHET also.*)

NON PROPHET

Some of the Big Kids GARBLE

ALL

We were overcome with signs

BARUCH

We found their bodies in the morning They were shot through with stars

Blackout.

END OF PLAY

ROUND 1

An ancestor on one side.

ROUND 2

A Ignatius Agnello
B Leo D. Nakamura
E Jessica Alma Keating
F Calvin Barton Upton
G Thomas A. Da Mota
H Amy Joan Nesbett
I Eunice Angela Adler
J Shannon T. Babcock

ROUND 3

A Kevin Andrew O'Keefe
B Martine Karin Zhao
E Terence Addo
F Valerie A. Phelps
G Patrick Adam Ranier
H Ebenezer O'Brien
I William Joseph Droppers
J Gregory M. Amadeo

ROUND 4

A Michael Thomas Sweeney
B Fanny Foster Hoskins
E Syed Salman Abad
F Thomas A. Song
G Robin Lucille Pincer
H Fabian Dawson Jr.
I Ginger La Fevre Adams
J Tatania G Szurlowski

ROUND 5

A Takashimi Yoshida
B David Glenn Haas
E Vincent Fallon

F Elmer George Hammond
G Douglas L. Douglass
H Ching T. Kang
I Maria Fowler Keller
J Richard J. Naples

ROUND 6

A Max Walcott Wagner
B Anthony Favuzza
E Julio Salas Portillo
F Bonnie Ruth Kaplan
G Glenn James Washington
H Liddy N. Abrahamson
I Hector Marshall Simmons
J Dierdre Wakefield

ROUND 7

An ancestor on the other side.

Then the Lord said unto me,
the prophets prophecy lies in my name:
I sent them not,
neither have I commanded them,
neither spake unto them:
they prophecy unto you a false vision and divination
and a thing of naught and the deceit of their heart

Therefore thus saith the Lord concerning the prophets that prophecy in my
name;
I sent them not
neither have I commanded them
neither spake unto them:
they prophesy unto you a false vision
and divination
and a thing of naught:

the deceit of their heart
they say: Sword and famine shall not be in this land...
by Sword and Famine shall those prophets be consumed!

Therefore thus saith the Lord of hosts concerning the prophets: Behold
I will feed them with wormwood

and make them drink the water of gall

Hearken not unto the words of the prophets that prophecy unto you:
they make you vain: they speak a vision of their own heart
and not out of the mouth of the Lord

They say Ye shall have peace
and they say unto every one that walketh after the imagination of his own heart,
no evil shall come upon
you.

Jay Smith (foreground), James Stanley, T. Ryder Smith in
the Clubbed Thumb production at the Ohio Theater

*T. Ryder Smith, left, and Jay Smith in the Clubbed Thumb production
at the Ohio Theater*

Elliotte Crowell in the Clubbed Thumb production at the Ohio Theater

Laura Flanagan. left, and Jennifer R. Morris in
the Clubbed Thumb production at the Ohio Theater

Tales of a Chronicler

An Introduction to Quiara Alegría Hudes' *Elliot, A Soldier's Fugue*
by Liz Jones & Asher Richelli

When Quiara Alegría Hudes applied for the P73 Playwriting Fellowship in the spring of 2004, her writing samples stood out immediately, as bold and poetic as her name. Over the next few months, we immersed ourselves in Quiara's works, rollicking through the heartbreaking humor of *The Adventures of Barrio Grrrl!*, luxuriating in the poetry of *Yemaya's Belly,* and sitting upright at the first ten pages of what was to become *Elliot, A Soldier's Fugue* – ten pages that convinced us that committing a year of resources to Quiara and to this play was not just a good idea, it was necessary.

The narrative landscapes in *Yemaya's Belly, The Adventures of Barrio Grrrl!* and *Elliot, A Soldier's Fugue* are informed in part by the experiences and stories of people Quiara knows intimately. *Yemaya's Belly* was sparked by tales that Quiara was told by her father, while *Barrio Grrrl!'s* heroine was inspired by Quiara's younger sister. In writing *Elliot,* Quiara grappled with the changes that her cousin Elliot endured during and after his 2003 tour in Iraq. Although he returned with what Quiara calls that same "cheeseburger" smile, the beloved family son changed forever during his months at war. This transformation set Quiara on a search for answers about her family's history in the U.S. military. Quiara traveled home to Philadelphia where she interviewed Elliot's father, who is a Vietnam veteran, and other family members. To her surprise, her uncle and cousin opened up, revealing painful memories and details that made their way into the final draft of the play.

In *Elliot,* as in her other plays, Quiara is as much of a theatrical "chronicler" as she is a playwright. Through Quiara, the stories of her family, friends and acquaintances become available and relevant to the larger culture. But Quiara does not merely take their words and experiences verbatim; rather, these stories serve as the inspiration around which she carefully crafts her unique theatrical worlds. In so doing, she fuses reality, poetry and magic realism, transforming, in the case of *Elliot,* the words of her uncle into theater that has both a universal and personal resonance. After being interviewed by Quiara about his experience in Vietnam, her uncle admitted that he "hadn't felt lighter in years." It is a testament to Quiara's writing that her plays liberate those whose stories she tells by imparting their personal tales and turning them into a life-force that buoys up subject and audience member alike.

Quiara's passion for these very real stories gives her plays strong grounding despite her works' experimental style. Although the characters that appear in *Barrio Grrrl!* and *Yemaya's Belly* speak about magical worlds, they are rooted in a reality that they long to escape. The principal character in *Barrio Grrrl!* dreams of fighting a secret society of alchemists that labels women "whores," while in *Yemaya's Belly* Jesús hopes to leave his village so that he can stay in the fanciest hotels and even meet the American president. In these two plays, Quiara charts the rites of passage of her protagonists through near-death dream sequences, dancing and music. The cultures that distinguish her characters from everyone else around them also provide a protective arsenal. Comforting food, incantations and herbs soothe Jesús in *Yemaya's Belly* and Ana in *Barrio Grrrl!*; in their desperate moments, they find solace in ritual and song. But Quiara's protagonists are not fantasists. They may dream of magical worlds where ointments cure both soul and body but they know that more than magic is needed to survive; their magic realism is one that is more psychological than fantastical. They are young men and women who, before becoming adults themselves, fight off the adult world with cartoon-bright pluck. Throughout, the energy and fizz of these characters is contrasted by the somber reality that they know they must eventually face and, in part, even accept. Quiara's inspired book for *In The Heights*, a new musical that opened off-Broadway in February 2007 and that focuses on young Latinos living in Washington Heights, is yet another example of her ability to connect cultural rituals to important coming-of-age moments.

Many of these tropes – the coming-of-age story and the soothing incantations of a motherly figure – also appear in *Elliot, A Soldier's Fugue*. Yet this play is markedly different from *Barrio Grrrl!* and *Yemaya's Belly* in a number of ways. Here, the characters' relationships are conveyed more by silences than by exchanged words. Although it is a play about family, in *Elliot*, no family members ever address one another; the only time that characters have a direct conversation is in a flashback that takes place in the past. The somber tone that pervades *Elliot, A Soldier's Fugue* is not surprising. This play is, after all, about war. But it is a war play that is neither polemic nor stridently political. The characters in *Elliot, A Soldier's Fugue* are not mouthpieces; they are dramatizations of flesh-and-blood people who lived through some of this country's worst military conflicts. The play chronicles the harrowing rites of passage of three men at war and, at the same time, it accomplishes the extraordinary: it successfully eschews political discourse about the hot-button topic of the Iraq War in favor of an emotional and personal tale.

A masterful conglomerate of words, ideas and history, *Elliot* makes the political personal. Quiara has said that, while her political feelings about the war are strong, she did not intend to use *Elliot, A Soldier's Fugue* as a platform for her views. The play is not about right-wing or left-wing politics. Still, it would be simplistic to call *Elliot* apolitical theater. There is no question that, in writing this intimate portrayal of war, Quiara has written a play that speaks to larger political themes. At performances of *Elliot, A Soldier's Fugue*, audience members ranging from military veterans to high school teachers pointed to *Elliot* as an object lesson in the choices available for inner-city teenagers with limited resources. Most importantly, it portrays the desperate choices made by young men at war and their need to make a human connection even in the most inhuman situations.

Elliot, A Soldier's Fugue is a departure for Quiara not only because of its themes but also because of its structure. Whereas *Barrio Grrrl!* and *Yemaya's Belly* are linear, with *Elliot*, Quiara has fashioned a play that weaves together three non-chronological monologues and a series of brief letters to explore three generations of Puerto Rican men. Like the pieces of a puzzle, each monologue and letter reveals the significance of family heirlooms and childhood memories. In college, Quiara majored in music; not surprisingly, music informs the structure and language of *Elliot, A Soldier's Fugue*. Although the play is non-linear, it follows the rigid structural tenants of a fugue. In a fugue, the principal subject is repeated successively in similar form at different pitch levels by different parts or voices. So Quiara opens her play with Elliot, as the young soldier looks at himself in the mirror and considers his active duty in Iraq. Pop then enters, writes a letter and, like his son, thinks about his military experience. The play's remaining voices enter one by one, each beginning by stating this same theme. The remainder of the fugue develops the play further using all of the voices and, usually, multiple statements of the theme. This narrative device gradually uncovers the similarities that transcend the generational gap separating the three men. Moreover, like an opera's recitative or a musical composition's overture, the snippets of letters and monologues build to Elliot's final glorious monologue, in which he pinpoints "the time in life [he was] happiest". Elliot's words – a sort of *aria* – echo the joy, sadness, fear and resignation of not only this 18-year-old Marine but also of his father, grandfather and mother. It is a heartbreaking theatrical coup through which Quiara intertwines everyday jargon with lyrical flourishes.

There is a temptation to categorize *Elliot* and Quiara's other plays within some great flow-chart of playwriting. Her plays are non-traditional plays. They are Latina/o plays. Similarly, there is a tendency to pigeonhole Quiara as a Latina playwright, a female playwright, a new playwright. But Quiara (and her work) is all of these things. Quiara becomes her own artist (and each play by Quiara, its own theatrical experience) through the intersection of her culture and background. In her writing, Quiara seeks to explore the experiences of her Latina/o characters, and the obvious point to make would be to say that she gives voice to those who have often been left out of the theatrical conversation. But it is not just the fact that the characters in *Elliot*, *Yemaya's Belly* or *The Adventures of Barrio Grrrl!* are Latina/o that makes them interesting. It is the specificity and authenticity of Quiara's depictions, which stem from her loyalty to and love for the individuals and cultures that inspire her work, that make her characters and theatrical worlds unique. From Ginny's sorrowful reminiscences to Yemaya's singing, the characters in each of her plays trust the audience in the same manner in which Elliot and his father trusted Quiara when she first sat down to record their military experiences. In each of her works, Quiara writes with the mind of a sensitive chronicler and the heart of a poet and invites her audiences to lean forward into the warmth of Ginny's garden or the magical ocean of *Yemaya's Belly* and witness a genre-defying mixture of serious drama, breathtaking lyricism and philosophical meditation.

ELLIOT, A SOLDIER'S FUGUE

by Quiara Alegría Hudes

ELLIOT, A SOLDIER'S FUGUE

ORIGINAL PRODUCTION PRODUCED BY
PAGE SEVENTY-THREE PRODUCTIONS, INC.

Elliot, A Soldier's Fugue was premiered by Page 73 Productions in New York on
January 4, 2006, under the artistic direction of Liz Jones, Asher Richelli, Nicole
Fiz and Daniel Schiffman, at the Culture Project. The production was directed
by Davis McCallum. The cast was as follows:

ELLIOT..Armando Riesco
GINNY...Zabryna Guevara
POP..Triney Sandoval
GRANDPOP..Mateo Gómez

The set design was by Sandra Goldmark, costumes designed by Chloe Chapin,
music by Michael Freedman, and lighting designed by Joel Moritz.

An early version of the play was produced at Miracle Theatre in Portland, Or.,
in September 2005, directed by Olga Sanchez.

CAST OF CHARACTERS:

ELLIOT..serving in Iraq, 1st Marine Division, 19

POP..............Elliot's father, served in Vietnam, 3rd Cavalry Division, various ages

GRANDPOP.....Elliot's grandfather, served in Korea, 65th Infantry Regiment of
Puerto Rico, various ages

GINNY......Elliot's mother, served in Vietnam, Army Nurse Corps, various ages

SET
The set has two playing areas. The "empty space" is minimal, it transforms into
many locations. It is stark, sad. When light enters, it is like light through a
jailhouse window or through the dusty stained glass of a decrepit chapel. The
"garden space," by contrast, is teeming with life. It is a verdant sanctuary, green
speckled with magenta and gold. Both spaces are holy in their own way.

PRODUCTION NOTES
Fugues
In the "fugue" scenes, people narrate each other's actions and sometimes
narrate their own. For instance:

     ELLIOT
     A boy enters.

        (ELLIOT enters.)

     GRANDPOP
     Clean, deodorized.
     Some drops of water plummet from his nose and lips.
     The shower was ice cold.

        (ELLIOT shivers.)

Elliot's action should mirror what the narrator, Grandpop, says. The narrator
steps in and out of the scene as necessary.

Pop's letters
Pop's letters are active and alive. They are not reflective, past-tense documents. They are immediate communication. Sometimes the letters are shared dialogue between Pop and Grandpop, but it should always be clear that it is Pop's story being spoken.

Music
Flute. Bach, *danzónes*, jazz, etudes, scales, hip-hop beats. Overlapping lines.

Interview voices
Should not be pre-recorded; distribute among the ensemble at your discretion. In the New York premiere, each interview voice was distributed among the entire ensemble to create a choral effect. In Atlanta, one actor embodied one interviewer, for a more conversational feel.

Other
Please do not use actual barbed wire or vines in the wrapping scenes. The stage directions in these moments are an important part of the soul of the piece, but should not be staged literally. Finally, the moments where Pop and Elliot say "bang" should not sound like someone shooting a gun or imitating a sound effect. Just say the word "bang."

For Elliot, Ginny and George.

With special thanks to Ray, Davis, Paula, and mom.

ELLIOT, A SOLDIER'S FUGUE
by Quiara Alegría Hudes

1. FUGUE

(The empty space, very empty. A pair of white underwear is on the ground. That's all we see.)

GINNY
A room made of cinderblock.
A mattress lies on a cot containing 36 springs.
If you lie on the mattress, you can feel each of the 36 springs.
One at a time.
As you close your eyes.
And try to sleep the full four hours.

POP
A white sheet is on the mattress.
The corners are folded and tucked under.
Tight, like an envelope.

GRANDPOP
Military code.
The corner of the sheet is checked at 0600 hours, daily.
No wrinkles or bumps allowed.

ELLIOT
A man enters.

(ELLIOT enters in a towel. It's 2003. He's 18.)

GRANDPOP
Clean, deodorized.
Some drops of water plummet from his nose and lips.
The shower was ice cold.

(ELLIOT shivers. He picks up the underwear.)

GINNY
He performs his own military-style inspection.

271

(ELLIOT looks at the front and back of the underwear. No apparent stains. He sniffs them. They're clean.)

ELLIOT

Nice.

(ELLIOT puts them on under the towel, removes the towel.)

POP

There's little bumps of skin on his arm.
His pores tighten.
His leg hair stands on end.
Cold shower spray.

(ELLIOT drops to the ground and does 10 push-ups. He springs to his feet and seems invigorated.)

ELLIOT

One two three four five six seven eight nine ten. Rah!

POP

The mirror in the room reflects a slight distortion.

(ELLIOT peers into the mirror – the audience.)

GINNY

The chin.
The teeth.
Uppers and lowers.
The molars.
The one, lone filling.

(He clenches his jaw, furrows his eyebrows. Holding the face, he curls a bicep, showing off a round muscle.)

ELLIOT
(to the mirror adversary)

What? You want to step? You're making Subway hoagies. I'm a marine. Who are you?

(He shakes out that pose. Now, he smiles like a little angel into the mirror.)

ELLIOT
(to the mirror mommy)
Mami, quiero chuletas. Pasteles. Morsilla. Barbecue ribs. *Sorullito.* Macaroni salad.
Sopa de fideo. When I make it back home, you gonna make me a plate, right?
A *montón* of ribs. But no pigs feet. Ain't no other Puerto Rican on this earth be
cookin no pigs feet.

*(ELLIOT shakes out that pose. He leans in, an inch away from the mirror. He
pops a pimple. He wipes it on his underwear. He scrutinizes his face for more
pimples. There are none. He fixes his nearly-shaved hair. He stands in a suave
posture, leaning sexy. He blows a subtle kiss to the mirror.)*

ELLIOT
You know you like it. Navy nursee want *mi culito?*

*(He turns around, looks at his butt in the mirror. He clenches his butt muscles and
releases. Then he does this about 10 times in a quick succession, watching the
mirror the whole time. He stops.)*

POP
Blank.
He's nervous about something.

GRANDPOP
He will board the ship to Iraq at 0700 hours.

*(ELLIOT starts to put on his uniform under... The room is empty. A towel is on
the floor.)*

GINNY
A room with steel doors.
Steel walls, steel windows.
The room sways up and down.
Hammocks on top of hammocks swing back and forth.

GRANDPOP
The room is inside a boat.
That's on the ocean to Vietnam.

GINNY
The floors of the USS Eltinge are inspected at 0530 daily.

POP & GRANDPOP
Military code.

No dirt allowed.

GINNY

But the floor is wet.
It's the Pacific Ocean, seeping inside.

POP

A young man enters.

(POP enters. It's 1966. He wears a uniform and catches his breath.)

GINNY

The 0400 deck run was hot.
The shower will be warm.
640 muscles will relax.

GRANDPOP

Military code.
No bare chests.

(POP untucks his shirt, unbuttons it, throws it to the floor.)

POP
(imitating a drill sergeant under his breath; faux
southern accent)
Keep up the pace, Ortiz. You can't hear me, Ortiz? Are you deaf, Ortiz?
Corporal Feifer, is Corporal Ortiz deaf?

GRANDPOP

Military code.
No bare feet.

(He takes off his boots, peels off his socks.)

POP

You're the best damn shot in the marines, Ortiz. You could kill a fly. Does
your momma know what a great shot you are?

GINNY

Reflect honor upon yourself and your home country.

(He peels off his undershirt.)

POP

Where are you from, Ortiz? What's your momma's name? Eh? Is she fat like you? Your momma got a fat ass, Ortiz?

(ELLIOT is fully dressed. He salutes the mirror.)

ELLIOT

Lance Corporal Elliot Ortiz Third Light Armored Recon Battalion First Marine Division. Mutha fucka.

(POP finds a paper and pencil. He taps the pencil, thinking of what to write. ELLIOT checks inside his duffel bag.)

GINNY

The duffel is heavy full of boots and pants.
A map of Iraq.
A Bible with four small photographs.

GRANDPOP

Military code.
No electronic devices.

ELLIOT

Got my walkman.

GRANDPOP

Military code.
No valuables.

ELLIOT

My Nas cd. Jay Z. Slow Jams. Reggaetón 2002.

POP

April 12, 1966…

(ELLIOT opens a little green Bible, looks at photos.)

ELLIOT

My photos. Mom. In your garden.

(He kisses the photo. Finds a new one.)

Grandpop. Senile old head.

(Taps the photo. Finds a new one.)

Pops. With your beer-ass belly.

POP
(writing)

Dear Pop...

ELLIOT
(still to the photo)

When I get home, we gonna have a father and son. Chill in mom's garden.
Drink some bud light out them mini cans. I don't want to hear about no "leave
the past in the past." You gonna tell me your stories.

*(ELLIOT puts on headphones and starts bobbing his head to the hip-hop beat.
POP continues to write under... The room is empty. A towel is on the floor.)*

GINNY

A tent.
No windows, no door.
Walls made of canvas.
A floor made of dirt.
The soil of Inchon, Korea is frozen.

GRANDPOP

16 cots they built by hand.
Underwear, towels, unmade beds.
Dirty photos.

GINNY

That is, snapshots of moms and daughters and wives
That have dirt on them.

GRANDPOP

A boy enters.

*(GRANDPOP enters. It's 1950. He's wearing heavy soldier clothes. He rubs
his arms for warmth. He puts on additional clothing layers.)*

GINNY

His breath crystallizes.
His boots are full of icy sweat.
The 0500 swamp run was subzero.

(GRANDPOP blows into his hands for warmth. He bends his fingers.)

GRANDPOP

One two three four… five. My thumb is as purple as a flower.

(He pulls a black leather case from his cot. He opens it, revealing a flute. He pulls out pieces of the flute, begins to assemble them, cleaning dirt from the joints.)

GRANDPOP

Ah, this Korean dirt is too damn dirty. We lost another man to frostbite this week. These guys deserve some Bach. Light as a feather,

POP
(finishing the letter)

Your son,

GRANDPOP

free as a bird.

POP

Little George.

(GRANDPOP puts the flute to his lips, inhales, begins to play. The melody of a Bach passacaglia. POP folds up the letter, puts it in an envelope. Addresses the envelope.)

GINNY

Military code.
Make no demands.
Military code.
Treat women with respect.
Military code.
Become friends with fellow soldiers.
No rude behavior.
Pray in silence, please.

(POP drops the letter, lays down, sings himself to sleep. It overlaps with GRANDPOP's flute and ELLIOT's head-bobbing.)

POP

1234
We're gonna jump on the count of four

(MORE)

If I die when I hit the mud
Bury me with a case of bud
A case of bud and a bottle of rum
Drunk as hell in kingdom come
Count off
1234[3]

(*ELLIOT skips forward a few tracks on the walkman. He finds his jam. Head bobbing, feeling it.*)

ELLIOT

Uh, uh.
And when I see ya I'ma take what I want so
You tryin to front, hope ya
Got ur self a gun
You ain't real, hope ya
Got ur self a gun

Uh, uh, uh, uh.	POP
I got mine I hope ya… uh, uh	1234
You from da hood I hope ya…	We're gonna charge on the count of
You want beef I hope ya…	If my heart begins to bleed
Uh, uh, uh, uh.	Bury me with a bag full a' weed
And when I see you I'ma	A bag full a' weed and a
Take what I want so	Bottle of rum
You tryin to front, hope ya…	Laugh at the devil in kingdom come
You ain't real, hope ya…	Count off
Uh, uh, uh, uh.[4]	Bud bud bud bud
	Bud bud bud bud

(*It is three-part counterpoint between the men. Lights fade, counterpoint lingers.*)

2. PRELUDE

(*The empty space. A flashbulb goes off.*)

SPORTSCASTER VOICE

Thanks, Harry. I'm standing outside the Phillies locker room with hometown hero Lance Corporal Elliot Ortiz. He'll be throwing out tonight's opening pitch.

---

[3] Based on traditional military cadences
[4] From Nas, *Got Yourself A Gun*

ELLIOT

Call me Big El.

SPORTSCASTER VOICE

You were one of the first marines to cross into Iraq.

ELLIOT

Two days after my eighteenth birthday.

SPORTSCASTER VOICE

And you received a Purple Heart at 19. Big El, welcome home.

ELLIOT

Philly!

SPORTSCASTER VOICE

You're in Philadelphia for a week and then it's back to Iraq for your second tour of duty?

ELLIOT

We'll see. I got until Friday to make up my mind.

SPORTSCASTER VOICE

Did you miss the city of brotherly love?

ELLIOT

Mom's food. My girl Stephanie. My little baby cousin. Cheese steaks.

SPORTSCASTER VOICE

Any big plans while you're home?

ELLIOT

Basically eat. Do some interviews. My mom's gonna fix up my leg. I'm a take my pop out for a drink, be like, alright, old head. Time to trade some war stories.

SPORTSCASTER VOICE

I hope you order a Shirley Temple. Aren't you 19?

ELLIOT

I'll order a Shirley Temple.

SPORTSCASTER VOICE

Big Phillies fan?

ELLIOT

Three years in a row I was Lenny Dykstra for Halloween.

SPORTSCASTER VOICE

A few more seconds to pitch time.

ELLIOT

Hold up. Quick shout out to North Philly. 2nd and Berks, share the love! To my moms. My pops. I'm doing it for you. Grandpops – videotape this so you don't forget! Stephanie. All my friends still out there in Iraq. Waikiki, one of these days I'm going to get on a plane to Hawaii and your mom better cook me some Kahlua pig.

SPORTSCASTER VOICE

Curve ball, fast ball?

ELLIOT

Wait and see. I gotta keep you on your toes. I'm gonna stand on that mound and show ya'll I got an arm better than Schilling! Record lightning speed!

3. PRELUDE

(The garden. GRANDPOP opens a letter and reads. POP appears separately.)

GRANDPOP & POP

May 24, 1966

POP

Dear pop,
It's hot wet

GRANDPOP

cold muddy

POP

miserable. Operation Prairie has us in the jungle, and it's a sauna.

GRANDPOP

One hundred twenty degrees by 1100 hours,

                                POP
you think you're gonna cook by 1300. Then yesterday it starts to rain.

                             GRANDPOP
Drops the size of marbles –

                                POP
my first real shower in weeks. Monsoon. They said,

                             GRANDPOP
"Get used to it." Corporal shoved a machete in my hand and told me to lead.

                                POP
He's the leader, but I get to go first!

                             GRANDPOP
I cut through the vines, clear the way. We get lesions,

                                POP
ticks,

                             GRANDPOP
leeches.

                                POP
At night we strip down, everybody pulls the things off each other. We see a lot
of rock ape.

                             GRANDPOP
They're bigger than chimps and they throw rocks at us.

                                POP
They've got great aim! You just shoot up in the air, they run away.

                             GRANDPOP
At night you can't see your own hand in front of your face.

                                POP
I imagine you and mom on the back stoop, having a beer. Uncle Tony playing
his guitar. My buddy Joe Bobb,

                             GRANDPOP
from Kentucky,

POP

he carries all his equipment on his back, plus a guitar, and he starts playing these hillbilly songs.

GRANDPOP

They're pretty good.

POP

I think Uncle Tony would like them. I pulled out your flute and we jammed a little. C-rations, gotta split,

POP & GRANDPOP

Little George.

4. PRELUDE

(GINNY in the garden.)

GINNY

The garden is 25 years old. It used to be abandoned. There was glass everywhere. Right here, it was a stripped-down school bus. Here, a big big pile of old tires. I bought it for one dollar. A pretty good deal. Only a few months after I came back from Vietnam. I told myself, you've got to *do* something. So I bought it. I went and got a ton of dirt from Sears. Dirt is expensive! I said, when I'm done with this, it's going to be a spitting image of Puerto Rico. Of Arecibo. It's pretty close. You can see electric wires dangling like right there and there. But I call that "native Philadelphia vines." If you look real close, through the heliconia you see anti-theft bars on my window.

Green things, you let them grow wild. Don't try to control them. Like people, listen to them, let them do their own thing. You give them a little guidance on the way. My father was a mean bastard. The first time I remember him touching me, it was to whack me with a shoe. He used to whack my head with a wooden spoon every time I cursed. I still have a bump on my head from that. Ooh, I hated him. But I was mesmerized to see him with his plants. He became a saint if you put a flower in his hand. Secrets, when things grow at night. Phases of the moon. He didn't need a computer, he had it all in his brain. "I got no use for that." That was his thing. "I got no use for church." "I got no use for a phone." "I got no use for children." He had use for a flower.

(MORE)

There are certain plants you only plant at night. Orchids. Plants with
provocative shapes. Plants you want to touch. Sexy plants. My garden is so
sexy. If I was young, I'd bring all the guys here. The weirdest things get my
juices going. I sit out here at night, imagine romances in the spaces between
banana leaves. See myself as a teenager, in Puerto Rico, a whole different body
on these bones. I'm with a boyfriend, covered in dirt.

When I was a nurse in the Army Nurse Corps, they brought men in by the
loads. The evacuation hospital. The things you see. Scratched corneas all the
way to. A guy with the back of his body torn off. You get the man on the cot,
he's screaming. There's men screaming all around. Always the same thing,
calling out for his mother, his wife, girlfriend. First thing, before anything else,
I would make eye contact. I always looked them in the eye, like to say, hey, it's
just you and me. Touch his face like I was his wife. Don't look at his wound,
look at him like he's the man of my dreams. Just for one tiny second. Then, it's
down to business. Try to keep that heart going, that breath pumping in and
out, keep that blood inside the tissue. Sometimes I was very attracted to the
men I worked on. A tenderness would sweep through me. Right before dying,
your body goes into shock. Pretty much a serious case of the shakes. If I saw a
man like that, I thought, would he like one last kiss? One last hand on his ass?
Give him a good going away party.
Just things in my mind. Not things you act on.

With George, though. We had a great time when he was in the evacuation
hospital. I stitched his leg up like a quilt and we stayed up all night smoking
joints. Everyone in the hospital was passed out asleep. The first time George
got up and walked to me. I took his head in my right hand and I kissed him so
hard. That kiss was the best feeling in my body. Ooh. You see so much death,
then someone's lips touches yours and you go on vacation for one small
second.

Gardening is like boxing. It's like those days in Vietnam. The wins versus the
losses. Ninety percent of it is failures but the triumphs? When Elliot left for
Iraq, I went crazy with the planting. Begonias, ferns, trees. A seed is a contract
with the future. It's saying, I know something better will happen tomorrow. I
planted bearded irises next to palms. I planted tulips with a border of cacti. All
the things the book tells you, "Don't ever plant these together." "Guide to
Proper Gardening." Well I got on my knees and planted them side by side. I'm
like, you have to throw all preconceived notions out the window. You have to
plant wild. When your son goes to war, you plant every goddam seed you can
find. It doesn't matter what the seed is. So long as it grows. I plant like I want
(MORE)

GINNY (cont.)

and to hell with the consequences. I planted a hundred clematis vines by the kitchen window, and next thing I know sage is growing there. The tomato vines gave me beautiful tomatoes. The bamboo shot out from the ground. And the heliconia!

(She retrieves a heliconia leaf.)

Each leaf is actually a cup. It collects the rainwater. So any weary traveler can stop and take a drink.

5. PRELUDE

(The garden. GRANDPOP opens a letter and reads. POP appears separately.)

POP

October 7, 1966

GRANDPOP

Dear dad and all the rest of you lucky people,

POP

Got my next assignment. All those weeks of waiting and boredom? Those are the good old days! They marched us to Dong Ha for Operation Prairie 2. I'm infantry. Some guys drive, go by tank. Infantry walks. We walk by the side of the tank. Two days straight, we've been scouting for body parts. You collect what you find, throw it in the tank, they label it and take it away. Where they take it? You got me. What they write on the label? It's like bird watching. You develop your eye.

GRANDPOP

Don't show this letter to mom, please. And don't ask me about it when I get home. If I feel like talking about it I will but otherwise don't ask.

POP

Today this one little shrimp kept hanging around, chasing after the tank. Looking at me with these eyes. I gave him my crackers I was saving for dinner. I made funny faces and he called me dinky dow. That's Vietnamese for crazy, I guess. Dinky dow! Dinky dow! He inhaled those crackers then he smiled and hugged my leg. He was so small he only came up to my knee.

6. FUGUE

(The empty space. Two wallets are on the ground.)

GINNY

In my dreams, he said.
Everything is in green.
Green from the night vision goggles.
Green Iraq.
Verdant Falluja.
Emerald Tikrit.

(ELLIOT enters. He puts on night vision goggles.)

ELLIOT
(to imaginary night patrol partner)
Waikiki man, whatchu gonna eat first thing when you get home? I don't know.
Probably start me off with some French toast from Denny's. Don't even get
me near the cereal aisle. I'll go crazy. I yearn for some cereal. If you had to
choose between Cocoa Puffs and Count Chocula, what would you choose?
Wheaties or Life? Fruity Pebbles or Crunchberry? You know my mom don't
even buy Cap'n Crunch. She buys King Vitaman. Cereal so cheap, it don't
even come in a box. It comes in a bag like them cheap Jewish noodles.

GINNY

Nightmares every night, he said.
A dream about the first guy he actually saw that he killed.
A dream that doesn't let you forget a face.

ELLIOT

The ultimate Denny's challenge. Would you go for the Grand Slam or the
French Toast Combo? Wait. Or Western Eggs with Hash Browns? Yo, hash
browns with ketchup. Condiments. Mustard, tartar sauce. I need me some
condiments.

GINNY

Green moon.
Green star.
Green blink of the eye.
Green teeth.
The same thing plays over and over.

(ELLIOT's attention is suddenly distracted.)

ELLIOT

Yo, you see that?

GINNY

The green profile of a machine gun in the distance.

ELLIOT

Waikiki, look straight ahead. Straight, at that busted wall. Shit. You see that guy? What's in his hand? He's got an AK. What do you mean, "I don't know." Do you see him?
(ELLIOT *looks out.*)
We got some hostiles. Permission to shoot.
(*Pause.*)
Permission to open fire.
(*Pause.*)
Is this your first? Shit, this is my first, too. Alright. You ready?

GINNY

In the dream, aiming in.
In the dream, knowing his aim is exact.
In the dream, closing his eyes.

(ELLIOT *closes his eyes.*)

ELLIOT

Bang.

(ELLIOT *opens his eyes.*)

GINNY

Opening his eyes.
The man is on the ground.

ELLIOT

Hostile down. Uh, target down.

(ELLIOT *gets up, disoriented from adrenaline.*)

GINNY

In the dream, a sudden movement.

ELLIOT

Bang bang. Oh shit. That fucker moved. Did you see that? He moved, right? Mother f. Target down. Yes, I'm sure. Target down.

GINNY

Nightmares every night, he said.
A dream about the first guy he actually saw that he killed.

(POP enters, sits on the ground. He's trying to stay awake. He looks through binoculars.)

GRANDPOP

In my dreams, he said.

GINNY

Walking toward the guy.

(ELLIOT walks to the wallet.)

GRANDPOP

Everything is a whisper.

GINNY

Standing over the guy.

(ELLIOT looks down at the wallet.)

GRANDPOP

Breathing is delicate.

GINNY

A green face.

GRANDPOP

Whisper of water in the river.

GINNY

A green forehead.

GRANDPOP

Buzz of mosquito.

GINNY

A green upper lip.

GRANDPOP

Quiet Dong-Ha.

GINNY

A green river of blood.

(*ELLIOT kneels down, reaches to the wallet on the ground before him. It
represents the dead man. He puts his hand on the wallet and remains in that
position.*)

GRANDPOP

Echo Vietnam.

POP

Joe Bobb. Wake up, man. Tell me about your gang from Kentucky. What,
back in the Bronx? Yeah, we got ourselves a gang, but not a bad one. We help
people on our street. Like some kids flipped over an ice cream stand. It was
just a nice old guy, the kids flipped it, knocked the old guy flat. We chased after
them. Dragged one. Punched him til he said sorry. We called ourselves the
Social Sevens. After the Magnificent Sevens.

GRANDPOP

Nightmares every night, he said.
A dream that doesn't let you forget a voice.
The same sounds echoing back and forth.

POP

Guns? Naw, we weren't into none of that. We threw a lot of rocks and bottles.
And handballs. Bronx Handball Champs, 1964. Doubles and singles. Hm?
What's a handball?

GRANDPOP

The snap of a branch.

POP

Shh.

GRANDPOP

Footsteps in the mud.

POP

You hear something?

GRANDPOP

Three drops of water.
A little splash.

(POP grabs his binoculars and looks out.)

POP

VC on us. Ten o'clock. Kneeling in front of the river, alone. He's drinking.
Fuck, he's thirsty. Joe Bobb, man, this is my first time. Oh shit. Shit. Bang.
(Pause.) Bang.

GRANDPOP

Whisper of two bullets in the air.
Echo of his gun.
A torso falling in the mud.

POP

Got him. I got him, Joe Bobb. Man down. VC down.

(POP rises, looks out.)

GRANDPOP

Hearing everything.
Walking to the guy.
Boots squishing in the mud.

(POP walks to the second wallet.)

Standing over the guy.
The guy says the Vietnamese word for "mother."
He has a soft voice.
He swallows air.
A brief convulsion.

Gasp.
Silence.
Water whispers in the river.

POP & ELLIOT

Military code.
Remove ID and intel from dead hostiles.

(POP kneels in front of the wallet. It represents the dead man. He reaches out his hand and touches the wallet. ELLIOT and POP are in the same position, each of them touching a wallet. They move in unison.)

POP

The wallet
The body
The face
The eyes

(ELLIOT and POP open the wallets.)

ELLIOT

The photo
The pictures
Bullet

(ELLIOT and POP each pull a little photo out of the wallets.)

POP

Dog tags
The wife

ELLIOT

The children

(They turn over the photo and look at the back of it.)

Black ink

POP

A date

POP & ELLIOT

Handwriting
A family portrait

(They drop the photo. They find a second photo. Lights fade.)

7. PRELUDE

(The empty space. A flash bulb goes off. ELLIOT is in a TV studio. Harsh studio lighting is on him.)

PRODUCER VOICE

ABC evening local news. And we're rolling to tape in three, two…

ELLIOT

(tapping a mike on his shirt collar)

Hello? What? Yeah. So where do we start?
(He presses his fingers against his ear, indicating that a producer or someone is talking to him through an ear monitor.)
My name? Elliot Ortiz.
(Listens.)
Sorry. Lance Corporal Elliot Ortiz, 3rd Light Armored Recon Battalion, 1st Marine Division.
(Listens.)
What? How was I injured?

PRODUCER VOICE

(impatient)

Someone fix his monitor. Don't worry, Mr. uh, Ortiz. Just tell us the story of your injury, would you?

ELLIOT

Okay. Well. I was on watch outside Tikrit. I don't know. I feel stupid. I already told this story once.

PRODUCER VOICE

You did?

ELLIOT

Just now. In the screen test.

PRODUCER VOICE

Right, right. That was to acclimate you to the camera.

ELLIOT

It loses the impact to repeat it over and over.

PRODUCER VOICE

Was it scary?

ELLIOT

People say, oh that must be scary. But when you're there, you're like, oh shit,

(MORE)

291

ELLIOT (cont.)

and you react. When it's happening you're not thinking about it. You're like, damn, this is really happening. That's all you can think. You're in shock basically. It's a mentality. Kill or be killed. You put everything away and your mentality is war. Some people get real gung ho about fighting. I was laid back.

PRODUCER VOICE

Yes, Mr. uh Ortiz. This is great. This is exactly it. Let's go back and do you mind repeating a couple sentences, same exact thing, without the expletives?

ELLIOT

Say what?

PRODUCER VOICE

Same thing. But no shit and no damn.

ELLIOT

I don't remember word for word.

PRODUCER VOICE

No problem. Here we go. "But when you're there, you're like, oh shit, and you react."

ELLIOT

But when you're there you're like, oh snap, and you react.

PRODUCER VOICE

"You're like, damn, this is really happening."

ELLIOT

You're like, flip, this is really happening.

PRODUCER VOICE

Flip? Do people say "flip" these days?

ELLIOT

You're like, FUCK, this is really happening.

PRODUCER VOICE

Cut!

ELLIOT

It's a marine thing.

8. PRELUDE

(GRANDPOP in the garden.)

GRANDPOP

Of everything Bach wrote, it is the fugues. The fugue is like an argument. It starts in one voice. The voice is the melody, the single solitary melodic line. The statement. Another voice creeps up on the first one. Voice two responds to voice one. They tangle together. They argue, they become messy. They create dissonance. Two, three, four lines clashing. You think, good god, they'll never untie themselves. How did this mess get started in the first place? Major keys, minor keys, all at once on top of each other. *(Leans in.)* It's about untying the knot.

In Korea my platoon fell in love with Bach. All night long, firing eight-inch howitzers into the evergreens. Flute is very soothing after the bombs settle down. They begged me to play. "Hey, Ortiz, pull out that pipe!" I taught them minor key versus major key. Minor key, it's melancholy, it's like the back of the woman you love as she walks away from you. Major key, well that's more simple, like how the sun rises. They understood. If we had a rough battle, if we lost one of our guys, they said, "Eh, Ortiz, I need a minor key." But if they had just got a letter from home, a note from the lady, then they want C major, up-tempo.

"Light as a feather, free as a bird." My teacher always said the same thing. Let your muscles relax. Feel like a balloon is holding up your spine. He was a gringo but he lived with us rural Puerto Ricans. Way in the mountains. He was touring in San Juan with his famous jazz combo, fell in love with a woman, never left. We accepted him as one of our own. He was honorary Boricua. "Light as a feather, free as a bird." I said, you know, if I get any lighter and freer, I'll float to the moon. But that's how you learn. By repeating. Over and over. At Inchon my right hand was purple with frostbite, I developed a technique for left-hand only. In Kunu-Ri? Every night we took our weapons to bed, like a wife. One night I shot myself in the shoulder. So I mastered the left-hand method.

Elliot always wanted to know. "*Abuelo*, tell me a story." About life in the service, about Puerto Rico. "*Abuelo*, how old were you when? How old were you when this, when that?" *Carajo*, I don't remember! All I know is what music I was playing at the time. When I started school, when I was a boy, helping

(MORE)

293

GRANDPOP (cont.)

mom in the house, it was etudes and scales. The foundations. The first girl I "danced with," it was *danzónes* around that time, mambo with a touch of jazz. But In Korea, I played Bach only. Because it is cold music, it is like math. You can approach it like a calculation. An exercise. A routine.

At the airport, I handed the flute to little George. I thought, he needs a word of advice, but what is there to say? I sent him to boot camp with a fifty dollar bill and a flute. That he didn't know how to play. But without it my fingers grew stiff. I started losing words. Dates. Names of objects. Family names. Battles I had fought in. I started repeating words as if I was playing scales. Practice. Bookmarks to remind myself. "Inchon, Inchon, Inchon." "Korea, Korea." "Bayamón." "Howitzer." "Evergreen."

9. PRELUDE

(The garden. GRANDPOP opens a letter and reads. POP appears separately, in a good mood.)

POP

November 30, 1966

Did you ever notice a helmet is an incredibly useful item? I got a wide range of artistic and practical uses for mine.

GRANDPOP

Today I took a bath, if you want to call it that, out of my helmet. The newer ones have two parts.

POP

If you take the metal part out, you can cook in it. Tonight we had two cans of tuna. A hamburger in gravy. Hess' contribution?

POP & GRANDPOP

Ham with lima beans.

POP

Everyone empties out their cans. Make a little blue campfire with some minor explosives. Voila,

GRANDPOP

helmet stew.

POP
So that's our Thanksgiving feast. The guys are singing carols. They're in the spirit!
Jingle bells
Mortar shells
VC in the grass
Take your Merry Christmas
And shove it up your ass

10. FUGUE

(The empty space. Two cots are there. ELLIOT lies on the ground. GRANDPOP, GINNY and POP wrap ELLIOT's legs in barbed wire. They entangle ELLIOT in this position, trapping him. ELLIOT lies helpless.)

GINNY

A road outside Tikrit.
A mile short of Saddam's hometown.

GRANDPOP

Cars are allowed out, but not back in.

POP

The boy was standing guard.

GRANDPOP

He saw an incoming car.

GINNY

The headlights approached.

POP

He fired into the car.

GRANDPOP

The horn sounded.

POP

The car collided into the barricade.

GINNY

The concertina wire slinkied onto his legs.

GRANDPOP

Two seconds ago.

ELLIOT

Sarge! Sarge! Waikiki!

GINNY

Seventy four thorns dig deep into his skin.

POP

Seventy four barbs chew into his bone.

GRANDPOP

It is not a sensation of rawness.

GINNY

It is not excruciating pain.

POP

It is a penetrating weakness.

GRANDPOP

Energy pours out of his leg.

GINNY

Like water from a garden hose.

ELLIOT

Sarge!

POP

The boy knows he is trapped.

GRANDPOP

He doesn't know he is injured.

GINNY

He does a military style inspection.

(ELLIOT *reaches up his pants leg.*)

GRANDPOP

His hand enters the warm meat of his calf.

ELLIOT

Oh shit. Stay calm. Put the tourniquet on. Lay back. Drink a cup of water.

(ELLIOT pulls a strip of cloth from his pocket. He wraps it like a tourniquet around his thigh. Tight.)

GINNY

Forty one percent of all injuries are leg wounds.

POP

Military code.

GRANDPOP

Carry a tourniquet at all times.

GINNY

Instructions in the event of rapid blood loss.

GRANDPOP

One.

ELLIOT

Stay calm.

POP

Two.

ELLIOT

Put the tourniquet on.

GRANDPOP

Three.

ELLIOT

Lay back.
Four... Four?

GINNY

Drink a cup of water.

                              ELLIOT
Someone get me a cup of water.

                              POP
Stay

                              GRANDPOP
Calm
Put

                              POP
Tourniquet

                              GINNY
Lay

                              GRANDPOP
Back
Drink

                              POP
Cup

                              GINNY
Water

                              ELLIOT
Hello? Stay calm. Put a beret on. Fall away. Drink a hot tub. Fuck. Stay with
me, Ortiz. Big El going to be okay. Hello? Big El okay. Right?

                              POP
Fast forward pictures.

                              GINNY
Mom

                              POP
Pop

                              GRANDPOP
Grandpop

                              POP
Fast forward.

298

                         GINNY
Grandpop

                         GRANDPOP
Pop

                         POP
Mom

                         GINNY
Rapid shutter motion.

                         GRANDPOP
Frames with no sound.

                         GINNY
Moving lips, no words.

                         ELLIOT
Mom

                         POP
Pop

                         GRANDPOP
Grandpop

                         ELLIOT
Stay calm. Lay back. Smoke a cigarette.
        (He pulls a cigarette out of his pocket.)
Anyone got a light?
        (He smokes the unlit cigarette.)

                         POP
Instructions if wounded while alone.

                         GRANDPOP
Call for help.

                         POP
Signal commander.

                              GINNY
Call for your corpsman.

                              POP
Identify yourself.

                              ELLIOT
Sarge! Waikiki! Big El down. Big El down.

                              POP
His blood congeals in the sand.

                              GRANDPOP
His fingertips are cool.

                              GINNY
He enters a euphoric state.

                              GRANDPOP
The boots,

                              ELLIOT
Beautiful.

                              POP
The barbed wire,

                              ELLIOT
Beautiful.

                              GINNY
The stars,

                              ELLIOT
Beautiful.

                              GINNY
In the event of extended blood loss.
Reflect on a time you were happy.
When have you felt a sensation of joy?

                              ELLIOT
Mom…
Pop…

300

(ELLIOT remains injured under… POP enters and lays on a cot.)

GRANDPOP

An evacuation hospital.
Made of a Vietnamese monastery.
Ancient windows with no glass.

GINNY

Through the window, views of Vietnam.
That look like views of Puerto Rico.
Mountains.

ELLIOT

Mountains.

GRANDPOP

Waterfalls.

ELLIOT

Waterfalls.

GINNY

All different colors of green.
Rock formations.
A few bald spots from the bombs.

GRANDPOP

The wood floor is covered with cement.
The cement is covered with water and blood.
The cement is cool.
The blood is cool.

ELLIOT

Cool.

(ELLIOT nods off, going into shock.)

GINNY

A woman enters.

(GINNY enters, approaches POP's cot.)

Hey.

POP

Nurse Ginny. Still on duty?

GINNY

Shh. Don't wake the babies.

POP

Can't sleep?

GINNY

Yeah.

POP

Me too.

GINNY

Nightmares. Weird stuff, I kept seeing your leg. I thought I should check up on you.

POP

It itches, but you know. The guy next to me's got no left leg at all.

GINNY

I was thinking, a private physical therapy session.

POP

Sounds good.

GINNY

Clean you up.

> (GINNY *lifts up his pant leg. There is a big gauze patch there. She slowly pulls back the gauze.*)

POP

That's as far back as it goes. The rest is stuck to the gauze.

GINNY

We're all out of anesthetic. I'll be gentle.

> (*She works on his wound. He is clearly in physical pain.*)

GINNY

Twenty eight stitches.
Two diagonals.
The first time she touched the man's wound,
A pain pierced up through her index finger.
Through her knuckle.
Wrist.
Forearm.
Elbow.
Humerus.
Shoulder.
The pain jolted in her veins.
Exploded in her vital organs.
Pancreas, lungs, brains, spleen.
Planted itself between her legs.
She touched the blood on his skin and had the desire to make love to the wounded man.

POP

Ay dios mío. Fuck.

GINNY

Think of the time in life you were happiest.

POP

Why?

GINNY

You forget the pain.

POP

It's not pain. It fucking itches!

GINNY

Sorry.

POP

Sorry.

(Pause. GINNY covers the wound. She pulls down his pant leg. She sits on top him.)

GINNY

Is it too much weight?

POP

Please, crush me to death.

GINNY

There's too many bells and whistles in hospitals. To be a nurse is easy. Give a dog a bone.

POP

Reach into my pocket.

GINNY

Lance Corporal Ortiz.

POP

Go ahead.

(She puts her hand into his pocket. She feels around.)

GINNY

What am I looking for?

POP

You'll know when you find it.

(She removes her hand from his pocket. She's holding a joint.)

Medicine.

GINNY

Anesthetic.

(GINNY lights the joint. They pass it back and forth. Between inhales, they touch each other.)

GRANDPOP

Through the window, views of Vietnam.
That look like views of Puerto Rico.
Mountains.
Green.

(MORE)

Stars.
Bamboo.
Little huts up the mountainside.

POP
(stoned)
I got one. I was a little boy in Puerto Rico. Bayamón. I had this ugly scrappy dog. We used to run around scaring my dad's roosters. One of the roosters got pissed and poked the dog's left eye out.

GINNY
What was his name?

POP
Jimmy.

GINNY
Jimmy? Jimmy!

(ELLIOT shivers.)

ELLIOT
Ugghhh…

POP
Shh. Did you hear something? The operating room.

GINNY
No, it's the monkeys. There's a whole family of them that live in the tree.

POP
They're not rock ape are they?

GINNY
What's rock ape?

POP
Big, brown, and ugly.

GINNY
Rock ape!

(They laugh. She suddenly gets off of him and walks to a far corner of the room. She still has the joint.)

GINNY

Tonight you're going to do like Jesus did. You're going to get up and walk on water. Defy all the odds. And I'm going to do like a circus tamer. Like someone who trains dogs or exotic animals. If you're a good tiger and you do your trick and you don't bite, you get a reward. If you do your dolphin tricks, I give you a fish.

POP

Seafood is my favorite.

GINNY

Walk to me. See if you can make it.

POP

Not even a hand out of bed?

GINNY

If you want a taste of this ripe avocado, you got to pick it off the tree all by yourself.

(POP struggles to get up. This is a difficult, painful process. He slowly makes his way across the room.)

POP

Shrapnel.

POP
In the ligaments.
In the soft-hard knee cap.
In the spaces between stitches.
Shrapnel from a mortar bomb.
Splinters that fragment within you.
Wobbling within your guts.
Creating ripples in your bloodstream.

ELLIOT
Stay

Back
Lay

Home

(POP arrives at GINNY. He falls into her. They kiss.)

Signal
Elliot Ortiz

(GINNY and POP stop kissing.)

306

POP
Do you heal all your patients this way?

                                                    Elliot Ortiz.

GINNY
Let's go outside and watch the monkeys.

POP
No, really. You do this a lot?

                                                    Elliot Ortiz.

GINNY
Think you can make it outside?

POP
Give me a hand this time.

                                                    Ortiz.

GINNY
There's a gorgeous view of the moon.

(They exit, slowly, carefully, in each other's arms. They pass in front of ELLIOT, who is shivering.)

                        ELLIOT
Mom?
Pop?

11. PRELUDE

(The empty space. ELLIOT wears big radio station headphones.)

                    RADIO VOICE
You're listening to WHYY, member supported radio, welcome back. I'm having a conversation with Elliot Ortiz, a North Philadelphia native who graduated from Edison High in 2003. So, Elliot, you're seventeen years old, just finishing boot camp, and the President declares war. What was going through your mind?

                        ELLIOT
I was like, okay then, let's do this.

                    RADIO VOICE
You were ready. Is it exciting to be a marine?

ELLIOT

People say, oh, it's like a video game. Oh, it's like the movies. Naw. Base is the most depressing place ever. You wake up, go outside, you see rocky sand mountains. That's it. Rocks. Sand. You gotta drive 30 minutes to find a Wal-Mart. I just mainly stay on base, rent a lot of movies.

RADIO VOICE

But not base, let's talk about Iraq. Did you see a lot of action?

ELLIOT

Yeah.

RADIO VOICE

Were there times you were scared?

ELLIOT

The first time I heard a mortar shell. That scared the crap out of me. Literally.

RADIO VOICE

And you were injured. Tell me about that.

ELLIOT

It's a long story.

RADIO VOICE

What sticks out in your mind? About the experience?

ELLIOT

I got two corrective surgeries. They'll send me back if I want.

RADIO VOICE

To Iraq? Will you go?

ELLIOT

I mean, my leg is still messed up but. I'm not trying to stay here and work at Subway Hoagies. "Pardon me, sir, you want some hot peppers with that roast beef?"

RADIO VOICE

What do the troops think about politics? Do they support the war?

ELLIOT

Politics? Nobody cares about that. People drink their sorrows away. You hear people running down the hallway like, "F this!" "F that!" "Kill raghead!"

RADIO VOICE
(slightly changed tone)

Editor flag last remark.

(back to interview)

Both your father and grandfather served in the military.

ELLIOT

My pop was in Vietnam, marine corps. Three purple hearts.

RADIO VOICE

It must be something else to trade war stories with your father.

ELLIOT

He doesn't bring up that stuff too much.

RADIO VOICE

Some say there's a code of silence after returning home.

ELLIOT

My mom's got a box of his old letters, his uniform, dog tags. Our basement flooded and everything is in piles down there. But I was like, mom you gotta find that stuff.

RADIO VOICE

What about your grandfather?

ELLIOT

He was in Korea. He was a flute player. He'll be like, "I played Mozart in the north when everyone had frostbite." He's got two or three stories that he just tells them over and over. He's got old-timers.

RADIO VOICE

Alzheimer's?

ELLIOT

Right.

RADIO VOICE

You must have felt a great deal of pressure to enlist.

ELLIOT

Naw, I didn't even tell them. I just went one day and signed the papers.

RADIO VOICE

Just like that.

ELLIOT

Dad was actually kind of pissed, like, "The marines is no joke. The marines is going to mess with you."

RADIO VOICE

So why go then?
        (No answer.)
Why did you enlist?

ELLIOT

I was like, dad was a marine. I want to be a marine. I really did it for him.

12. PRELUDE

(The garden. GINNY holds a large yellow envelope stuffed full of papers. She pulls out one sheet at a time.

(GRANDPOP appears separately, reading a letter. POP appears separately. He is incredibly happy, slightly drunk.)

POP

April 4, 67

To my pop back in the Bronx aka "Little P.R.",
The evac hospital was like Disney Land. Real beds.

GRANDPOP

Clean sheets.

POP

Fresh pajamas. The women there? I met this one nurse, Ginny. Nurse Ginny. So let me ask you.

GINNY

"Nurse Ginny."

310

POP

How old were you when you fell for mom?

GRANDPOP

Did you know right away she was your woman?

POP

I'm serious old man, I want answers. Got back to the platoon this morning.
The guys were still alive, which is a good feeling. We had a big celebration.

GINNY

"Helmet stew."

POP

Hess' mom sent a package with wood alcohol. Stuff she made in the bathtub.
Awful stuff.

GRANDPOP

We got drunk.

POP

Joe Bobb pulled out his guitar. I pulled out your flute. I made a big official
speech, told them the whole story. You're a decorated veteran,

GINNY

"Bird watching."

POP

you served in Korea, back when they kept the Puerto Ricans separate.
How you played the same exact flute to your platoon. Then when I enlisted
you handed me the flute and said,

GRANDPOP

"You're a man. Teach yourself how to play."

POP

Joe Bobb showed me a hillbilly song. I showed him a *danzón*. The keys are
sticking, it's the swamp. Low D won't budge, two of the pads fell off. Here's
my little plan I'm putting together.

GRANDPOP

Get home safe.

POP

Marry nurse Ginny.

GINNY

"C-rations."

POP

Have a son, give him the flute. One flute, three generations. Aw man, right now Joe Bobb is throwing up all over. The smell is bad. It's the wood alcohol.

GRANDPOP

Tell mom my leg is okay.

GINNY

"Date unknown."

POP

And sorry I didn't write for so long.

13. PRELUDE

(The garden, at night. ELLIOT stands in the garden. Pop's letters are on the ground.)

ELLIOT

My little green Bible. Every soldier has something you take with you, no matter where you go, you take that thing. Waikiki had a tattoo of his mom. Mario had a gold cross his grandma had gave him. He wore it around his neck even though it was against the rules. I kept the Bible right inside my vest pocket. I had a picture of Stephanie in it, like a family portrait with all her cousins. My senior prom picture with all the guys. A picture of mom and pop. I looked at those pictures every day. Stared at those pictures. Daze off for like two hours at a time. *(Pause.)* The first guy I shot down, I kept his passport there.

One night, I don't know why, I was just going to kill my corporal. He was asleep. I put my rifle to the corporal's head and I was going to kill him. All I kept thinking was the bad stuff he made us do. He was the kind of guy who gets off on bringing down morale. Like making us run with trench foot. Trench foot is when your feet start rotting. Because of chemical and biological weapons, we didn't take our boots off for 36 days straight. When I finally took

(MORE)

ELLIOT (cont.)

my boots off, I had to peel my socks from the skin. They were black, and the second they came off, they became instantly hard. Corporal made us run with trench foot. Run to get the water. Run to get the ammo. Everyone was asleep and I was ready to pull the trigger. Waikiki woke up and saw what I was doing.

He kicked my arm like, "Eh, man, let's switch." So I looked at my pictures and slept, he went on watch. The next day me and Waikiki were running to get the water and he was like, "Eh, man, what were you doing last night?" I was like, "I don't know." He was like, "It's alright. We'll be out of here soon."

After I got injured, when my chopper landed in Spain. They pulled me out of there. They cut. My clothes were so disgusting they had to cut them off my body. My underwear was so black. The nurse had to cut it up the sides and take it off me like a pamper. The second she did that, it turned hard like a cast of plaster. You could see the shape of everything. Everything. It looked like an invisible man was wearing them. She threw it like a basketball in the trash. When the guys had finally found me, they had stuffed my leg full of cotton rags. The nurse counted one two three then ripped all the cotton out. I thought I was gonna die. I broke the metal railing right off the stretcher.

They didn't have underwear to put on me so they put a hospital gown instead. The kind that opens in the back and you can see the butt. I was still on the runway. The chopper took off, my gown flew up over my face, but my hands were tied down so I couldn't do nothing. I was butt naked in the middle of everybody. Next thing I know, someone pulled the gown away from my face and I saw this fine female looking down at me. When I saw her, it was like angels singing.
(He imitates angels singing.)
Like, aaaaaaah. So what's the first thing that's gonna happen to a guy? She saw it. I was so embarrassed.

The sponge baths I got while I was over there? They give you a sponge bath every other day. The first time. Once again, it was another fine female. It was four months since I seen one. Most female officers, out in the field, they don't look like this one did. So something happened, you know what happened. She was sponging me down and saw it and was like, "You want me to leave the room?" After three days she got used to it. She would be chatting, changing the subject. When you catch a woody with an officer, who you have to see everyday in Spain? The day I left she was like, "Yo, take care of your friend."

When I first landed in Philly Chucky and Buckweat met me at the airport. They
(MORE)

ELLIOT (cont.)

came running up to the gate like, "Did you kill em? Did you kill em? Did you have a gun? Did you have a really big gun?" I was like, nah, don't you worry about none of that. Don't think about those things. I was trying to forget, but that's how they see me now. That's what I am. That's how Stephanie sees me.

And the guys.

On the airplane flying home. All I could think was, I have to talk to pop. Hear his stories. He used to tell stuff from the war but looking back, it was mostly jokes. Like he swallowed a thing of chewing tobacco and puked for three days. He took a leak off a tank and a pretty Vietnamese lady saw him. He never sat me down and told me what it was like, for real. The first night I got here, I was like, pop, I need to hear it from your mouth. That was Monday. He was like, we'll talk about it Tuesday. Wednesday rolled around, I'm like, pop I'm only home a week. Did you have nightmares, too? Every single night? Did you feel guilty, too? When you shot a guy? Things he never opened up about. Finally I got him real drunk, I'm like, now's the time. I was like, did you shoot anyone up close? Did you shoot a civilian? Anything. He threw the table at me. Threw his beer bottle on the steps. Marched up the stairs, slammed the door.

Seeing mom, it takes so much stress off. She laid me down, and worked on my leg in an old fashioned way. Went to the herb store, got all her magic potions. The gauze bandage, it hardly came off. I could peel it back like a inch. The rest was infected, stuck to the gauze. At night, it itched so bad I had to scream. Mom laid me down in her garden, she told me to relax. Breathe in. Breathe out. Breathe like a circle. She told me to close my eyes and imagine the time I was happiest in my entire life. Then I felt her fingers on my leg. That felt so good. Hands that love you touching your worst place. I started to cry like a baby. I don't know why. It's just, I forgot how that feels. Like home. The tears were just coming. She put aloe and all sorts of stuff in there. I could tell she was crying too. She knows I been through a lot. She understands.

(GINNY enters. She begins to braid vines around ELLIOT's body, from the garden. She wraps his body in intricate, meticulous ways. She adds leaves and other flora. This is a slow process. It lasts until the end of the scene.)

ELLIOT

It's a hard question. Of every second in your life, nail down the best one. I started playing memories, like a movie in my mind. The prom. Me all slicked out with the guys, in our silver suits. Matching silver shoes. Hooking up with

(MORE)

ELLIOT (cont.)
Stephanie. All the different places me and Steph got freaky. In her mom's
house. On top of the roof for New Year's. This one time I took Sean fishing
down the Allegheny. He farted real loud. He ripped a nasty one. All the white
dudes, in their fisherman hats, they were like, "Crazy Puerto Ricans. You scared
the fish away."

The first time I ever went to Puerto Rico. With mom and pop. We drove
around the island with the windows rolled down. I was like, damn, so this is
where I come from. This is my roots. This one time we stopped at Luquillo
beach. The water was light light blue, and flat like a table, no waves. Mom was
like, "Pull over, George, and teach me to swim." We swam in there like for five
hours. Pop was holding mom on the surface of the water. He would hold on,
like, "You ready? You ready?" She was like, "Ay! Hold on, papi! I'm gonna
sink!" And he would let go and she would stay, floating, on the top. She was
so happy. It looked like they were in love. Then you could see the moon in the
water. It was still day but she floated on the moon. I could live in that day
forever. See them like that every day.

After mom fixed my leg, she was like, "I got a gift for you. Something
important." She gave me a fat yellow envelope. Crusty and old. She was like,
"Burn this or read it. It's up to you." I sat out in the garden, started pulling
letters out of the envelope. It was all of pop's letters from Vietnam.

(POP enters the garden.)

POP
Date unknown

ELLIOT
I read every one. All night, I didn't hardly move.

POP
Dad,
I just want to say I'm sorry.

ELLIOT
I was like, pop, I fucking walked in your shoes.

POP
I threw your flute away.

ELLIOT
Pop, we lived the same fucking life.

315

POP

All these thoughts were going through my head like thinking about the Bronx, you, mom.

ELLIOT

It's scary how much was the same. Killing a guy. Getting your leg scratched up. Falling in love.

POP

They got Hess and Joe Bobb.

ELLIOT

Nightmares. Meds. Infections. Letters to your father.

POP

One instant. Their bodies were covered with dust. Tree bark. Their eyes.

ELLIOT

Even ripping them up, taping them back together. It was like the feeling from Puerto Rico, but not a peaceful feeling.

POP

It was like shoot someone, destroy something. I threw your flute in the river.

ELLIOT

You see all the shit you can't erase. Like, here's who you are, Elliot, and you never even knew.

POP

You can't sit around and feel sorry for yourself or you're gonna die. I had to do something, so that's what I did.

(POP's letter is done.)

ELLIOT

Pop's up on the second floor, got the AC on, watching TV. Probably smoking weed. Probably doesn't even know I seen his letters. I know he won't even come to the airport tomorrow. He'll just be like:

(POP speaks directly to ELLIOT.)

POP

Well, you chose it so good luck with it. Don't do anything stupid.

(ELLIOT is tangled in vines. Lights fade.)

14. FUGUE

(The empty space. Three duffel bags are on the floor.)

GINNY

A runway.
The Philadelphia airport tarmac.
July 2003 is dry and windy.
Two seagulls fly even though the ocean is miles away.
Luggage carts roll in one direction,
Taxiing planes in another.
The windows are sealed to airtight, noisetight.
People crowd around the departure monitors.

ELLIOT

A man enters.
(ELLIOT enters.)
Cologne is sprayed on his neck.
A clean shave.
(ELLIOT looks at his watch.)
0700 hours.
Thinking in military time again.
He fixes his short hair.
(ELLIOT fixes his short hair.)
Grabs his life.
(ELLIOT picks up a duffel bag.)
Inside his bag are two fatigues his mother ironed this morning.
Fresh *sorullito* from grandmom.
Still warm, wrapped in two paper towels.
Grease-sealed in a plastic bag.
A naked photo from Stephanie.
In the photo she is smiling and holding in her stomach.
Her skin is brown.
The hair on her body is brown.
She is blinking, her eyes half closed.

GINNY

San Juan Bay.
A boarding ramp.
A transport ship to South Korea

(MORE)

Via Japan via Panama Canal.
September 1950 is mild.
The water is light light blue.
And flat like a table, no waves.

GRANDPOP

A boy enters.

(GRANDPOP enters. He stands beside ELLIOT and picks up another duffel bag. GRANDPOP waves goodbye to his family, offstage.)

Slacks pressed.
Hair combed.
Family standing at the rails.
His wife wears a cotton dress.
Sweat gathers in her brown curls.
On her hip, Little George.
His five year old son.

A boarding ramp.
Corrugated steel.
His first ride on the ocean.

(GRANDPOP picks up his duffel and freezes.)

GINNY

A runway.
The Newark Airport tarmac.
August 1965 is unseasonably cool.

(POP enters. He stands beside ELLIOT and picks up a duffel bag.)

POP

A boy enters.

(He looks at his watch.)

9:15 a.m.
He will never get used to military time.
He grabs his life.
At the bottom of his duffel, good luck charms.
A red handball glove.

(MORE)

                         POP (cont.)
A bottle of vodka from the Social Sevens.
Two pencils and paper.
A long corridor.
A gray carpeted ramp.
A plane to Parris Island
To a ship to Vietnam.

(POP picks up his duffel and freezes.)

                         ELLIOT
The bag
The duffel
The photo
Stephanie
Teeth
Jazz
Calvin Klein
Fubu
Flute
Helmet
36 springs
Ink
Heliconia
Handwriting

(ELLIOT grabs his duffel, steps forward.)

He walks down the gray carpeted ramp.
Boards the plane to Camp Pendleton.
Where he will board his second ship to Kuwait.
Where he will cross the border north into Iraq.
Again.
Happy he has an aisle seat.
Going back to war.

END OF PLAY

Armando Riesco (left), Triney Sandoval, Zabryna Guevara, Mateo Gomez in the P73 production at the Culture Project

Triney Sandoval (top), Zabryna Guevara, Armando Riesco in the P73 production at the Culture Project

From left: James Martinez, Teddy Cañez, Mateo Gomez in the P73 production at El Museo del Barrio

From left: Teddy Cañez, Sheila Tapia, James Martinez (foreground), Mateo Gomez in the P73 production at El Museo del Barrio

Profiles

2007 marks my 5ᵗʰ year as a full-time NYC resident, and – during various extended subway rides – I began to reflect upon those whose work has particularly inspired and energized me during my first half-decade here. Then I began to wonder, what inspires those who inspire? Then I came up with ten questions. (See "Contributors" section following for the skinny on who's who here if you don't know 'em).

– B. Stowe

Where are you originally from?

Alec Duffy (AD): Winchester, Massachusetts, outside of Boston. And later, Minnesota.

Cynthia Croot (CC): I grew up in Maryland in a small community along the Severn River (take the Hog Farm Road exit).

Davis McCallum (DM): I'm from Atlanta, Georgia.

Kenneth Schlesinger (KS): I grew up on both coasts, so I like to consider myself a Californian trapped in a New Yorker's body.

Lear deBessonet (LB): I grew up in the Deep South – Baton Rouge, Louisiana.

Mike Daisey (MD): I'm from far northern Maine – Fort Kent, on the Canadian border, at the end of U.S. Route 1.

Pavol Liska (PL): I was born and raised in Slovakia.

Kelly Copper (KC): I'm a radio gypsy. My dad was a disc jockey and so we moved all over when I was a kid. I was born in Gainesville, Florida.

Polybe + Seats (P+S): We are from Castle Rock, Colorado (Stacey McMath); Ann Arbor, Michigan (Jessica Brater); Northampton, Massachusetts, (Miriam Felton-Dansky, Katya Schapiro); and Brooklyn (Catherine Wallach).

Susan Bernfield (SB): I grew up in Palo Alto, California.

Zhen Heinemann (ZH): Augsburg, West Germany.

How long have you lived in NYC? If you are not a native of the City, why did you originally come here? Do you have a "New York Moment" – something that happened to you that you feel defines what it means to survive/exist here, either as an artist or a human being?

SB: I've been here for 20 years, and it has never gotten old, and when I look up and see certain NYC landmarks, or walk by them, I still feel incredibly joyful and free and can't believe I'm lucky enough to actually live here. I used to watch *Family Affair.* I was obsessed with the idea that kids could live in an apartment. When I was 16 – this is so embarrassing – the movie *Fame* came out and I have to admit that that was the point of no return. That year my dad was on sabbatical, I spent the first part of my junior year of high school in Connecticut. I used to take the train in to the city all by myself, get to Grand Central, walk to Shubert Alley and just stand there. For hours. It doesn't get more freakish than that.

KC: I've lived in New York since 1993. I was working as a talking puppet telephone on a children's reading series. My boss was Slim Goodbody, this guy who wore a unitard with his internal organs painted on it. I was walking on 42nd Street to the West Side Highway in my bib overalls and this guy in a van pulled over and asked me to get in the car and suck his yoohoo. It's something that really seems now like it comes from another time, before Disney.

PL: I've lived in New York since 1995. One weekend I came down to New York from school and Kelly took me to see the Wooster Group's *Frank Dell's Temptation of Saint Anthony*, Reza Abdoh's *Quotations from a Ruined City*, and Richard Foreman's *My Head Was a Sledgehammer*. I couldn't make the same theater after that weekend.

CC: 10 years here. It's really quite personal, everywhere you look. Existing here as a human being or artist seems to be about foundation and connection. Focusing on your center, your base, is vital, but I think you really need to forge frequent, generous, intimate connections. Sometimes the connection is profound – like with a lover, but sometimes it's just commiserating with someone about the cold, or helping them get their stroller down the stairs in the subway. It invigorates me to transgress the silence and anonymity.

DM: I came to New York in 2000. When I was just starting here, my closest collaborator was Noah Haidle, who's since become a very fancy playwright. We decided that we wanted to create a play about the Dakota Building, and we got a bunch of actors together, and everyone worked for free, and we rehearsed in all sorts of dumpy spaces, and we got kicked out of a church once for being too noisy. We went to the Dakota Building and pretended to be interested in buying an apartment, and turned it all into a ramshackle play, which we did as part of a residency at HERE. I have good memories of that first year in NYC, even though it was a kind of an ad hoc, scrappy, guerrilla-theater type process. Amazing what a little nostalgia can do.

MD: I've been here since summer of 2001, and in fact the story of moving to NYC and what it has meant to me is some of the principal story threads in *Invincible Summer* – 9/11 happened just after the summer I moved here, and had a huge impact shaping and defining me as a person in the context of this community.

LB: I've been here almost 5 years, since summer 2002. For a year I had a job working as a waitress at an illegal poker club. I worked one 14-hour shift a week and could make my whole living in that one night. I wasn't making enough money serving Cokes, so I started offering shoulder massages for $1 per minute and made a bundle. When the club got busted, the *New York Times* curiously mentioned, "supposedly this poker club was also offering massage to patrons" – I appreciated the shout out.

ZH: I've been in NYC for almost three years. I'm constantly trying to think of things that won't be offensive to whisper to New York so that I can get a foothold and feel that I have some kind of space or place here.

P+S (Jessica): Catherine Wallach is our only native New Yorker. The rest of us came here for college. Besides constantly scanning street garbage for potential props, I'd say my most defining moment as a New York theater artist was when I got stuck in one of those tall, rotating subway exits with a school desk-chair I was transporting for our set on a sweltering day at the end of June because we couldn't afford a taxi. A bunch of high school boys were walking in and after making various noisy and profane exclamations, they helped jiggle me out.

KS: This will date me – but I always considered working in New York to be like the *Dick Van Dyke Show*: you put on a tie, then go to an office where you make jokes all day. For the most part, this has turned out to be true.

What kind of – if any – influence has NYC, be it the City itself, the energy, proximity to other artists, etc., had on your own work?

MD: New York is the best city in America to be an artist in – the collision of live arts and industry, the clashing cultures, the social dramas being played out in the neighborhoods and architecture – it's marvelous. It's like being in a zoo, and I love going to the zoo. Humans are a very interesting species of animal, in New York probably more so than elsewhere.

DM: I love living in NYC and have a hard time imagining leaving it. I love going to the theater, and seeing other people's work. When I'm rehearsing a play at night, and I can't go to the theater, I feel like I'm missing everything that everyone is doing. Of course – let's be honest – it's disappointing most of the time, but when something comes along that really grabs out, it reminds you why you thought a life in the theater would be a rich and rewarding way to spend your life. If the jackpot were more common, theater wouldn't be nearly as addictive.

KC: The City really deepened me as an artist. You're in an environment where you're constantly challenged and changed by what you see. People still — despite everything – come here from all over the world to show their work. It's an amazing place. On the flip side, I would also say that the city itself – the financial difficulty of it – has influenced our work. You're forced to deal with limitations. If you can only rehearse in your studio apartment, say – and you can't make any noise or you'll get evicted, (and that has happened more than once) – you're forced into these other areas. It can result in despair, or it can break the work open. Pavol and I have taken some very obscure paths in our quest just to keep working in the face of restriction.

LB: When I first arrived here, I had never been through a real winter before, and hadn't learned any deflective city-skills. I'd walk up to a homeless person and give them a hug, for example, which led to some really crazy encounters. To be honest, New York has caused me a lot of suffering, which I think was crucial for my development as an artist and as a human.

CC: The work I've done in South Africa, Syria, Alaska, all came from connections in this arts community. I love the energy here, but I also love to retreat from it, to go away to a place markedly different, drink the water, sleep in the sheets, come back to the city like a stranger. I also love how politically engaged you can be here if you choose. Because of my interest in conflict resolution and social justice, I'm particularly well-fed as an activist here.

P+S (Jessica): The proximity to other artists is a huge, huge reason to make art here. I don't think you'd have these kind of human resources anywhere else.

SB: I think I wouldn't be me in any way, shape or form if I wasn't here, so … does that answer the question? Even though I think we'd all have more impact if we lived and worked in a smaller community, there's still more of an attraction to doing it here … it's totally counter-intuitive in a lot of ways.

ZH: New York makes you really bust your ass to try to do what you want to do. I always feel like I'm slacking because New York constantly reminds me to work harder.

Did you have an early theater/performance memory that has continued to influence your work and/or was the catalyst for your turning to theater/performance initially; i.e., is there a "before xxx" and "after xxx" in your personal history?

P+S (Jessica): My dad is a theater professor, so my parents always took me to see plays as a kid. I particularly remember a production of *A Midsummer Night's Dream* at the Royal Shakespeare Company that I saw when I was about 5 years old. The set was these gigantic flowers that opened up and revealed the fairies inside – the dream of any 5-year-old girl.

CC: I have a hokey memory of being about 5 or 6 and seeing some guy on television – a little black and white television my parents had up on a shelf – seeing this old guy on a hillside very upset, and being so moved that I started to cry. My mom told me it was *King Lear*, and the man was Laurence Olivier. Funny, right? I haven't seen that performance as an adult, but have been told that it's a bit hammy. At 5, I was mesmerized.

LB: I started making my plays in my backyard (and forcing the neighborhood kids to be in them) when I was really little, about 5 – so to some extent it's what I've always wanted to do.

AD: *Man of La Mancha* was one of the first I remember seeing. I pissed my second grade teacher off the following day by singing "I am I, Don Quixote!" all through the class.

ZH: I'm not sure what lead me to theater. I was blessed enough to be exposed to many of the arts as a child, but it may have had to do with *Cats*. Specifically the costumes and those super large pieces of garbage in the set.

KS: As an adolescent, I saw Alan Bennett's *Habeas Corpus* in London, which blew me away with its theatrical magic and zest for language.

SB: A musical of course, *Sunday in the Park with George*, by Stephen Sondheim and James Lapine. I listened to this thing constantly, and I was driving my roommates crazy, so finally I dragged them all into New York to see a Saturday matinee. And I think that it was kind of a primer for me on what theater can do. George is sketching in the park; he draws a tree, it appears onstage. He erases it, it disappears. It's a pretty simple theatrical conceit, but it's just perfect in how it expresses what he's doing, and it's purely theatrical

DM: When I was at Princeton, Stephen Wadsworth came to the McCarter to do *Changes of Heart*, an 18th Century comedy by Marivaux, and I was the rehearsal intern. I was completely spellbound, and walked home to my dorm in a complete daze each day, and came to all the performances and sat next to Stephen and his assistant, and by the end of the run I knew that I wanted to be a director.

PL: I spoke earlier about "the weekend" that changed how I made theater. But after several years of trying to make theater imitating those people I quit making theater altogether. What got me back after several years, and revitalized my interest in performance, was seeing my 8-year-old niece and her schoolmates do a show in front of their parents. It showed me why people make theater at all, in the most primitive, basic way, why we dress up, put on make up, play at being someone else, dance, etc., which we tend to forget in our modern preoccupation with originality and the next best, and most attention-grabbing gimmick. Now I always try to return to the most elementary impulse behind making theater.

KC: There was something so effortful and beautiful about those kids on stage that really re-focused both of us back to a more elementary theater aesthetic. And a more primitive joyfulness. What is it that makes people perform in front of other people? I think that exerts a real fascination.

What other theater artists, if any, do you admire and/or are inspired by?

AD: I love Meredith Monk. I like so much that she was as brave as she was, and ambitious, and uncompromising in creating her own sound/movement world that is like no other.

CC: Certainly Pina Bausch, Marcel Dzama (his images are like stage plays), Chuck Mee, Tadeauz Kantor, Samuel Beckett, Anton Chekhov, Kathy Acker, Wallace Shawn, Suzan-Lori Parks, I think Ivo von Hove does wonderfully compelling work, I've been staggered by some of the moments I've seen created by Philippe Genty, Arienne Mnouchkine, Robert Woodruff, the Wooster Group, Theatre de Complicite ... but I'm most inspired by the actors with whom I work. They are so damn brave.

DM: Chuck Mee, Sarah Ruhl, Michael Freidman, Moises Kaufman, Christine Jones, Tracey Bersley, Ellen Beckerman, Pam McKinnon, Hannah Cabell, Aysan Celik, Quiara Hudes, Maria Dizzia, Tom Nelis, Henry Stram, Jeremy Shamos, Zelda Fichandler, Mary Zimmerman, Noah Haidle.

KS: Laurie Anderson, Robert LePage, Ingmar Bergman.

MD: Aaron Landsman, Sheila Callaghan, Anne Washburn, and Heidi Schreck, whose work inspires and fills me with hope.

PL: Richard Foreman, Christoph Marthaler, Kassys, Elizabeth LeCompte, Reza Abdoh, Kelly Copper, John Collins, David Herskovits, Amber Reed, Richard Maxwell, Sarah Michelson, Ryan Gilliam, Anne Bogart, Young Jean Lee, Chuck Mee, Kantor, Grotowski, Stanislavski, Julie Atlas Muz, Brian Kulick, William Forsythe, Merce Cunningham, Eric Dyer, Jim Findley, Tim Etchells, STAN, Anne, Zack, Bobby, Fletcher, and many, many more.

KC: I would second all of Pavol's picks. What are in short supply are mentors. I've been lucky enough to have had two major ones in my life: Leonardo Shapiro, who ran the Trinity/La MaMa Program that brought me to New York. He was an amazing teacher. And Mac Wellman—who has now really taught and fostered an entire generation of young, inventive theater writers. Richard Foreman has also been a big mentor for people; I know many directors, including Pavol, who watched his rehearsals, worked in his theater. Also, Ryan Gilliam, who runs Downtown Art, has inspired us, and opened her space to us and let us make *No Dice* there this past year. The mature artist who really generously opens his mind and practice and shares his resources with a younger generation – those people are essential. And few.

P+S: Polybe + Seats is greatly indebted to Mabou Mines. Jessica is also a big fan of Target Margin.

ZH: A wholehearted believer that life and all art can be read as performance – Marina Abramovich, Julie Atlas Muz, Cindy Sherman, Renee Magritte, Frida Kahlo.

What do you have coming up – or have recently completed – performance-wise, either in NYC, or elsewhere?

LB: I'm directing my version of Brecht's *Saint Joan of the Stockyards* at PS122 in June featuring an original bluegrass/rock score by Kelley McRae that I'm really jazzed about. I'm also directing *Hair* at UVA in April and developing some new pieces with my collaborator, Deborah Stein. I'm working hard now to get Tickets for the People off the ground, a program I started with the Culture Project in 2006.

MD: In January, I performed *Invincible Summer* at the Public as part of "Under the Radar" festival, curated by Mark Russell. In April I'm at American Repertory Theatre in Boston with a new monologue, and in June at Berkeley Rep with *Great Men of Genius*, my series about Brecht, Barnum, Tesla and L. Ron Hubbard.

CC: I'm creating an event up at SIPA (the School of International and Public Affairs at Columbia University) in partnership with the student-run Forum on Political Violence. We're calling it "Insurgency/Counterinsurgency" and we're commissioning new work from five playwrights, with performances in April. This Summer, I'm directing *Julius Caesar* at the Colorado Shakespeare Festival, and this Fall I'll be directing one of the Suzan-Lori 365s at the Brick Theater in Brooklyn.

KS: In February, the Theatre Library Association presented its second Symposium, "Performance Reclamation: Research, Discovery and Interpretation" at NYU. It discussed the library's creative role in reconstructing "lost plays," obscure musicals, or dance works. TLA partnered with the Mint Theater, Encores! and Jacob's Pillow in our most ambitious undertaking to date.

DM: *Jane Eyre* (Bronte/Teale) for The Acting Company, *The Clean House* (Sarah Ruhl) for Cleveland Playhouse, *West Moon Street* (Wilde/Urbinati) for Prospect Theater Company, *The Turn of the Screw* (James/Hatcher) for Westport Country Playhouse, *Melancholy Play* (Ruhl) for 13P.

AD: I'm directing a week of Suzan-Lori Parks plays in June, as part of the 365 Days/365 Plays festival. We're going to perform them in community gardens in each of the five boroughs, with lots of music, composed by percussionist Michael Wimberly. I'm also directing a new piece of mine called *Dysphoria* for the Ontological Theater's Summer Residency, in August.

PL: In late January, we showed our newest piece, *No Dice*, at Downtown Art as part of "Under the Radar" Festival.

KC: Hopefully, we'll find some opportunity to take *No Dice* or *Poetics* on the road this summer as well.

P+S: We kicked off the new year with a week of 365 Days/365 Plays at various locations in Williamsburg. In February we did a reading of a new play by Katya Schapiro called *Better Angels*, and in April we are taking *The Charlotte Salomon Project* to the University of Michigan as part of the inaugural events for their new Walgreen Theater Center.

ZH: I was honored to work on Julie [Atlas Muz]'s show at PS 122 in February. Also in February, I performed at the CUNY Segal Theatre as part of the NoPassport conference there, and I'm working on a large-scale interactive show that will come up in the Spring or Fall of this year at chashama's 44th Street location.

SB: New Georges is producing a gorgeous play called *God's Ear*, by Jenny Schwartz, which Anne Kauffman is directing at the East 13th Street Theatre. And we're part of the whole 365 Days/365 Plays thing; our week was March 19. And I'm continuing to work on several of my own pieces, my solo musical (singing again!) *Tiny Feats of Cowardice* is going to be read up at the Adirondack Theatre Festival this summer, and hopefully there'll be some movement on some of my other pieces.

What do you like about the current state of theater in NYC, particularly alternative or "off-Off-Broadway" theater and performance? What do you not like about it? What would you most like to change about theater here and how would you go about doing it?

CC: I'm not sure there is a whole lot to like about the current state of theater, *per se*. Sure, I like that we are all scrapping and clawing and making stuff, but it is just plain hard to make work here.

DM: I like the sense of interconnectedness, and feeling like after six years of being in town, I know the landscape and the personalities of downtown theater. I like that the price is low, and that audiences expect something thrilling and unusual to happen. I like that the theater blogs here have successfully democratized the conversation about downtown work.

P+S (Miriam): I like that there is a community that supports indie theater and that all these new festivals have grown up to support it, and that people are coming to Brooklyn more to make theater and to see it.

AD: I like a lot of the companies doing work here. There's some thrilling stuff happening: Radiohole, Collapsable Giraffe, Banana, Bag & Bodice, among others.

MD: I love that we have a downtown scene, and that there's enough of an ecosystem that work can grow and develop in that hothouse.

KC: A lot of work that just feels necessary and clear and pure is out there now. I've been more excited by stuff I've seen in the last two years than I have been since I moved here 13 years ago. It feels like vital times.

SB: I think there's so much energy, so many artists, it's really one of the most fertile times in my memory. Which makes me feel really optimistic. I'm continually amazed that there are so many people who just … wanna do it, keep on doing it, despite the escalating price of everything, especially real estate, and just how hard it continues to be.

KS: I'm always overwhelmed by the sheer vitality and breadth of originality in New York's theater scene. However, I value language as much as visuals – so I can be disappointed at lack of attention to text.

MD: I do wish that the alternative theater was not so opposed to the tools of narrative – subtracting narrative from plays doesn't automatically yield art, and I think sometimes that's a math that gets employed. In the opposite direction, I think the industry of theater is a dangerous game of zero-sum musical chairs, and the pursuit of "success" kills more interesting endeavors than I can even find breath to enumerate.

P+B (Miriam): I don't like that the real estate is impossible, though there's not much to be done about that since the government has decided not to support the arts.

LB: I would like the NEA to step up and invest seriously in the arts, but in lieu of that, I would like Tickets for the People to expand to include any willing theaters in the city.

AD: At the risk of sounding whiny, I wish there were more resources to support this work (and, by extension, my work). I also wish audiences for this work weren't just other theater makers, which is a result of a combination of non-outreach on the part of us theater-makers, but also of non-interest in experimentation on the part of the populace.

KC: If I say I wish there was more funding out there I'll sound like a douche, but I wish there was. And I wish that it funded what people are actually making rather than being grants specifically geared toward some administrator's pet concerns – like the show must have a "post-9/11" theme or must involve international collaborators or use found space ... why not just fund that artist's work?! Period.

LB: I think the economics of making off-off work are totally unacceptable. The financial constraints limit the work in so many ways. Making extended collaboration – a rehearsal process longer than 4 weeks – really difficult, dictating who has the luxury of entering the profession in the first place, making it nearly impossible to pursue a diverse audience.

DM: I wish downtown shows paid a living wage, and that the runs were longer than the standard showcase 16 performances, so that a successful show could really gain momentum, and start to pull a wider audience. I hate losing actors to TV and commercials and film. I don't like feeling that downtown theater is the bottom of the food chain, and anyone might come along at any point in your rehearsal process and poach your actors away from you.

PL: There is very little money and acclaim to go around. This doesn't bother me at all anymore. I have learned to ignore it, for the most part, and just focus on the work, and what gives me pleasure about the work.

CC: I'd love to see some real estate guru buy up a whole complex of apartments with a huge performance space in the basement, and give it over to a cabal of artists just to see what happens. Or walk down Lorimer one night to find thirty people squatting in little luminous pup-tents at McCarren pool, forming an artist collective and taking over the building. Or create a group to re-purpose office buildings after hours and stage a cycle of midnight performances in Citibank branches.

SB: I always feel – or I hope – that we can make change happen just by doing the work, making the kind of theater we want to see and have some sort of vision for, and trying to get audiences in to see it. It's kind of radical that we're bothering to do this, at least it helps get me through the day to think that it is! After all these years I'm finally starting to see what our place is, what our role is – or could be – in that, and it's encouraging me to be more articulate about our aesthetic and, I hope, make stronger choices.

CC: More collective spaces. More collaboration. More invention. Subsidies. Government support. People taking more time to create. Not just three weeks of rehearsal – but three years of rehearsal and then work in permanent rep. Time to steep. Deeper relationships. More risk. Less TV.

Was there a single-most remarkable – memorable – influential – inspirational theater-performance piece you saw in NYC in 2006? If so, what was it, and why?

DM: *Spring Awakening* at the Atlantic – superb directing, mind-blowing music, out-of-this-world design from Christine Jones, Kevin Adams, and Susan

336

Hilferty. *Trouble in Paradise* at Hudson Guild Theater – great balance between Wooster Group irony and something else, more human. Incredible acting from Shamos, Hellman, etc. *No Child* at Barrow Street – entrancing, transporting, moving. No stuff. Just actor and audience.

MD: I saw Heidi Schreck's *Creature* read at Soho Rep's Writer/Director Lab, which is a wonderful organization, and I think that piece haunted me more than any other this year

ZH: Taylor Mac's *Red Tide Blooming* at PS122 made me excited, as does *Bad Ass Burlesque* at the Bowery and all of Marina's restagings at the Gugge. Oh! And Ron Athey's *Dissociative Sparkle* – xoxox to Ron for that experience!

P+S: (Katya and Miriam): We loved *Not Clown* at Soho Rep.! **(Miriam):** I thought *Not Clown* was that incredibly rare piece of theater that critiques the current political climate in a complex, non-didactical, entertaining way, and that it was beautifully staged and imaginatively written. **(Catherine):** the most remarkable performance I saw this year was by the cast of *Sweeney Todd* – they were everything an ensemble should be – they supported and highlighted each other. **(Jessica):** I thought that Target Margin's *Faust* – especially the first part – was fantastic. The translation was very lively and it was great to have the opportunity to see all of the whole big thing! David Greenspan was marvelous as *Mephisto*, especially in his final speech, and David Herskovits' directing, per usual, made me feel like I was watching a play on the moon or something like that.

AD: Young Jean Lee's *Songs of the Dragons Flying to Heaven* at HERE was a highlight. She inspires me to be more raw and revealing in my own writing. The play has such a brutal honesty in the way it treats the internal contradictions we are all subject to.

CC: I guess it was that little cabaret piece down at the South Street Seaport, *Absinthe*. Not because it was brilliant theater, but because it dealt very tangibly with the body on stage, instead of apologizing for it. And it made me want to make a really difficult, political, aggressive piece in the style of cabaret.

KS: I think these are from 2005, but they must be mentioned: Ivo van Hove's *Hedda Gabler* at New York Theatre Workshop, which imbued the play with an irresistible physicality, stunning images, and a cast actually corresponding to the ages of the characters (late 20s). Matthew Bourne's *Play Without Words* at BAM interpreted Losey's film, *The Servant*, with ingenious sets and movement so compelling you wanted to be up there with the cast.

PL: ERS's *Gatz*. It was an event, an actual experience, not just a show. It wasn't needy like most theater; it didn't slobber all over the audience with a desperate need to be loved and appreciated.

KC: I would have picked *Gatz*, too, but I think we saw it in 2005. We saw Kassys's *Komer* (from The Netherlands) which showed last January at "Under the Radar." That was amazing, too. That is the one show I think about most often from 2006. It was so simple. The language was as banal as any soap opera, but ... I had to go back to see it three times.

SB: I just felt so privileged to see Meryl Streep in *Mother Courage* in the Park. It was such a stunning example of performance, and not just of a great artist, blah blah blah, but more than that – of what a human being can do. Like this was the ideal of human activity, the pleasure she took in just being out there and chewing it up; forget that it's Meryl Streep and all that conjures up, what I felt I was watching was a human being who was doing what she was absolutely born to do.

Worst. Theater experience. Ever. What comes to mind? (Not necessarily in NYC.)

SB: The list. Is so. Long.

KS: I will always declare something the second-worst thing I've ever seen, conjuring up images of the ultimate House of Torment. I am respectful of actors' work, so try not to disturb them onstage – but admit that I've let the door slam.

CC: A production of *Pippin*. I believe I was caught leaving on video tape by the camera person documenting. Oh, it was painful.

LB: When I was 19, I stage-managed an original musical in Switzerland that was extraordinarily toxic. Sort of "Waiting for Guffman: Europe."

PL: Richard Caliban's *Teatro Slovak*. I didn't think anything could offend me, but this show managed to offend every single fiber of my being. I'm in therapy to forget that experience. This is just a personal thing, and I apologize to everyone who worked very hard on that show, as well as to those who love the show.

KC: That was a surreally bad time. We went to see it because it was billed as this collaboration between an American director and Slovak actors, but it wasn't. It was New York actors acting out every conceivable Eastern European stereotype ... it was like watching some kind of minstrel show. They were all getting drunk and talking about beating their women.

P+S (Jessica): There are so many bad ones, but I hate to trash them in print because hats off to anybody who subjects themselves to a life in the arts. I did walk out of an oddly histrionic performance of a Moliere play that I saw in Italy – that was up there.

ZH: I think my worst theater experiences have all been forgotten.

DM: I have blocked them all out. I really have. I don't remember painful things. My world is kept a beautiful place.

What was your most influential or memorable read of 2006?

Black Swan Green by David Mitchell. Random House, 2006, ISBN: 0812974018. *"Best read of 2006, unquestionably"* – *Davis McCallum*

Essays on the Blurring of Art and Life. Allan Kaprow and Jeff Kelley, editors. University of California Press, 2003. ISBN: 0520240790. *"The best thing I have read all year"* – *Kelly Copper*

The Final Days. Carl Bernstein and Bob Woodward. Simon & Schuster, 2005. ISBN: 0641796994. *"Oh man, what a page turner!"* – *Susan Bernfield*

Lulu Meets God and Doubts Him by Danielle Ganek. Penguin Group, May 2007. ISBN: 0670038660. *"It's like* The Devil Wears Prada, *but set in the gallery world, and with a less obnoxious heroine"* – *Catherine Wallach, Polybe+Seats*

Mountains Beyond Mountains by Tracy Kidder. Random House, 2004. ISBN: 0812973011. *"The biography of Dr. Paul Farmer. I recommend everyone read it for a good kick in the ass" — Lear deBessonet*

No Man's Land by Duong Thu Huong. Hyperion, 2005. ISBN: 1401366643. *"Although Huong is permitted to live in Hanoi, her works are not available in Vietnam. In most countries, she would be celebrated as a national writer of the stature of Toni Morrison or John Steinbeck" — Kenneth Schlesinger*

On Killing by Lt. Col. Dave Grossman. Back Bay Books, 1996. ISBN: 0316330116. *"About what happens to the human body and psyche when under physical attack" — Cynthia Croot*

Paradise Lost by John Milton. Barnes & Noble Books, 2004 (among a gazillion other publishers, publication years, and editions). ISBN: 1593080956. *"It's a really sexy book!"* — *Katya Schapiro, Polybe+Seats*

Reefer Madness by Eric Schlosser. Houghton Mifflin Co., 2004. ISBN: 0618446702. *"From the author of* Fast Food Nation*"* – *Zhenesse Heinemann*

Shame, by Sam Cohen. Xlibris, 2000. ISBN: 0738822302. *"I couldn't recommend it highly enough"* – *Mike Daisey*

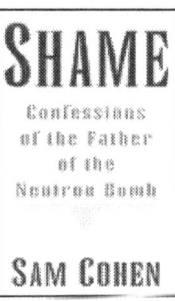

Party!

Tiffany Clementi as Sheila Callaghan in August Schulenburg's Brantley, Lightning, *directed by John Hurley.* New York Theater Review *fundraiser at the Brick Theater, Williamsburg, Brooklyn. October 2, 2006*

Party Night For *NYTR*

On Monday night, October 2, 2006, *NYTR* threw a party at the Brick Theater to help raise money for the 2007 edition and to, well, throw a party. Biondo played, Brian Boyles & Gary Keenan performed, Sheila Callaghan sang, and four playwrights contributed original Tiny Plays on a topic near if not dear to us all: critics.

Who Did What

The Stage Manager
Heather Cohn

The Actors
E. Calvin Ahn
Mark Bovino
Joe Carnutte
Chris Carpenter
Jody Christopherson
Tiffany Clementi
Stephanie Dodd
Jason Grote
Emily Hyberger
Paige Lussier
Feliciano Martinez
Joe Mathers
Dina Prioste
Mac Rogers
Abby Royale
Johanna Saum
August Schulenburg
Alexis Soloski
Jennifer Gordon Thomas
Ana Valle
Pieter Van Winkle
Cotton Wright

The Guy Who Knows Where Everything Is
Michael Gardner

The Photographer
Punam Bean
www.punambean.com

The Benefit Staff
Stephanie Dodd
Emily Hyberger
Dan McCoy
Laura Riley
Kimberly Stowell

The Host Committee
Emily DeVoti
Jason Grote
Rob Handel
Alyssa Simon
Caridad Svich

Special Thanks
Michael Gardner and the Brick Theater
www.bricktheater.com
Susan Bernfield and New Georges
www.newgeorges.org

Produced by
Brook Stowe & Jody Christopherson

August Schulenburg (left), Joe Mathers, Cotton Wright backstage at the Brick

Even the orchestra is beautiful: Billyburg's Biondo blows up a storm

MC Susan Bernfield of New Georges

Jennifer Gordon Thomas (left), Mac Rogers in Love Letter, *written and directed by George Hunka*

The ensemble cast of Sheila Callaghan's Masterpiece, *directed by Kelly O'Donnell*

Jason Grote, Alexis Soloski in Adam Szymkowicz's The Mind of the Critic, *directed by Kip Fagan*

Armitage Shanks & the Floozy
Sophocles Papavasilopoulos (top, left) as the Floozy; Sheila Callaghan as Armitage Shanks

Contributors

SUSAN BERNFIELD (Profiles) – is the founder and artistic director of New Georges, which has been producing and developing new plays downtown since 1992. In that capacity, she has produced 28 new plays – most recently, Sheila Callaghan's *Dead City* in May 2006 and Jenny Schwartz's *God's Ear* in May 2007 and 10 festivals of new and alternative work; received an Obie among other awards; and serves on the board of directors of A.R.T./New York. Susan is also a playwright and solo performer whose work has been developed and presented at theaters across the country. She lives in Manhattan.

SHEILA CALLAGHAN (Cover Design) – Sheila is a playwright who does design on the side to feed herself, including work for the playwrights' collective 13P, the Flea Theater, the Lark Play Development Center, the web version of *American Theatre* magazine and the debut edition of the *New York Theater Review*. Sheila is not very tall and has all her fingers and toes. At Christmas, she slides down chimneys and delivers ironic gifts to cynical people. She wishes she could skeet-shoot. Visit Sheila's work at www.savagecandy.com. She lives in Brooklyn.

KELLY COPPER (Profiles) – is the progeny of a disc jockey and a librarian. For the past 10 years she has been at work with Pavol Liska and Nature Theater of Oklahoma making things – sometimes even making sandwiches. She is also a suspicious affiliate of the bad-ass gang of playwrights known as Joyce Cho. She lives in Manhattan.

CYNTHIA CROOT (Profiles) – is a NYC-based theater director known for her innovative international collaborations (Suzan-Lori Parks' *Venus*, Windybrow, Johannesburg; Palestinian playwright Natalie Handal's *Details of Silence*, Symphony Space NYC; Brazilian poet Haroldo de Campo's *Act of the Possessed*, Guggenheim Museum); experimental work (*Buzz* from John Hersey's *War Lover*, P.S. 122); and classical and contemporary productions (Perseverance Theatre; Colorado Shakespeare Festival; New York's Town Hall). Cynthia earned her MFA from Columbia University and is one of the lead organizers of THAW (Theaters Against War). This summer she will return to the Colorado Shakespeare Festival to direct *Julius Caesar*. She lives in Brooklyn.

MIKE DAISEY (Profiles) – is a solo performer whose monologues include *21 Dog Years*, *Great Men of Genius*, *The Ugly American*, *Monopoly!*, *Invincible Summer*, *I Miss the Cold War*, *Wasting Your Breath*, and *Stories From the Atlantic Night Cafe* Currently he's a commentator for National Public Radio's *Day To Day*, a contributor to *Wired*, *Slate*, and *Salon*. Mike's writing also appears in the anthology *The Best Tech Writing 2006*. His first book, *21 Dog Years: A Cubedweller's Tale*, was published by the Free Press and he is working on a second book, *Great Men of Genius*. He lives in Brooklyn.

LEAR DE BESSONET (Profiles) – is Artistic Director of Stillpoint Productions and has assisted Martha Clarke, Anne Bogart, and Marianne Weems. Lear was recently featured in *Time Out New York*'s "25 People to Watch 2006." Upcoming: *transFigures* at the Women's Project in April 2007 and *Saint Joan of the Stockyards* at PS122 in June 2007. New York devising/directing credits include *Bone Portraits* (Walkerspace), *Death Might Be Your Santa Claus*, *The Eliots* (Center Stage), *transFigures* (Calvary Church), and *The Female Terrorist Project* (HERE). Lear is an alumnus of the Soho Rep Writer/Director Lab, a Drama League Directing Fellow, and a Jefferson Scholar. She lives in Brooklyn.

ALEC DUFFY (Profiles) – is a writer-director who has been creating original music-theater work in New York for the past seven years. His play, *The Top Ten People of the Millennium Sing Their Favorite Schubert Lieder*, produced in 2005 at the Bank Street Theater in New York and at the Victory Gardens Theater in Chicago, is published in the collection, *Plays and Playwrights 2006*. Upcoming projects include the Public Theater's 365 Days/365 Plays Festival, Alec's original play, *Dysphoria*, premiering at the Ontological Theater in August 2007, and a Sloan Project Commission from Ensemble Studio Theatre. He lives in Manhattan.

GARRETT EISLER (Essays) – is a freelance theater critic for the *Village Voice* and *Time Out New York*. His blog, *The Playgoer*, (playgoer.blogspot.com) received nationwide and international attention for its coverage of the *Rachel Corrie* controversy in 2006. Garrett holds an MFA in Directing, is currently a Ph.D. candidate in Theater History at the CUNY Graduate Center, and was a Critic Fellow at the Eugene O'Neill Theater Center's Critics Institute. He lives in Manhattan.

ZHENESSE STANIEC HEINEMANN (Profiles) – Zhen's performance installations, *You Will Know by the Lines of My Skin*, *MMC (Maiden Mother Crone)* and *Human: Deli Style* have been presented and supported by chashama in NYC. She has performed at Galapagos, The Slipper Room and New York University. Zhen recently performed in Julie Atlas Muz's *Divine Comedy of an Exquisite Corpse*, the NoPassport conference at CUNY's Segal Theatre, and in the 2007 SCOPE Art Fair. Zhenesse holds Masters degrees from the University of Southern California (Playwriting) and New York University (Performance Studies). She lives in Manhattan.

QUIARA ALEGRÍA HUDES (Plays) – Quiara's new original musical, *In the Heights* opened off-Broadway in February 2007, with a book by Hudes and music and lyrics by Lin-Manuel Miranda. Other plays include *Yemaya's Belly* (Portland Stage, Signature Theatre, People's Light, Clauder Prize), and *The Adventures of Barrio Grrrl!* (Miracle Theatre). Her work is published by Dramatists Play Service. Quiara was born and raised in West Philadelphia,

PA, received a B.A. in Music Composition from Yale, and an M.F.A. in Playwriting from Brown. She lives in Manhattan.

GEORGE HUNKA (Introduction) – is a theater writer who spent much of 2006 writing about theater and drama for the *New York Times, Time Out New York* and other publications. His own drop in the ocean of New York theater last year was the premiere of his play, *In Public* in October, the first production of his *theatre minima* group (more information at: www.theatreminima.org). George continues to write about theater on his blog, *Superfluities*, at www.ghunka.com, and in other publications. He lives in Brooklyn.

JEFFREY M. JONES (Plays) – is a playwright whose works include *A Man's Best Friend, 70 Scenes of Halloween, Nightcoil*, a series of collage plays (*Der Inka Von Peru, Tomorrowland & Wipeout*), a series of *Crazy Plays, 12 Brothers* (with Camila Jones), and two musicals, *Write if You Get Work* (score: Dan Moses Schreier) and *J.P. Morgan Saves The Nation* (score: Jonathan Larson), many of which are published by Broadway Play Publishing. Jeffrey also is co-curator of the Obie-winning Little Theatre @ Tonic, and holds an annual Pataphysics workshop at the Flea Theater. He lives in Brooklyn.

LIZ JONES (Plays) – is a Founder and Producing Director of Page 73 Productions. Previous positions include: Manager of Development and Communications for National Corporate Theatre Fund, Company Manager for the 2001 National Tour of Camp Broadway, Events Management Associate for the 2002 Tony Awards, and Associate Producer for *Stage Blue*, the bi-coastal celebration of Yale's contribution to the theater industry. From 1996 to 2000 Liz worked on the artistic staff of Manhattan Theatre Club. She is a member of the Board of Directors of A.R.T./NY and holds a BA from Yale in American Studies and an MFA in creative writing from Sarah Lawrence College. She lives in Brooklyn.

PAVOL LISKA (Profiles) – came to Oklahoma from Slovakia when he was 18 years old. Since 1995 he has lived and made work in New York with his partner, Kelly Copper, and their company, Nature Theater of Oklahoma. Their current work, *No Dice*, will tour to Rotterdam, Graz and Hamburg this Fall, and will have its official premiere in New York at Soho Rep in January 2008. He lives in Manhattan.

ALAN LOCKWOOD (Essays) – Alan's writing on theater appears in the *New York Press* and the Brooklyn *Rail*, as do his pieces on music, dance, and visual arts. A selection of these and other works is available at nonserviampress.org. While attending FSU, the writer Janet Burroway's delight in Samuel Beckett's *Molloy* spiced a first reading of that novel; later rewards were reaped at Lincoln Center after a Gate Theatre performance of *Waiting for Godot* alongside James

Knowlson, when his biographer exclaimed that the author fancied white Beaujolais, and in former Grove publisher Barney Rosset's anecdotes, such as hosting Beckett in New York for the making of *Film*. Alan lives in Brooklyn.

DAVIS McCALLUM (Profiles) – has directed new plays by Chuck Mee (*A Perfect Wedding, Big Love*), Quiara Hudes (*Elliot, A Soldier's Fugue*), Noah Haidle (*Women & Criminals, The Dakota Project, A Long History of Neglect*), Adam Bock (*The Thugs*), Peter Morris (*Marge*), and Sarah Ruhl (*Melancholy Play, Eurydice, The Clean House*). Other credits include *The Belle's Stratagem* for the Oregon Shakespeare Festival; *The Turn of the Screw* and *Jane Eyre* for The Acting Company; and *Unbound: The Journals of Fanny Kemble*, which he co-created with Laura Marks, for Prospect Theater Company. He lives in Brooklyn.

POLYBE + SEATS (Profiles) – produces plays and projects that experiment with language and structure toward the development of a new poetics for the theater. The name comes from one of Gertrude Stein's plays and Polybe's ideas are based on Stein's writing for and about the theater. Polybe kicked off 2007 by premiering a week of new plays by Suzan-Lori Parks in the 365 Days/365 Plays festival with the Public Theater/New York Shakespeare Festival. In April 2007, *The Charlotte Salomon Project: Life? or Theater?* will travel to the University of Michigan as part of the inaugural events for their new Wallgreen Drama Center. Polybe will begin work on a new devised piece about mermaids and the collapse of the global fishing market in the summer of 2007, when they will also produce a number of Gertrude Stein's "children's plays" with children in the Brooklyn community at Brooklyn's Greenpoint Reform Church. Polybe + Seats is based in Brooklyn.

ASHER RICHELLI (Plays) – is a Founder and Producing Director of Page 73 Productions, a non-profit theater dedicated to early-career playwrights. His professional experience in the theater includes working as Assistant Company Manager and Company Manager at Lincoln Center Theater and as a management associate for commercial theater producer Ben Mordecai. Asher holds a BA (*magna cum laude*) from Yale and a JD from New York University School of Law (Sol Kopehlson Award for Excellence in a Note on Labor Law). Asher has practiced law as a finance attorney at Shearman & Sterling LLP. He lives in Manhattan.

KENNETH SCHLESINGER (Profiles) – was appointed CUNY York's Acting Chief Librarian in February 2007. He had been Director of Media Services at LaGuardia Community College since 2000. Previously, Kenneth worked in both libraries and archives at Hostos Community College, Thirteen/WNET, Time Inc., the Museum of Television & Radio, NBC News, and the Kurt Weill Foundation for Music. He received a Master's degree in

Information and Library Science from Pratt Institute, and an M.F.A. in Dramaturgy and Dramatic Criticism from Yale University. Kenneth is co-editor of the *Symposium Proceedings for Performance Documentation and Preservation in an Online Environment* (Theatre Library Association, 2004). He lives in Manhattan.

CRYSTAL SKILLMAN (Plays) – is the author of *The Ride*, (nominated for an NYIT Award) and *The Telling* (Rising Phoenix Rep); *4 Edges* (Amphibian Productions); *The Flow* (E.S.T/ Sloan Project); *Ballad of Phineas P. Gage* (HERE); *In the Wild* (Perishable Theatre's Women Playwriting Festival); and *Tooth* (E.S.T). Crystal is currently working on the book/lyrics for the new musical *That's Andy* (www.thats-andy.com) and her new play, *The Vigil or the Guided Cradle*. Crystal is a member of the MCC Theatre Playwrights' Coalition, E.S.T, Rising Phoenix Rep and the Dramatists Guild. She lives in Brooklyn.

BROOK STOWE (Essays) – is producer/director of the way-underground documentary, *In Process: Creating Performance in NYC*, which chronicles the work of downtown hipsters Alec Duffy, Taylor Mac and Julie Atlas Muz. His play, *Late to the Republique* was produced recently by Brooklyn's Wallis Knot. Brook is currently at work on a trilogy of one-act plays set in the seedy Los Angeles suburbs he knows all too well while simultaneously pursuing his dream of becoming the American Baudrillard. Sometime in 2007, Brook is committed to taking a vacation. He may even leave New York City for a few days. Until then, he lives in Manhattan.

CARIDAD SVICH (Essays) – is a playwright-songwriter-translator and editor of Cuban-Spanish, Argentine and Croatian descent. She is the author of over forty plays and fifteen translations. Recent premieres: *Thrush* (a play with songs) at Salvage Vanguard Theatre in Austin, Texas; *Iphigenia...a rave fable* at 7 Stages in Atlanta, and *Antigone Arkhe* at The Women's Project/NYC. Caridad is resident playwright of New Dramatists and founder of the theater alliance NoPassport. Her catalogue can be found at www.alexanderstreetpress.com. She holds an MFA from UCSD. Her website is www.caridadsvich.com.

ADAM SZYMKOWICZ (Plays) – is currently studying with Marsha Norman and Christopher Durang at Juilliard in the Lila Acheson Wallace American Playwrights Program. In 2004, he received his playwriting MFA from Columbia University where he was the Dean's Fellow. Other plays include *The Relationship Game* (reading at Playwrights Horizons), *One Wednesday at West Haddam High* (Manhattan Theatre Source), *Open Minds* (reading at Epiphany Theatre) and *Deflowering Waldo* (Hartt School, Bloody Unicorn Theatre Company). Adam is a member of the Dramatists Guild. For more info, visit Adam online at: www.adamszymkowicz.com. He lives in Brooklyn.

ANNE WASHBURN (Plays) – Anne's other produced plays include *Apparition, The Ladies, The Communist Dracula Pageant,* and *The Internationalist. Apparition* is published in *New Downtown Now* (University of Minnesota Press, 2006; edited by Young Jean Lee and Mac Wellman); *The Internationalist* is published by Playscripts.com. Anne is an Associated Artist with Obie-award winning groups 13P, The Civilians, and New Georges, and is a member of New Dramatists. MFA: NYU. She is currently working on a commission from Yale Rep. She lives in Brooklyn.

Last Word

Hoyt Schermerhorn A/C   *Brooklyn*